GRAVE PURSUIT

CAROLYN RIDDER ASPENSON

SEVERN RIVER PUBLISHING

Severn River Publishing
www.SevernRiverBooks.com

ISBN: 978-1-64875-704-4 (Paperback)

ALSO BY CAROLYN RIDDER ASPENSON

The Rachel Ryder Thriller Series

Damaging Secrets

Hunted Girl

Overkill

Countdown

Body Count

Fatal Silence

Deadly Means

Final Fix

Dark Intent

Foul Play

Trusted Lies

Grave Pursuit

Killer Headline

Jenna Wyatt Series

How They Were Taken

Never Speak of It

Before the Next One Falls

The Dead Don't Tell

To find out more about Carolyn Ridder Aspenson and her books, visit
severnriverbooks.com

For Ricky Viet Dang
RIP
We will keep you in our hearts always.

PROLOGUE

He watched them.

The woman moved with unassuming confidence, unaware of the eyes tracing her every step. Sometimes he followed from a distance, far enough to remain invisible. He knew the precise cadence of her stride, the subtle shift of her weight, the unconscious tilt of her head as she inhaled the crisp morning air. Every breath, every movement, was a study. A slow, delicious anticipation of ownership.

Other times, he positioned himself close enough to breathe her in, to catch the fleeting scent of rose and sweat trailing behind her as she ran. She glided along the trail like a bird in silent flight, muscles coiled, movements precise. Not fragile. Controlled. Lethal in her smoothness, dangerous in her calm.

She was fascinating to him to the point of obsession.

His fingers twitched against the camera's grip, aching to immortalize the moments, every one of them. Not to study her, but to own her image, to command it. He wanted so desperately to strip her of control and rebuild her in his vision. But it wasn't time. Still, he hungered to reach for her. To press his hand against the small of her back, to pull her into the darkness she didn't yet know lived behind her name.

But restraint mattered more. The hunger to reach for her, to feel the fragile pulse beneath her skin, clawed at him, a physical ache. But purpose was a colder, sharper thing, demanding patience, demanding perfection.

Desire couldn't overpower purpose. She wasn't ready. Not yet.

He studied the man next. The one who remained slightly far enough away to be an annoyance. Vigilant, composed. Always scanning. That surprised him. He had expected her to be the threat, the one who watched corners and tracked movement. But the man had discipline carved into his bones.

He didn't feel it with him: the visceral jolt, the spark, the heat. The man triggered nothing. No connection. No longing. But understanding him was essential to perfecting his timing with her. Timing demanded precision, and the plan required no surprises.

Click.

The shutter snapped. The woman's form captured in perfect profile, haloed in the dying afternoon light.

Click.

A second shot. Her face turned, mouth parted as if preparing to speak, though no one stood beside her.

The others? Pawns. Simple pieces. All already marked, but no one understood. No one acknowledged them, but they would. Soon.

She didn't matter. Not really.

But she started the game.

A game impossible for him to lose.

Checkmate.

1

———

The trail curved ahead, packed dirt fractured by patches of loose gravel with a fringe of brittle pine needles lining the edge. Georgia winters rarely delivered snow, only a chill that hung in the air and crept into your bones that made everything feel a little heavier, a little harder. My lungs burned before I hit the first mile. Not from the cold, though that sucked, but from stubbornness. I refused to start slow. I never did. Especially not with him.

Kyle's stride extended ahead of me. His fluid, efficient, maddeningly perfect stride he'd taught himself for efficiency and speed. Chasing down drug traffickers required a fitness level paramount to a Marine. He moved like someone born to do it. His elbows tucked, posture upright, and every inch of him in sync with the ground beneath his feet. He wasn't even trying. I hated that I noticed it. Hated more that it mattered. My legs couldn't cover the same ground in one step, and the gap between us widened. Not far. But enough.

He meant nothing by it, but that didn't matter either.

Everything felt like a competition. And I didn't like to lose, not even to the man I loved.

Damn it.

I clenched my jaw, pushed down the burn in my legs, and leaned into the effort. My ponytail slapped against my neck with each step, a rhythmic sting that only fueled my irritation. I matched my breathing to my cadence, narrowed the gap, and waited. As the trail leveled out, I surged. My arms pumped harder. My feet hit the dirt with more intent. I passed him with a smirk I didn't bother hiding, cutting just close enough to make a point. Even if that point didn't last more than a few seconds.

With a smile plastered on my face as I passed him, I then hollered, "And she takes the lead."

He looked over, and there it was. That half-smile. The one that told me he knew what I was doing and had let it happen. Like it was cute. Like I was cute. Like he had given me a shot at winning before he jogged past without breathing hard. His brow lifted, smug and unbothered.

I wanted to shove him into the nearest tree.

His hands relaxed at his sides, and his whole body shifted, subtly and infuriatingly, like he was pulling back. Letting me have it, the win. At least momentarily. That lit something in me that had nothing to do with running.

I kept the lead for ten, maybe twelve steps, before the sprint ignited fire in my calves and wrapped heat behind my knees. My body screamed, so I backed off just enough to fall into something steadier. Controlled. A run, not a sprint. My breath evened, then caught again, sharp at the base of my throat. I didn't look at him. I didn't need to. He was already there beside me, his footsteps falling into rhythm with mine like he'd never left.

His breathing? Still calm. Of course, it was. He let out a quiet exhale, one of those effortless sounds that told me he was nowhere near his edge—and that he knew I was.

The trail tightened around us, boxed in by the tree line on one side and a shallow slope dropping toward a dry creek bed on the other. Most of the trees were bare, their limbs clawing at the breeze, swaying just enough to stir the silence. The sun cut through in slivers, making it look warmer than it felt. Up ahead, a couple came toward us, both red-faced and lost in their own pace with their earbuds shutting out the world. The man gave us a nod. The woman didn't even look in our direction. I imagined that mirrored how Kyle and I looked on our runs.

He stayed quiet. He always did during the first stretch because he knew I needed that space to settle, to calculate, to judge myself more harshly than anyone else could. I used the silence to inventory every mistake I had made. Every muscle I burned too soon, every breath wasted on pride, every stupid impulse I gave in to just to prove I could pass him.

I hated his letting me, but I hated more that I needed him to.

Our strides aligned again. Each footfall pressed into the dirt, quiet and purposeful, leaving behind faint prints destined to fade before the next runner even came through.

He checked his smartwatch. "We've got four miles left, and you already used your reserve energy." He shot me a sideways glance, mouth twitching like he had to force himself to keep the smugness from spilling out.

"I have more energy than that." My heavy breathing betrayed me. "Go ahead. I'll catch up."

"I think I'll stay with you. If I run ahead, you'll throw it in my face later."

"Aw, you know me so well."

He laughed.

I narrowed my eyes but didn't turn my head, saving my breath—and my pride. I would have laughed too, but I didn't want to waste the breath.

Sixteen minutes and forty-seven seconds later, we finished the run and walked back to the parking lot. Kyle bent at the waist to stretch his hamstrings while I tried not to collapse like a dying star.

I guzzled some water and told Kyle he should run without me next time.

"Why?" he asked. He pressed the button to start his truck. "It's fun to watch you lose your mind because you can't beat me."

He grinned as he reversed out of the parking spot, one hand on the wheel, the other tapping the dash like a drummer between sets.

I narrowed my eyes, tapping my bottle against the door like it was a weapon. I drummed my fingers on my thigh but didn't say a word.

He pulled onto the road. "You're plotting my death for that one, aren't you?"

"Yep."

"I figured." He nodded, then added, "You were slower than normal. Are you feeling okay?"

"I'm fine, Kyle. I just need to work out more."

"Have you had your physical yet?"

"You know I have a father, right? And I'm not talking about my real father or Lenny. I'm talking about Bishop."

He laughed. "It's my job to worry about you."

"Well, don't. Dr. Lawin and I are getting together next week."

"For your physical, I assume?"

"Yes, but I like to pretend it's a date." I smiled. "You know I have a schoolgirl crush on him." A faint, almost imperceptible scent always clung to the memory of his name, something clean and clinical, like antiseptic and nitrile gloves.

"Yes, I know. I also know Savannah and Lauren do too. I guess I should check this guy out."

"Don't bother. He's not your type."

Bishop set a disposable aluminum pan of pulled pork barbecue on his kitchen table. The smell made me salivate. I set my contribution beside it.

He stared down at it and then up at me, his eyes pleading. "Please say those beans don't need to go into the oven."

"Shut it, Bishop. I screwed up the beans once. One time, and I can't live it down."

"You caught Michels's kitchen on fire," he said, fighting back a smile. He tilted his head with mock sympathy and reached for a serving spoon like it was a shield.

Michels, with his stupid perfect timing, walked into the kitchen.

"Oh, hell," he said, glancing at the beans. "Rachel bring those?"

He leaned against the counter, arms crossed, smug as a cat that found the cream.

I threw my arms in the air, spun around, and stomped out the back door, muttering loud enough for them to hear every single expletive I didn't say. I walked outside, still cursing them both as I heard them laughing.

Ashley, Michels's wife, sat there with a big smile on her face. She had struggled since losing the baby and finding out about her split uterus, so seeing the smile brought me joy.

"Hey," she said. She patted the spot on the bench next to her. Her hand lingered on the wood as if she needed the grounding.

I sat beside her.

"Don't let them give you a hard time. The fire wasn't that big."

"Gee," I said with a chuckle. "How sweet of you to support me." I bumped her shoulder and shot her a mock scowl. "How are you?"

"Rach, I'm fine. Please stop worrying about me."

"I will never stop worrying about the people I love, Ash, so get used to it."

She leaned her head against my shoulder. "You are a great friend, but I promise you, I'm okay." She sat up and added, "Justin and I are considering adopting, but we haven't told anyone yet." Her fingers twisted the edge of her sweater as her eyes flicked to the yard, worried someone might have overheard.

For a second, I just stared. Then the grin hit me, but I bit my bottom lip before I could squeal like a deranged toddler. "That's great news. I promise not to say a thing until you do first." Then I babbled on like a baby. I wanted to hug her, but I kept my excitement hidden for the sake of the secret. "You two will be perfect parents, however it happens." I retracted that by saying, "Okay, maybe just you. Michels's gag reflex is too short to change a diaper."

"You have no idea," she said. "He gags if my hair is in the shower drain. He can't even unclog a toilet with a plunger, and you know what a man can do to a toilet."

"Please don't tell me to keep that quiet. Please."

A grin stretched across her face. "Use it how you please, daily if you'd like."

Zach Christopher, Fulton County's Assistant District Attorney and the significant other of our crime scene tech, Nikki, walked through the back gate. "Did I miss anything?"

"Just a few ribs on me," I said.

"That's too bad. I enjoy those." He grinned and headed toward the door. He looked way too relaxed for a man working for the DA's office, his tie crooked and his shirt half-untucked.

"They're getting serious," Ashley said.

"I think so too. I'm happy for her. He's a good guy."

"You only think that because he's a prosecutor."

"True."

Kyle pushed open the sliding glass door for Zach. He nodded toward me as he did, like he knew what we were talking about and dared me to deny it.

"You know you're next, right?"

"How 'bout dem Bears?" I used an old Chicago phrase to change the subject. I waved my hand in a "nothing to see here" motion and took a long sip of lemonade.

"Think what you want, but I see it in how your man looks at you."

I scoffed, glanced sideways at her, and gave a sharp shake of my head like she'd lost hers. I'd imagined marrying Kyle at least a hundred times, usually during those moments when my biological clock didn't just tick, it full on smacked me upside the head and shouted, "Get a move on!" But time rolled on, and that clock's battery was close to dead. Truth was, I didn't need to get married. I'd been down that road before, and it ended with my heart shattered and my husband bleeding out in front of me, killed by a gang member while I stood there, gun in hand, a second too slow. Maybe if I hadn't hesitated, he'd still be here. And while I knew it sounded like something a therapist would underline, bold, and circle twice, somewhere in the dusty corners of my mind, I started linking marriage with death. It wasn't rational, not really, but the cold, hard fact remained: every time I allowed myself to fully love, to truly commit, the universe seemed to demand a payment in blood. Which, as one can imagine, doesn't make marriage inviting.

"When Anderson kidnapped me and I wasn't sure I would live," Ashley said, "the only thing I could think of was my future with Justin. I imagined this house, two-point-five kids, everything I've always wanted. It's what helped me escape. Tragedy doesn't define us. It's what we do after that does."

I swallowed back the lump in my throat. "I know."

Kyle brought me a lemonade. "Thought you might want this since you're on call tonight."

I blinked up at him and took the drink, brushing my fingers against his briefly—just long enough to feel guilty. I took the drink and looked up at him. If Tommy, my deceased husband, and I had met Kyle together, they would have been best friends. I know Tommy would have wanted me to move on, to meet someone, and to be happy. Since both of us were in law enforcement, we discussed it many times. As much as I wanted to take that step, I couldn't get there, and Kyle understood.

Bishop walked outside and said, "Jimmy's running late."

"Did something happen with the kids?" Ashley asked.

"Not sure. Dispatch sent a text—"

My cell rang, cutting Bishop off. I answered as I normally would. "Ryder."

"Detective Ryder, this is Sergeant Jason Montgomery. Chief Abernathy needs you at the station."

"Right now?"

"Yes, ma'am."

"I'll be right there." I killed the call and looked up at Bishop as I stood.

"Just you?"

I shrugged. "Guess he doesn't want to ruin everyone's weekend."

2

Jimmy waited for me in his office. I tapped on his door and cracked it open. "Hey."

"Come on in."

I stepped inside, brushing loose hair from my face and dragging the fatigue of the day behind me like a backpack full of bricks. I dropped into a chair in front of his desk. "Bishop's crying in his beer because you didn't call him in."

"He's not on call."

"But we're partners."

He motioned for me to come around his desk.

Since it was clear he wasn't in the mood for jokes, I obliged.

He lifted a file folder from his desk. "This came for you."

His fingers tapped once, twice on the folder before sliding it across like it might bite.

I moved to take the folder, but he stopped me.

"They didn't mail it. Someone couriered it here. I just happened to be leaving when the courier arrived." He handed me the folder.

Jimmy acted too serious for me not to open it with caution. What I saw stopped my breath.

A single photo of a woman stretched across a king-sized bed, with her limbs arranged neatly, as if she'd fallen asleep that way. The folds of a crisp white luxury hotel robe draped her body. She appeared fine other than a single, clean slash across her throat. Someone with surgical training had executed the slash with precision. No jagged edges, no torn flesh. Just a precise, clinical line that didn't match the softness of the scene. No blood stained the robe, none soaked the sheets, and not a trace touched her skin.

My stomach clenched as if someone had punched me from the inside. My fingers curled tight around the folder's edge, knuckles white. I closed the file and handed it back to him. "It came for me?"

He nodded. His lips pressed together in a tight line, his eyes still fixed on the folder like it might explode.

"I need Bishop."

"Call him in."

Bishop studied the photo and then looked at Jimmy over his readers. "Just this?"

"Just that," Jimmy said. "Rachel said she doesn't know the woman. Do you recognize her? Maybe from a previous investigation?"

He examined the photo again. "No."

Cathy had prepared a spread of food from the cookout, but it sat untouched on the table in Jimmy's office.

Jimmy eyed the food. "Can either of you think of anyone in particular who would do something like this?"

"You mean people we've arrested?" Bishop asked.

"Yes, or anyone from any aspect of your lives."

I bit my bottom lip, crossed the small office, then retraced my steps and scrutinized the photo again. "I've arrested hundreds of people during my career, many of them in Hamby, Jimmy. It could be any of them or none."

"Can you recall anything with a similar theme?"

"Dead woman in a luxury hotel robe on a hotel room bed with her throat slashed?" I paused and then shook my head. "Not that I can remember." I looked at Bishop.

"Nothing similar either, Chief. Not before or after Rachel started with the department."

"We don't have any hotels in Hamby," I said. "So, is this really ours?"

"The photo came for you," Jimmy said. "And until we know the hotel location, this is ours."

"Got it, Chief," I said. "I'll call in Bubba. We'll need him to find that hotel." I dialed his shortcut and placed the call on speaker.

Bubba answered on the second ring. "I'm almost there. I was deep into a mission in GTA VI, and time just slipped away. I'm bringing beans in case yours catch fire again."

"It doesn't matter. We need you at the department."

"Should I stop and get Bishop or anyone else?"

"Bishop's here. I'll call the others in," Jimmy said. "We're going to need all eyes on this one."

"What's going on?"

"Someone delivered a photo to Rachel. We need you to look at it."

"I'll be right there."

———

Bubba sat at the investigation table, bouncing his leg rapidly. He studied the photo while the rest of us watched him. "There's nothing online?" he asked. "Like an email or something?"

"You mean of the photo?" Jimmy asked.

Bubba nodded.

We quickly checked our email but found nothing.

"Then we're SOL for any metadata or traces of its origins, timestamps, or any embedded information about the photo or the camera."

"That's what I thought," Jimmy said. "Can you work your magic and find the hotel?"

"Probably," he said. "But it could be AI."

"It looks too good for that," I said.

"For the AI you'd use, probably, but there are advanced programs that can create lifelike images."

"Can you check that too?" Bishop asked.

He nodded. "Let me try a few things first. It won't take long to run it through TinEye, and a couple OSINT plugins I wired into Intel Owl, and maybe a background fragment matcher I cobbled together last year when I was bored."

"English, please," Bishop said.

"I'll use a program that breaks the image into foreground, mid-ground, and background, and scans public and semi-private databases to check for visual overlap."

"Like what?"

"Like if someone pulled the background from a real estate listing, or a travel blog, or swiped it off a Pinterest board, we'll know."

"Or if it's an actual image from the location?"

He nodded. "Then I'll check to see if it's AI because AI composites love to borrow from the internet. But if this background already exists somewhere else online, and the person in this picture isn't in that version, we'll know it's a fake."

He stood and stepped to his portable standing desk, where he left multiple laptops, a desktop, and a printer. He clicked a few times on the desktop, scanned the photo, then zoomed in on a section of the wall behind the subject in the photo.

I walked behind him to watch.

"See this texture?" He pointed to a crack in the plaster just under the light switch.

"The crack? Yes."

"If that shows up in another photo with a different subject or no subject at all, it means they dropped the victim in digitally."

Everyone stood and crowded behind Bubba.

"What's that on the robe?" I asked.

"It's the number two. I had to blow it up to read it." He blew up the photo again. "Looks hand-stitched."

"Which means something," Bishop said.

"Can you determine if the person is AI?" Jimmy asked.

"Maybe, but I can't promise."

Jimmy grimaced. "Why?"

"It just depends on the details of the photo. AI leaves fingerprints. Normally, I can scan for compression noise inconsistencies, symmetry flaws, eyes that don't align, teeth that look like marble, pixel-level weirdness in the pupils, that kind of thing. Most of the time, AI gets the big stuff right but trips up on the fine print."

"Like?" Bishop asked.

"They'll have five fingers and no thumb."

Bishop grimaced.

"But her face is blurred," I said.

"Right. If she's real, she'll have a digital footprint somewhere. Her socials, public record, stock photo archive, even something as simple as a wedding announcement. If she doesn't exist anywhere, that's not proof she's fake, but it makes her suspect." He tapped the keyboard keys faster than my eyes could follow. "It's going to take me a little time," he said.

The door opened, and Susan pushed a metal mail cart into the room. The barbecue smell hit me first.

"I got it all," she said.

"How'd you know?" Jimmy asked.

"Savannah called. I told her I'd come get everything. She couldn't bring it all with those two babies of yours."

I smiled, thinking of Scarlet and Carter, my non-biological niece and nephew. Those two could certainly be a handful, but they brought me too much joy to care. "Is she coming here?"

She shook her head. "She said she doesn't want to spend her weekend with dead people."

"Probably wise," I said.

She set up the spread, and I noted my beans were on the right. Even though Susan wasn't there for my unfortunate bean event, word traveled fast in the department.

She put together a plate for Bubba and set it on his desk. Bubba, deep into his screen, didn't notice.

Detective Lauren Levy arrived last and headed straight for a plate. "I'm starving. Someone fill me in while we eat, please?"

"How was traffic?" I asked.

"Garcia says it's worse than Chicago, and he's right. It took two hours to get to the airport because of the Braves game, and two to get back."

"That's because they're losing and everyone's leaving," Bishop said.

"People," Jimmy said. "I think we'd all like to get home to our significant others."

"Not me," Bubba said. "But only because I don't have one."

I would have felt sorry for him, but I didn't think he cared about having a significant other.

"I don't understand why Rachel received it," Levy said.

"Agree," I added. "We discussed this before you got here, but I'm at a loss." I pushed my empty paper plate toward the center of the table. "It doesn't make sense. Why send it to me specifically? Not the department. Not the chief. Me."

Bishop sat back and folded his arms across his chest. "Rach, you wouldn't win any awards for being nice to criminals. Are you sure there's no one who might do this? Maybe as a prank?"

"Right," Michels said. "To distract you—or us—from something else they're doing."

"Could be someone trying to rattle you," Levy added, licking barbecue sauce from her thumb before tossing her napkin aside. "It wasn't an accident it came to you."

Jimmy ran his hand through his hair. "Think about it again, please. Are you sure it's not connected to anything back in Chicago? Anyone you crossed still out and walking around?"

"Anyone who didn't make it to court?" Michels asked.

"If they didn't make it to court, then I didn't arrest them," I said. "And if they did, they're either locked up or dead. I don't know anyone with this kind of reach who's still above ground." I stared at the plate, the remains of baked beans congealing into something less than edible. Not that they weren't questionable in the first place, but I'd never admit it. "It doesn't feel like Chicago. And it doesn't feel like Hamby either. This is polished. Expensive. Whoever did this wanted to make a point without making a mess. Those aren't my people, for lack of a better term."

"For sure. Your people are wealthy with serious mental issues," Michels said, "or the scum of the earth with serious mental issues."

He had a point.

"What about Tommy?" Levy asked quietly.

I looked up. "He's been dead a long time. If they were going to come after me, they would have already."

"Maybe someone from his past just got out and is trying to send a message. You were married. Could be enough."

Jimmy nodded. "That tracks. Plenty of old grudges out there."

"Even so," I said, "who from his cases would still have the resources and the nerve to pull this off? I went through the list more than once after his murder. There wasn't anyone with this kind of method."

"Unless they were off the radar until now," Bishop said. "Or someone else took up the cause. Family member. Friend. Partner."

Susan entered the room pushing a plastic bin on a cart, nodded at Jimmy, and started cleaning. She moved quickly, stacking empty plates, wiping barbecue from the table, and dropping napkins and bones into the trash. No one spoke while she worked. No one needed to.

I glanced at Bubba who was still hunched over his desk, fingers tapping, eyes locked on the screen. If he heard any of it, he gave no sign. He also hadn't touched his food. I doubted he even knew it was there.

Susan looked up. "Is everyone good in here?"

Jimmy nodded. "Appreciate it, Susan. Go on home."

She gave a quick smile and wheeled the bin out.

Jimmy stepped forward and cleared his throat. "We need to take the next steps as if this is real. Doesn't matter if it's a stunt, a warning, or the opening to something worse. We can't treat it like noise."

The thought coiled through my mind, tightening with each loop. I didn't like how naturally the strategy came to me. As if part of me already knew it was a game. One I'd been drawn into before I realized I was even a piece on the board. I straightened in my chair to force down the twist in my gut.

Bishop planted his hands on the table. "What do you want us to hit first?"

"You and Rachel dig into known enemies. Start with Rachel's closed cases, anyone paroled, released, or who had family making noise afterward." He looked at me. "I'll see if I can get someone to send us Tommy's biggest cases." He paused. "Excluding the one he was investigating before his death."

There was no reason to check that one. Everyone who might have sought revenge was already dead.

Bishop gave a tight nod. "You want us checking old IA reports too?"

Jimmy nodded. "Internal Affairs is always an option. Anything that puts a target on your back. I don't care if it's ten years cold or didn't go past the rumor mill. If someone had a reason to hold a grudge, I want their name."

"Most of my casework in Chicago was digital," I said. "If you'll call the precinct and get the files to me, I can sort through the priors easier."

Jimmy looked to Michels and Levy. "You two call Miller at APD. He owes me a favor. Find out if they've received any calls from a hotel. If there's even a sliver of video from any luxury hotel in Atlanta, I want it."

Levy reached for her tablet. "That seems like a long shot, Chief."

"And a lot of research."

"It is."

I scribbled a few notes on the edge of my tablet. "If someone meant for this photo to rattle me, I want to know why now. Why not a year ago? Two? What triggered this?"

"Something set them off," Bishop said. "A case reopening. A release. Anniversary."

"Or maybe you popped up in the wrong place," Levy added. "Something current crossed their path. Maybe they didn't know where you were until now."

Jimmy looked at me. "We'll keep eyes on your place until we sort it out. I don't like coincidences."

I nodded. "Me neither."

"All right," Jimmy said, standing straight. "This gets top priority. I want all of it documented. If this is the beginning of something, I don't want to get caught reacting."

Bishop pushed back from the table. "Then let's start digging."

We broke. Chairs scraped. The plates, bones, and jokes vanished. No one laughed. Everyone shifted into work mode. The moment passed, but the tension sat in my spine like steel.

Bubba leaned back with his eyes still focused on the screen and cracked his knuckles. Before we all could leave, he said, "It's not AI, the hotel part, but someone photoshopped in the woman. She's not AI either. I ran every filter, overlay, and shadow analysis tool I have. Compression artifacts are clean, lighting angles match across all layers, no misaligned irises, no fake texture bloom."

"So, the background? The hotel is real?" I asked.

"Yeah, and I know the place."

That got everyone's attention. Bishop set down his cup, and Levy straightened from her half-lean.

"Where?" Jimmy asked.

"I'm not one hundred percent sure yet, but it looks like the St. Regis in Buckhead. The layout, fixtures, everything matches. I stayed there a few years ago for DEFCON South. It's high-end."

"You can confirm that?" Jimmy asked.

"Give me a few minutes. I want to run some comparisons to their marketing shots and booking sites. See if I can find a match."

"Is it possible they used a photo online then?" Levy asked.

"Yes."

"I'll call APD," Michels said.

"And I'll call the St. Regis," Levy said. "Give us five."

They stepped into the hallway.

Levy returned a minute later. "Nothing from the St. Regis. No 911 calls. No welfare checks. Nothing from that hotel in the last two weeks."

"I didn't think there would be," I said.

"Still had to check," Jimmy replied.

Michels returned. "Atlanta PD hasn't had a single report from the St. Regis. Not even a noise complaint. They've got three female bodies. Two Caucasians who are known addicts, one African American."

"What about from other hotels?" Jimmy asked.

"Nothing."

"So, either this woman didn't die there," Bishop said, "or she didn't die at all."

Levy spoke. "The photo isn't real, but the woman in the photo is, so it happened somewhere."

"Could be a screenshot from a movie," Michels said. "Or from a previous case anywhere in the world."

"Look," Bubba said.

We gathered around him again. He clicked through high-res images of the Astor Suite on a travel site. "There. Same light sconces. Same drapes. Even the marble tiling. It matches like I said, but I'm not sure yet if the photo came from online or was taken by our guy." He tapped again on his screen. "Hold on." He split the screen, overlaying our crime photo with the booking image.

"The camera angle's different, but yeah. That's the same room," Bishop said.

"It's got to be a fake then," I said. "I mean from their marketing materials or something."

"Bubba," Jimmy said, "can you zoom in on the body? I know the head's blurred, but let's take another look at it."

He zoomed in again, eyes narrowing. "There. Wrist. Left hand. Tattoo. I think it's a compass rose with an emphasis on east."

I exhaled. "That mean anything to anyone?"

Bishop shook his head. Levy did the same.

"Could be a travel thing," Bubba said. "Some influencer crap. Minimalist ink is trendy."

"Can you run it through image databases? See if someone posted a similar tattoo online?"

"I can, but that'll take time. And the odds are low unless it's super unique or tied to a profile photo."

"Still worth it," I said.

He nodded and started the search. The silence stretched while we watched the screen blink through matches. A few minutes later, he said, "This is going to take a while."

We waited an hour, tossing out theories and thoughts while Bubba worked his magic.

Finally, he said, "She either doesn't post, or she uses filters, or it's not her tattoo."

"Could it be fake?" Bishop asked.

"Could be. Temporary decals have come a long way. But hang on."

He zoomed in again. "No ink shine. No light break at the edges. Skin looks flat. Almost matte. That's not healed ink."

Michels sported several tattoos. "Let me get a good look. I can tell a fake from a real one from a mile away."

Bubba shifted the light contrast again.

"Yeah, this looks like a transfer," Michels said. "Texture's wrong. The edges are too perfect. Real tattoos shift with the skin. This one doesn't."

Levy stepped closer. "You sure?"

Michels dipped his chin and looked up at her with his, *are you serious* look.

"Yeah. Someone applied it to make us think it belonged to her."

The landline beeped. Jimmy answered.

"A man called in to report his wife missing," the officer said. "It's been over twenty-four hours."

"He didn't report it right away?" I asked.

"No, ma'am."

"You take it," Jimmy said to me. The line clicked. "This is Detective Rachel Ryder."

"Yes, thank you. My name is Ray Abbott. My wife, Jennifer Abbott, left for a work conference in Atlanta two days ago. She was supposed to call when she checked in. She didn't. Her phone's been off since yesterday."

"Where was she staying?"

"She didn't say. Just said she was downtown."

"Where do you live?"

"In Hamby."

"Can you describe her for me?"

"Uh, yeah. Brown hair, hazel eyes. Five feet four, maybe 140 pounds, but I don't know. She hated telling me her weight, and I never asked."

"Does she have any specific defining characteristics? Maybe a scar or a tattoo?" I asked.

"A few tattoos, yeah. Why?" He sounded concerned. "There's a cross. She's got a cross on her left ankle."

We couldn't see her left ankle, but if it was her, we preferred to tell him in person. Everyone deserved to hear that kind of news face to face. They needed someone to empathize with them in person. "Could you please come into the department?" I asked.

"Did you find her? Please tell me you found my wife."

"We haven't located a body," I said. Which was true.

"Then how do you know she has tattoos?"

"Mr. Abbott, we have a photo of a woman, and we would like to make sure she isn't your wife."

3

Ray Abbott stood about five feet eight inches if he didn't hunch, which he had since first arriving. He slicked back his graying hair, but pieces of it popped up as if he'd dragged his hand through it multiple times. He appeared distraught, but that didn't mean the guy hadn't killed his wife.

It happened often, husbands murdering their wives and sometimes their children, but acting as if their world had ended, which it had, but not for the reason they hoped.

Law enforcement academies used people like Scott Peterson to train officers how to cut through the façade and get to the truth in situations like his. Peterson killed his pregnant wife, Laci Peterson, and maintained his innocence publicly, even appearing in media interviews expressing concern for his missing wife. However, investigators discovered he had been having an affair and had researched boat routes and fishing areas near where Laci's body was eventually found. Some continued to think he was innocent, especially women who offered to marry him—an entirely insane thought—but the evidence said otherwise.

Cases like that often involved the perpetrator trying to redirect suspicion by appearing as the grieving victim and cooperating with the media and police, while investigators gradually uncovered inconsistencies in their stories and evidence of their guilt.

It just took a little time. If Abbott murdered his wife, we'd eventually figure it out.

"I don't understand what's going on," he said in an interview room. "Why can't you just show me the photo?"

"We'd like to ask you a few more questions," I said. "It's procedure."

"So, you're going to drill me about my wife, and you don't even know if that's her in the photo?"

"I understand you're worried and upset," I said, "and we will show it to you, but we need you to answer our questions first."

"Why?"

"Out of respect for the woman in the photo."

He crossed his arms and scowled, but it quieted him.

Levy handled the hard stuff. "Mr. Abbott, where does your wife work?"

"She's a consultant for AmCo Engineering."

"And it's located where?"

"New York, but like I said, we live here in Hamby. She's contracted and works all over the country."

"Did AmCo sponsor the conference?"

"I don't know. She didn't tell me."

"Your wife is in the city for a conference, but she doesn't tell you anything about it?"

"We share our locations."

"Do you have an iPhone?" she asked.

"Android. Why are you asking me all these questions?"

"Is the Find My app turned on?"

He shrugged. "I don't know. I just check her location from time to time."

"And what does it say now?"

"Nothing."

"May I see your phone?" I asked.

He narrowed his eyes at me and then at Levy. "You think I did something to my wife, don't you?" He pounded his fist on the table. "Why the hell would I be here if I hurt her?"

I repeated my question. "Mr. Abbott, may I please see your phone?"

"Fine." He grabbed it from his pocket and tossed it across the table. "It's not showing her location. Go ahead and check."

He was correct, so they had either turned off the Find My app or not used it.

"Does she normally turn off her phone?" Levy asked.

"No, but it dies sometimes. Doesn't yours?"

We knew someone had altered the photo, but the woman in it was still herself. We just didn't know when someone took it. Levy addressed it. "Has anyone seen your wife in the past few days?"

"Uh, other than me? Sure. I guess. I mean, she goes to Starbucks every morning."

"Which one?"

"The one on Birmingham Highway."

"Do you have a photo of Jennifer?"

"Yeah, of course." He swiped through his phone and clicked on a photo. "Here. That's one showing her whole body so you can see the tattoo on her ankle." He handed me the phone.

The woman didn't have a tattoo on her wrist, which coincided with our theory about the fake tattoo. "I'll be right back." I walked out and contacted that Starbucks, then spoke to the manager.

"Sure," she said. "I'll be here for another hour."

I took a screenshot of the photo and sent it to the officer in that patrol zone, explaining what we needed. A few minutes later he let me know the woman in the photo had been there two days prior, in the morning, but not the day before or that day.

I returned the phone to Mr. Abbott. "Someone saw your wife at that location two days ago, but she hasn't been since."

"Because she went to a conference in Atlanta."

"Do you share a bank account?" Levy asked.

"Several," he said. "Do you want to check them?"

Levy wrote that down. "What about credit cards?"

"She has one for work she usually uses, but I don't have access to that one."

"Do you have a contact number for someone at her company?" I asked.

"Yeah, I've got a few." He searched his phone and gave us two contacts, her direct report and a peer.

"Have you tried to contact either of them?"

He shook his head. "I didn't want to seem like that controlling husband if she was there and her phone had died or something."

That struck me as odd. You're worried about your wife, but you won't contact someone she works with to see if they had been with her?

I excused myself again and made the calls outside the room.

Neither had heard from Jennifer Abbott. Both had figured she had decided not to attend since it hadn't been necessary, and they had let her know the day the conference started, two days prior, via text message, to which she hadn't responded.

Back in the room, I said, "We can't see the leg in our photo, but we have a tattoo on a wrist. Does Jennifer have one on her wrist?"

"No. She wouldn't get one there. She always said it was too obvious and not professional."

There was no way around it. Without a body, our only recourse was to show him the photo of the woman, slit throat and all. Levy warned him of the details of the photo before showing him.

His tense jaw instantly relaxed. "That's not her."

"How do you know?" I asked.

"That woman has long brown hair."

"As does your wife," Levy said.

"No. She got it cut last weekend. I just don't have a picture. It's just above her shoulders now."

Levy put out a BOLO, be on the lookout, for Jennifer Abbott and sent an officer to her house, telling Mr. Abbott they would perform a search upon his approval, to find anything that could tell us what had happened to his wife.

The odds were we wouldn't, or he would have already mentioned it, but we still had to try.

We met the team back in the investigation room.

"Great," Jimmy said. "Now we have two issues. A possible dead woman and a missing one, and my gut tells me they're tied together somehow." He eyed me. "Get Nikki here. We'll need her to test for fingerprints and DNA on the photo and envelope, then analyze the paper type, printing method, and ink composition. Make sure she checks for fibers, hair, or other trace evidence." He paused and placed his hands on his hips. "Oh, and see if she can determine the type of printer used."

"You realize no one tells Nikki how to do her job," Bishop said. "Right?"

Jimmy chuckled. "Fair point. She'll know what to do. Someone needs to contact hospitals and morgues in a wider radius around the hotel location for unidentified bodies or Jane Does. Look at detention centers too."

"Got it," I said.

"I'm not finished."

I didn't think he was.

"Check with coroners' offices for recent deaths that might match, even if they're not initially classified as homicides. Contact other law enforcement agencies to see if they have received similar photos. Post the woman's photo in law enforcement bulletins and missing persons networks."

I nodded as if he had singled me out, though I knew he meant it for everyone.

"Then I want you to check local print shops to see if anyone remembers printing unusual photos or anything that might lead us to the woman's ID. Get with the husband again and get contact information for anyone he can think of who's recently interacted or is close to his wife. Close friends, additional family members, coworkers, and neighbors. Interview them all about her recent behavior, relationships, and any concerns. Check her workplace for attendance records, recent conflicts, or changes in routine."

He looked at Bubba. "Can you examine Jennifer Abbott's social media accounts and recent communications? Then run the image through facial recognition databases beyond just missing persons. Driver's licenses, social media scraping tools, passport databases, whatever you can access on that computer of yours."

"On it, Chief," he said.

"We'll pull bank records and credit card statements to see if there's been any recent activity," Bishop said.

"Great. Also, check her phone records for the last known location and recent contacts. Get a list of places she frequents—gym, gas stations, that kind of thing—and review any security footage from them. Let's organize search parties for areas she visited both recently and regularly if anything comes up. If nothing does, re-interview the husband. Verify his alibi more thoroughly. Check security cameras, receipts, whatever you can find." Another pause and then, "Bubba, look for any history of domestic violence, recent marital problems, or financial issues."

"Yes, sir. I'll check his digital footprint too."

Jimmy paced the small room. "The key question is whether we're looking at evidence of an actual murder or an elaborate intimidation tactic. We need to determine if this photo represents an actual crime scene, a threat against Rachel, or psychological warfare."

"We need a body," Bishop said. "The fact that a real woman has gone missing right before we received a fake photo of a different woman doesn't sit right with me. They're connected, and we need to figure out how."

4

Nikki arrived twenty minutes later, ready to dive in.

"Do you need a list of what the chief wants?" Bishop asked.

She scanned the envelope and photo. "Only if he knows how to do my job better than I do."

Bishop nodded. "I'm not sure people trained to do your job know how to do it better."

She smiled. "I'd say Ashley and I are at the same level."

I agreed. "How long will it take?"

"Let's see." She pressed her lips together and then added, "I'll test for fingerprints and DNA on the photo and envelope. See what I can get from the photo paper. If I'm lucky, I'll find something like hair we can match to DNA in the system."

"He wants you to check for the printer type if possible."

"I can try, but that's not a quick job."

"Do what you can," I said. "Sorry about this."

"About what? Having me come in on a weekend to do my job? When was the last time any of us had a true weekend off?"

"Good point," Bishop said.

Three hours later, everyone met back in the investigation room to update Jimmy.

Jimmy stormed in, slammed the door behind him, and stood at the head of the table. "Where are we?"

Michels went first. "I contacted GBI first because, as you know, the Georgia Bureau of Investigation runs most of the state's 159 coroners' offices. Nothing that matches our missing person or victim in their system, either dead or alive. The other five, including Fulton, are drawing blanks as well."

"What about other agencies?" he asked.

"Levy already issued the BOLO," Michels said. "We used the GCIC's missing persons database to cross-reference with other cases but found nothing, so I contacted the Georgia Association of Chiefs of Police to distribute the info to other agencies and check if they had something. Chief, no one's got anything we can connect to these two women."

Bishop spoke next. "Most of the print shops are closed now, including the UPS stores, so I've got two officers set up to check tomorrow. We've contacted Mr. Abbott, and he's getting us a list of people to contact. He should have it first thing in the morning."

"Bubba's working on the tech-centered stuff," I said. "The cell phone pings, etc."

"Who signed the warrant?"

"Judge Nowak." I smiled. "Who else?"

"Go Cubs," Bubba said.

We all looked at him.

"Sorry, not the time to be funny?"

"It's always the time for a laugh when murder's the special of the day," Bishop said.

Nowak and I came from Chicago and shared a fondness for the Cubs. That simple connection worked miracles for me, and I appreciated it.

"Anything else?" Jimmy asked.

"I'm still working on my searches," Bubba said.

"Nothing, Chief," I said.

"Same," Levy said.

He nodded and checked his watch. "Thanks for the update. Go home, get some rest, and then we hit it hard tomorrow. Appreciate you all." He walked to the door, opened it, and left.

"Seven o'clock?" Bishop asked.

"Eight," I said. "Nothing's open at seven, and we wouldn't have enough to move with if it was."

"Eight it is," Levy said.

Bishop and I carried the heaviest loads and stuck around to finish up the assigned tasks. It took all of two hours to end up with nada.

He walked me out and hung out by my Jeep.

He leaned against my vehicle. "You think I'm right? They're connected."

"I don't believe in coincidences."

He nodded once. "Right there with you, partner. Think about why the perp dragged you into this tonight. That could be our biggest get to move this thing forward."

"Already on it, partner." I smiled, then opened my door. "See you at eight."

I turned out of the department lot and instantly replayed the night in my head. My phone stayed face down on the passenger seat. I should have called Kyle to let him know I was on my way, but like Abbott, Kyle had my location.

I had made a copy of the image, but I didn't need it. It had etched itself into my mind.

Why me? Why had it come to me instead of Jimmy or someone else? An icy dread, sharp as a winter wind, curled in my gut. The act had been intentional and highly personal, though I wasn't sure what it meant. Had someone wanted my attention? For what? I ticked through the options as my fingers flexed on the steering wheel. To threaten me? Lure me? Warn me? Or maybe just to be an ass?

Maybe someone I put away, someone whose name blurred into the hundreds I helped convict, finally got free and wanted to rattle my cage. But Bishop and I already cross-checked every Chicago parole, every obituary. And it wasn't because of Tommy's murder. That much I knew because everyone connected either rotted in a grave or stared through glass and bars three times a week.

Whoever sent that photo wanted to see how I'd respond. Would I chase the shadow? Dig into the pixels? Lose sleep over a corpse that might not even exist? That had to be it, or at least part of it. Someone had meant to pull me into a new game, hand-selected by them. Someone who studied me and learned enough to make their move. But was it real? Had they killed someone or found a photo from a previous crime scene?

Bubba would do his best to match the photo of the woman to other scenes, but as Lenny, my former Chicago boss and closest thing I had to a real father, including my real father, used to say, that was a long pull on a burned down cigar.

My gut said it wasn't about Jennifer Abbott. She'd gone missing, yes. But she wasn't the woman in the robe. That tattoo wasn't real. Someone manipulated the photo, even down to the lighting. Maybe Jennifer was bait. Perhaps she had no connection to it. I didn't like coincidences, but I hated being used even more.

A flicker of motion in my rearview mirror caught my attention. A car sped up close, riding my tail and matching my speed, holding tight through every curve. No headlights flashed. No turn signals blinked. It just hovered there, a dark silhouette against the night, its bright lights making it impossible to identify.

I kept my speed steady, made no sudden moves, and refused to panic. If it was some teenager trying to intimidate the wrong driver, they'd picked poorly. If it were someone *else*, they wouldn't tail me this obviously unless they wanted me to know they were there.

My grip shifted on the wheel, tighter as every one of my senses prickled.

It couldn't be Chicago. Not unless someone had risen from the dead. Tommy's killers had gone down hard. I made sure of that. Unless someone new had stepped up—a brother, cousin, someone with an axe to grind— there was no one left.

The image of Tommy sprawled across the sidewalk, his blood pooling from his head, snapped into focus. I just stood there as that POS shot him. I'd been too slow, one second too late, my hesitation costing everything. I hadn't pulled the trigger fast enough.

That guilt didn't fade. But facts were facts. Tommy's case didn't connect to the woman in the photo or Jennifer Abbott. Not unless someone crawled out of the woodwork we didn't know existed, drove down from

Chicago and enacted their revenge. It was always possible, just not probable.

The car behind me edged closer. I passed Hardscrabble Road. It stayed with me. I shifted lanes. Nothing drastic, just a slow veer to the right, my foot ready above the brake. The car followed without missing a beat. The driver knew the area. It matched every curve on the road without hesitation. Its headlights flooded my rear window. I couldn't see the driver.

"Come on," I muttered. "Get off my ass." I slowed my speed, then the car jerked left and rocketed forward. Its engine whined high as it darted around me and disappeared into the next bend. I checked for a license plate, but it didn't have one.

Asshole.

I caught the make and model as it passed. A late-model Chevy Malibu with a driver hopped up on testosterone and zero courtesy. The brake lights glowed briefly as it vanished onto a fork heading south, toward one of a dozen turnoffs between subdivisions and old farmland.

Still, I hadn't missed the details. Tinted windows. Matte finish. No dealership plate on the back. That car wasn't just *any* Malibu. It was a predator's vehicle: clean, unbranded, and stripped of any identifying marks, a phantom in the night, designed to deliver a message without leaving a trace. It could've been nothing. Might've been something. I hit the gas to find out.

Birmingham Highway curved hard through the hills long enough to lose someone in seconds, treacherous enough to flip a vehicle if you misjudged a bend. I took the turns fast with my eyes locked on where taillights might have lingered.

But I found nothing. No sign of the car. No fresh tire marks. Just the long, unbroken stretch of night ahead. Something wasn't right. The timing and the pressure. The way that car pushed hard enough to make me react but not enough to strike.

It had to be related to the photo, and they must have been watching, waiting for me to leave. Whoever sent that photo wanted me unbalanced. The sender reminded me I wasn't as insulated as I liked to believe. They'd studied me. Knew my habits. Knew how I would respond.

And they knew I'd chase. I braked to a stop at the next intersection, then I pulled out my phone and typed a note to myself: *Check traffic cam footage from Hardscrabble to Red Barn.* Because someone out there wanted me chasing shadows.

But I didn't play games blind.

Kyle sat on the rug in the living area in front of my old wooden trunk. He stretched his legs out in front of him and bent at the waist. "But you can't be sure they weren't following you." He reached his arms toward his toes and groaned.

I stood sipping a glass of wine. "I can't be sure I'll make it to work tomorrow either." I cocked my head to the side. "Why are you abusing your body like that?"

He pushed to a stand. "I've reached the age where my back hurts if I sit too long."

My eyes widened. "Okay, Bishop," I said with sarcasm. "Should we get you a cane?"

"Why? To trip you with when you pick on me?"

"You don't have the heart for that."

"You're right."

We sat next to each other on the couch.

"You're going to tell the team, right?"

"Yes, of course. I just don't think someone who goes to the trouble of manipulating a photo and then sending it to me is the same person who would follow me."

"What's that saying about assuming?"

"It makes an ass out of you?" I winked at him.

"Something like that." He brushed a hair from my face. "So, what's the plan?"

"To be announced when we figure it out. But the plan for tonight is to be here with you, relaxing for a few minutes and then going to bed."

"To..."

"Sleep, Kyle. To sleep."

The wicked, sexy smirk on his face dropped into a lower-lip pout. "That's disappointing."

I guzzled the last sip of my wine and leaned my head onto his shoulder. "You're so gullible."

Kyle and I had met during a drug investigation. His work with the Drug Enforcement Agency required him and my team to work together. That work relationship crossed the line into a one-night stand, something I swore I would never do, but ultimately, that turned into a committed relationship. We had talked about marriage a few times, and with many of our friends tying the knot, it flooded my mind more often than I'd expected. I used to think Tommy was it, my once-in-a-lifetime love. And in so many ways, he was. But loving Kyle didn't mean I loved Tommy any less, and loving Tommy didn't lessen my love for Kyle. What I had with him wasn't second best. It was something entirely different, but just as real, just as powerful. He opened a part of my heart I thought had closed for good.

And I didn't want to lose that. Call it crazy, but Tommy and I married, and I watched him die in front of me. What if marrying Kyle did the same? "You know what?" I stood and pulled on his arm. "I hate disappointing you."

5

———

I stopped at Dunkin' and grabbed a mix of two dozen donuts and a box of coffee for the team. Knowing it would be a long day, I asked them to add several shots of espresso into it and ordered a large triple shot coffee with cream for myself. I needed the energy burst, and when the crash came, I'd just do it again.

I slid the box onto the table in the investigation room. "Is Jimmy here yet?"

"He's in with the mayor," Michels said. He yawned. "Said to move forward and stay in touch."

I sipped my coffee. "Is he meeting about the photo?"

He yawned. "Don't know." He yawned again.

"We assisted in the search," Levy said. "They're still out there looking. Chief lined up off-duty patrol. I'd bet that's the reason for the meeting with the mayor. Overtime dollars are cutting into the budget."

"We've got a missing woman," Bishop said. "And a woman in a photo who appears to be dead. The mayor can take his budget and shove it where the sun don't shine."

No one argued.

I pulled out a chair and sat. "Everyone okay with my taking the lead until Jimmy assigns someone?"

Everyone agreed.

"Okay, we were all tired, and some of us had had a few beers last night, so let's review and see where we are. Levy, you start."

"I sent an officer to the Abbott residence to work with their search efforts. Jimmy brought in ten officers and the K9 unit. We searched multiple areas, but Michels and I left early knowing we had a long day ahead today. Michels and I are waiting for an update."

"No updates from GBI or any other agency, but they won't call unless they find something," Michels said.

"Like a body," I added.

"Right."

"Officer Handley's wife is a hospital administrator. He said there's a system called the Georgia Health Information Network where hospitals input admissions to their facilities," I said. "According to Handley, not every hospital or center takes part, but there's almost two hundred of them in the state, so it's a good start."

"Anything?"

"He texted me an hour ago and said there were ten Jane Does admitted to the hospital but none of them matched what little description we have."

"Thank God for tattoos," Levy said.

"Definitely. Since Chief told both me and Michels to hit up the coroners, I left it to him."

"Got them done before," he said. "But I can check again."

"Will they call if they get anyone?"

He nodded.

"Then I think we're good."

"I've got more to do, but I'm delegating most of it," Bishop said. "I'd like to go to the Abbott home and check things out."

"Delegate to us," Michels said. "I don't feel like picking my teeth all day."

"I brush my teeth," Levy said. "And floss."

Bishop asked them to tag along. We needed the husband's approval and help to get bank records, phone lists, and a list of Jennifer's frequented locations.

We finished the donuts and walked back to the pit, the area where the officers did their work. We called it the pit because that was what it felt like.

Jimmy caught up with us there. Walking toward his office, he dropped multiple f-bombs in between words like, the mayor, kiss my ass, budgets over victims, and other things I couldn't make out because of the mumbling.

He paced his small office while we all crowded near the desk, waiting for him to calm down.

I'd known Jimmy since first taking the job at Hamby PD, which I had done to honor a promise Tommy and I had made to each other. Retire in a small town and own horses. I had honored the part I could. The small town part. Though it hadn't stayed small.

Living and working in Hamby didn't go well with the good ol' boy network—especially the corrupt ones—but Jimmy had been on my side. After we took down the corruption in the department and local government, Jimmy received a promotion to chief, and things fell into place.

Bishop and I had found our rhythm, and I'd developed a close friendship with Savannah, a relationship I had not expected.

Savannah and I had nothing in common. Her Southern belle personality and my Chicago, rough around the edges one should have clashed, but they hadn't. Instead, we found a commonality in the middle. General respect for our opposites. She'd taught me how to handle and communicate with Southerners while I taught her how, occasionally, it was okay to drop the femininity and a few f-bombs.

And we hadn't looked back since.

"Jimmy," I said, treading carefully. "We can handle the rest without additional staff. The last thing you need is the mayor on your back."

"Screw the mayor," he said. "We've got two major investigations, and we need to hit them hard. Trust me, he now understands his reelection might depend on it. On us."

"That's a tool that's always worth pulling out," Bishop said.

"Damn straight."

We briefed him on our minimal updates.

He nodded. "All right, he wants us to use our community to move forward, which I'm not opposed to if handled properly." He pointed at me.

"The photo came to you. You're lead, and I need you to hold a news conference about it. We want you to talk to the press but also directly to the person who sent the photo without the press realizing. We can't give them ammunition. Hit this as a missing person without mention of the photo. Do you think you can do that?"

"No doubt," I said. "When are we doing this?"

"In fifteen. City Hall steps. Get ready." He pointed at my head. "And do something with that ponytail."

He hurried out while I stood there, frozen in shock. Finally, I scanned the others' faces. "What's wrong with my ponytail?"

Bishop and Michels shrugged. Levy crooked her finger. "Locker room. Stat."

Reporters, bloggers, and citizens crowded the steps of City Hall, some holding their microphones clustered like a bouquet of weeds. Photographers angled cameras at me from all directions. A chill seeped into my bones. I'd done multiple press conferences, but sometimes my mouth raced ahead of my brain and blurted things it shouldn't have. I sucked in a breath, prayed it wouldn't happen that way, and stood straight. I locked eyes with the reporters and hoped to choose each word deliberately.

I cleared my throat and stepped up to the podium. "Thank you all for coming. Last night, we received a call regarding the disappearance of local resident Jennifer Abbott from her husband, Ray Abbott."

A reporter yelled from the back. "Have you found a body?"

"Please refrain from interrupting until I have finished. I will take questions at the end." I watched the people closest roll their eyes but didn't care less. "Jennifer was last known to be heading to a professional conference in downtown Atlanta two days ago. As of now, we haven't located her or established communication."

Questions burst forward simultaneously. Had they not heard me? I held up a hand to slow them. "I understand your concerns, but I will take questions in a moment. First, I want to make something clear. We're taking every measure to find Mrs. Abbott. Sometimes missing-person cases are straightforward; however, other times, they're complicated by circumstances beyond our immediate view. It's important we distinguish clearly between assumptions and what we know to be facts."

A reporter thrust his microphone higher. "Detective Ryder, is there reason to believe Mrs. Abbott met with foul play?"

I gave up. I had planned a clever message to the person who sent the photo but winged it since the crowd couldn't contain their outbursts. "At this stage, we're keeping every possibility open. We have no evidence linking Jennifer Abbott's disappearance to any known crime. It's easy to look at situations like this and jump to conclusions, but clarity matters. A lot of what we deal with in law enforcement involves separating what's presented to us from what's real."

A woman in the front shouted her question. "Is there something you're not telling us, Detective? You sound like you're addressing something very specific."

I allowed myself a small, measured smile. "I am. I'm addressing speculation. I'm addressing misinformation. And importantly, I'm addressing anyone who may have information they haven't realized is valuable yet. Our priority is finding Jennifer Abbott safe."

"Do you believe someone out there knows exactly what happened?" another reporter asked.

"I do," I said clearly. "It would be unusual if someone didn't. But to be completely transparent, I think it's essential that person understands the stakes. Real people's lives are involved, not hypotheticals or staged scenarios. Real people, real consequences, and if someone comes forward, things will be much easier. We could even find Mrs. Abbott without harm."

"Is Jennifer Abbott in danger from someone in Hamby?" another voice called.

"There's no evidence supporting that. But I will say it again—if anyone watching this believes they know something, something they believe might connect even indirectly to Jennifer Abbott, please step forward. No detail is too minor. Perhaps a photo from your home security cameras or local business cameras. Everyone should check their cameras and submit anything they think might be related. Even if you think it's unrelated or insignificant, share it. Every piece, every connection, matters."

"Could this have something to do with past cases or enemies you or someone within the department has made, Detective Ryder?" a familiar face from the local news asked.

I'd been waiting for that one. The moment a detective's name gets tangled in past cases—like Bishop and I with two different serial killers—the media can't resist spinning the next story back to us. "We're law enforcement. We've all made plenty of enemies over our careers," I admitted. "Any detective has. It's an unfortunate occupational hazard. But at this time, we can't find any personal connection or association with any of us to Mrs. Abbott."

"But how can you be sure?"

"Valid question," I said. "The fact is, we can't, but this investigation is about Jennifer Abbott. This is about resolving a real disappearance involving a real person, and that's what we must focus on. If someone out there believes differently, I urge them to reconsider their perspective and focus on reality, not illusions."

Another reporter jumped in. "Can you explain that further?"

"I'm saying assumptions can be dangerous. When you're working on a puzzle, if you jam in the wrong piece just because you want it to fit, the entire picture ends up distorted. This isn't the time for forcing facts. This is the time for patience, diligence, and clear-headed investigation."

I paused, choosing the next words carefully. "Collectively, the team within Hamby PD sees the difference between what's real and what's not. We also understand that whatever the intention, confusion won't distract us. We're focused. We're ready."

I saw a slight shift among the reporters, something like a ripple of confusion. Good. The media wouldn't catch the nuances, but I hoped the intended recipient would.

"If Mrs. Abbott did not leave of her own accord, which we have yet to determine, we want you to know that anyone who believes they can manipulate perception is in for a rude awakening. Manipulation only works until the truth comes out. And we will find the truth."

A few murmurs rose, but it was time to cut the questions. I'd said the same thing multiple times, hoping I provided what they needed, an assurance we would do our best to find Abbott, as well as give the person who sent the photo a strong message.

I wrapped up clearly and deliberately. "Thank you for your cooperation and support. We'll update you the moment we have new information."

My eyes scanned the crowd, searching for a sign as I stepped back from the podium. If the sender of the photo watched, I hoped my message hit home. Jennifer Abbott's disappearance was real and critical, not some twisted puzzle. The woman in that manipulated photograph—whoever she was, whatever purpose she served—wouldn't derail our search. I made it clear: We knew the difference, and the connection. And they knew it.

I received a round of applause inside the pit. I laughed while giving them my best rendition of a Southern beauty queen wave, something Savannah taught me. In Chicago, I would have rolled my eyes and maybe flipped them off, assuming they had applauded with sarcasm.

"Good job," Jimmy said.

"Thanks. It's taken a few years, but I think I've finally got the reporters trained in how I work."

Bishop laughed. "Right."

Nikki knocked on Jimmy's doorway. "Ready for an update?"

"Only if it's going to find Abbott."

"Can't promise that," she said. She walked in and closed the door behind her.

I leaned against the credenza as Nikki adjusted the folder in her hands and cleared her throat. Jimmy sat behind his desk, arms crossed, face set. Bishop stood just inside the door, while Levy and Michels hovered near the window.

Nikki's expression gave little away, but I knew her well enough to read the frustration behind her controlled tone.

"I finished my analysis of the photo and envelope," she said, waving the folder in the air. "Fingerprints came back partial because of multiple smudges. Unfortunately, I got zero hits in AFIS."

Jimmy didn't move. "Not even a latent worth enhancing?"

"Nothing usable," she replied. "Too degraded. Probably lifted through latex. I found trace residue of that. Microscopic flakes consistent with nitrile-based latex. Suggests our person wore gloves."

"What about DNA?" I asked.

"No epithelial cells, saliva, or skin flakes. The envelope wasn't sealed with a tongue. The adhesive was dry stick. Whoever handled it knew how to avoid leaving a trace."

"What about the printer?" Jimmy asked.

"I analyzed the ink and printing method," she said. She flipped open the folder. "Ink is thermal transfer, consistent with consumer-grade HP inkjets. The alignment and dot pattern suggest an HP Envy model, maybe from the 6000 or 7000 series. I've contacted HP to see if they can narrow it down based on cartridge batch codes, but they said it could take a week or more."

Jimmy gave a sharp nod. "What about the paper?"

"Standard photo paper. No watermark. Manufactured by one of a dozen generic suppliers. I've sent microfibers to paper labs, but that'll take time, and the odds of a match are slim."

Michels scratched his head. "So, you're saying that whoever did this bought common stuff at a big-box store?"

"Likely. Nothing proprietary, nothing custom," Nikki said. "Even the envelope's stock-grade. No branding. No glue anomalies. Nothing that ties it to a geographic region."

"What about trace evidence?" I asked, hoping for anything.

She shook her head. "Aside from the latex? Nothing. No hairs, fibers, or pollen. It's clean. Honestly, someone did it too clean, which means someone did it purposefully."

Levy blew out a breath. "So, we've got a photo of a murdered woman, no ID, no location, no viable trace, no suspect, and no way to tell where it came from."

Nikki met her gaze. "To be clear, we've got a photo of a woman who appears dead, but we can't confirm if she is."

I nodded. "And we're still treating the body in the image as potentially altered, even if the body itself is real."

Jimmy tapped the desk. "Is there anything at all we can use to trace who made this?"

"If the HP data pans out," Nikki said, "we might get cartridge distribution info. Maybe. But without a serial number or IP hit tied to an online print job, it's a dead end unless someone steps forward. Or makes a mistake."

"And until then?" I asked.

She closed the folder. "Until then, we've got latex, generic supplies, and a whole lot of nothing. If we're going to link this to someone not already in the system, we need a miracle."

Jimmy called for Bubba, who a few minutes later, raced in sucking in breaths like he just ran a marathon.

"Okay," he said through pants. "You want an update, yes?"

Jimmy eyed him with a completely emotionless face. "If there's anything to update."

"Right. I've already cleaned up the woman's face as much as possible and run it through facial recognition like the DMV and passport databases. I got three hits with the DMV."

Bishop rubbed the back of his neck. "Let me guess: none of them are our Jane Doe."

"Unfortunately, no."

Jimmy raised an eyebrow. "How did you confirm?"

"I requested wellness checks on the women, and all came back alive and well, Chief."

"Anything else?"

"Nothing on socials, but that doesn't mean she's not there. The image is cloudy, and social sites don't work well with our technology."

"Shocking," Michels said.

"On a hunch, I went through Jennifer Abbott's socials thinking maybe she knew the victim, but I can't find anything that suggests she might."

Jimmy nodded. "Good effort."

"Mr. Abbott's digital footprint looks solid. No arrests, no domestic violence calls. His socials don't show much. Mostly he's tagged in stuff, but still nothing that might connect him to the victim. I'll start looking for matches on the temporary tattoo, but the chances of my finding anything are slim."

"Understood," Jimmy said, though we all heard the frustration in his tone. "Wish we had something to go on, but I appreciate your effort." He made eye contact with me. "Ryder, you're lead on this since the note came to you." He grabbed a file from his desk. "Let me know what's happening."

We followed him out and headed back to the investigation room, where Levy and Michels dove deeper into the search.

"Abbott is genuinely upset," Levy said. "I don't think he's involved in his wife's disappearance."

"I don't either," Michels said. "He let us search his house without supervision."

"And you found nothing," Bishop said. It wasn't a question.

"Nothing that would show she intentionally disappeared," Levy said. "But we need a team there to do a full search."

I agreed. "Set it up. I want you and Michels there." I turned toward Michels and added, "Can you update if you get any Jane Doe DOA calls?"

"Yeah. I've requested calls if one comes into the coroner's offices, the hospitals, and law enforcement. Want me to expand the search area?"

"Not yet. We'll need to re-interview Mr. Abbott. I want to make sure we have his whereabouts for the last two days before he reported her missing."

"We'll get that this morning. Anything else?"

"Just to verify, do we have anything on bank records and credit card statements for Jennifer Abbott yet?"

"Already done," Michels said. He smirked at me. "While you chatted with the media. I thought we could get info from the banks based on exigent circumstances, but our information isn't enough yet to lead us to believe she's in imminent danger. So I contacted Mr. Abbott who said he'd email his personal banker to get us approval to access their accounts. Except to the best of his knowledge, she left with nothing from the bank or even her house, so I can't help but think we won't find anything out of the ordinary."

"Technically, she packed a bag for a quick trip, but it's important to verify with the bank. She may have accounts her husband doesn't know about."

"We'll find out."

Bishop suggested he and I go to Abbott's home as well.

"I'll meet you there," I said. "I have something personal to attend to first."

6

___

I stepped into Bubba's office and closed the door. "Hey, got a minute?"

He stopped pounding his fingers on a desktop keyboard and looked over his glasses at me. "Sure."

"Can you check the traffic camera from Hardscrabble to Red Barn from when we left last night?"

He pursed his lips. "This is off the record, huh?"

I nodded.

He pulled up the first camera. "That's you."

"Keep letting it play."

"There." I pointed to a black car turning onto Hardscrabble shortly after I passed the road. "Pause the video."

"Who's that?"

"That's what I want to know. Can you enlarge the vehicle? I'd like to get a look at the driver if I can."

He enhanced the image, but as I had suspected, the car, a late-model Malibu had windows so dark they might as well have been painted black.

Bubba whistled and said, "Those windows have a serious tint."

"Better to follow cops with."

He checked the rest of the videos and forwarded through them hoping to see the vehicle again, but it had disappeared completely.

"Thanks," I said. "I'd appreciate it if you'd keep this between us for now."

"Really? Why?"

"It could be a coincidence. I'll say something if I see the vehicle again."

"Okay. I'll roll with that for now."

"Thanks, Bubba. Let me know if you get anything on Abbott."

"Will do."

I kept an eye out for the black Malibu on my way to the Abbott home. If it had followed me, it had only meant to put me on notice. If the driver had wanted to do something, he would have already.

"Where are we?" I asked Bishop outside the home.

He gave me a long look, and I knew he wondered why I had hung back at the station. "Everything okay?"

I nodded. "Just needed to check on something, but I'm good."

He eyed me with the curiosity I knew meant he didn't believe a word I'd said, but he knew not to push. I'd tell him eventually, if it mattered, and he knew that as well.

"They're getting the list of the places Jennifer Abbott goes regularly."

"Great. What about the additional search?"

"We wanted you here for that."

"Okay. Any updates on the search?"

"They've been at it most of the night. He got his fraternity brothers here at six o'clock this morning. They're out hitting her frequented places."

My eyes widened. "Please tell me they're not talking to people."

"I can't tell you that."

I pulled a Jimmy and dropped an F-bomb. "This can screw up everything."

He cocked his head to the side. "I know that, Rach. That's why I told him to call them off. Once I explained why, he did. They're on their way back now. According to him, they only hit up the gym and a coffee shop."

"The two most frequent places stalked by rapists and sex traffickers." I blew out a breath. "Great."

"What's got you all steamed up?"

I waved it off. "Lack of sleep. Too many deaths in this no-longer-small, small town. A manipulated photo sent specifically to me. Want me to continue?"

"Nope. Oh, FYI. Levy called Garcia, who called Lenny. They've got people running through your last few cases looking for something that might drop a clue about the photo."

"Good, but I don't think they'll find anything."

"Call Lenny. Levy said he's concerned."

"I will later. He'll know I'm busy."

We walked inside. The Abbotts lived in what someone from Hamby might call a modest home for the city. Given the income levels in Hamby, a four-bedroom home with a three-car garage ranked as middle class, though in Chicago, it ranked a hell of a lot higher.

We searched everything from books on bookshelves to under the mattress and in her makeup drawer. Though she had expensive tastes in clothing and jewelry, nothing pointed to a planned departure.

Abbott needed further explanation about why we didn't want his friends questioning businesses, saying it made no sense because they're all professionals with college educations.

"Did they graduate with criminal justice degrees?" I asked. "Attend any law enforcement academies? Go through interrogation training? Because asking questions is easy. Asking the *right* ones, in the *right* way, with the *right timing*—that's a whole unique skill set."

He opened his mouth, then closed it again. Finally, he muttered, "They're just asking if anyone's seen her."

My nod of acknowledgement was slow and deliberate. "Right. And do you think the people they're asking, her coworkers, baristas, gym staff, whoever, don't pick up on that desperation? Or worse, that frustration bubbling underneath because your friends think we're not moving fast enough?" I folded my arms. "You ever hear of confirmation bias? It's what happens when someone wants a certain answer and ends up twisting what they hear to fit that expectation. Your buddies aren't taking notes. Statements are not being recorded. They're not evaluating body language, vocal tension, evasive eye movement. They're hearing what they *want* to hear and reporting it back to you like gospel."

He frowned. "I just want to find my wife."

"And so do we, Mr. Abbott, but these things matter. They can make or break an investigation. You know why? Because if someone sees or saw her and is nervous or hiding something, they'll instinctively deflect or downplay. Civilians don't catch that. Law enforcement does. Police don't walk into those places waving a badge and barking questions. We observe first. We ask open-ended questions that make people talk. Then we shut up and let them fill the silence. That's how you get genuine answers. You let them reveal something they didn't mean to."

He looked like he wanted to argue, but I could see it registering.

"Listen, we get it," Bishop said. "You want to help. You want her found. So do we. But this isn't a lost dog flyer situation. This is an open, active missing persons investigation. And while we appreciate initiative, what we need is *control*. We need clean, unbiased accounts. Not summaries passed through five guys and a group chat."

"I understand."

"Please," I added. "Understand that doesn't mean we don't need their help. Checking parks, trails, getting permission to search through communities, that's where we need them. We've got a team out, which you know, and we can split them into groups with your friends."

He nodded. "They're on their way here now."

"Perfect," I said. "We'll get them set up."

"Mr. Abbott, we'd like a list of the places you've been over the past few days, since your wife left for her conference."

He blinked. "What? Why? Are you checking on me?"

I answered firmly. "Yes."

"But I reported her missing."

"We know, but we have to make sure you're not the one who did something to her, and once we can verify that, you'll be off the suspect list."

"Do I need a lawyer?"

"Only if you did something illegal," Bishop said.

"I love my wife."

"That's good to know," I said. "Listen, I get it. Marriage is hard. It's not always perfect. Ask Bishop," I said, hitching my thumb toward him. "He pisses his wife off daily."

"My wife and I have a good relationship. We don't fight. Really, we just want to be together. Things are good. She wouldn't just leave."

"And you wouldn't hurt her?"

He flinched. "What? Why the hell would you think I would when I came to you to report her missing? This is bullshit."

Bishop offered him a slight nod. "We have to ask the hard questions. If we don't, men like Scott Peterson wouldn't be in prison."

Ouch. That had to sting.

"Fine," he said through gritted teeth. "I'll give you the damn list. But I didn't hurt my wife, and you're wasting your time trying to prove I did when you could be looking for the real person."

He spoke as if he knew someone had hurt her.

"Do you believe someone's hurt your wife, Mr. Abbott?" I asked.

"What other reason would she be missing?" He walked into the kitchen. We followed.

Bishop and I headed on our tour of locations where both Abbotts had frequented, and, hopefully for Mrs. Abbott, over the past few days. We started at the Starbucks I had called previously.

"This is about the woman from the other night, right?" the manager asked.

"Yes."

"Cool. The same people work the morning shift, so you can talk with them, but only one at a time because this is our busiest time in the morning."

"Thanks. Where would you like us?" Bishop asked.

"How about the corner table over there?" She pointed to a table near the bathrooms.

"That works. We'll be waiting."

One by one, the baristas confirmed that Jennifer Abbott had been there, but not in a few days. Their details, though, hadn't matched.

"Yeah, corporate makes us write stupid notes on the cups now. She looked like she'd just gotten radioed for reals."

Bishop cleared his throat and asked, "Radioed for reals? Can you translate that into real English, please?"

"Sure, she, uh, she looked like someone pissed her off."

"Got it," I said.

"Yeah, so like, I did the whole say something positive crap my mom always pushes on me."

"What do you mean?" I asked.

She groaned. "Turn that frown upside down."

Bishop laughed. "I know that one."

"Of course you do," she said.

Walking out, Bishop said, "Talking to kids today isn't a conversation. It's a series of shrugs and acronyms. I might as well be interviewing a pile of hoodies."

I laughed. "Joe would call them a dark cavern where conversations go to die."

"Who's Joe?" he asked.

"A serial killer on a Netflix series."

His eyes widened slightly. "You watch serial killer shows?"

I exaggerated a wide-eyed look. "You don't?"

"Why watch what we so often live?"

"Fair point." I climbed into his vehicle. "So, she didn't skip her caffeine fix. I can relate to that. Let's hit the gym."

I typed the address into his GPS. "Turn left out of the parking lot."

He glanced at the screen. "Hamby Athletic Club. I know it."

"Wait, didn't you try working out there for a while?"

He nodded. "It's mostly high-intensity stuff. My back is too old for that kind of hell."

I laughed. "You're more of a lift and Stair Master kind of guy."

"Lift and treadmill."

"That tracks."

He pulled into the parking lot of the gym. "Want me to handle this one?"

"Nope. I want to stare at buff men shirtless and sweating."

He rolled his eyes. "Of course, you do."

The gym conversation, though easier for us to understand, landed the same. No one mentioned any change in Jennifer Abbott's routine. They didn't notice any strange behavior. No mention of anything off other than she had enjoyed the class that last day. According to staff, she usually complained the entire time.

We hit the list of friends Ray Abbott had written for us. Two of them were work from home moms who'd fallen into the multi-level marketing trap. They drove the pink cars and worked their careers like social media influencers, and it had worked.

One, Marissa Leverton, almost convinced me to buy their TimeWise Miracle Set, but Bishop cut it off before I did.

"Jen and Ray, they're the perfect couple, you know?" She handed me an eyeliner. "This would be beautiful with your eyes."

I pretended to care. Savannah would have been all over it, but I only wore makeup when she forced me.

"What do you mean by perfect?" I asked.

"Best friends. They did everything together when they weren't working, I mean. And they adore each other, but yeah, lately, I think things have been a little weird. She's been a little off, you know?"

"How so?" Bishop asked.

She capped the eyeliner, suddenly more focused on the memory than the makeup. "I don't know, really. It started small. She'd forget plans or say she was tired or had errands, but it felt like she just didn't want to go home. And when she talked about Ray, it was like—" she paused, searching for the right word. "Like she was trying to convince herself everything was still good. You know when someone says *he's just stressed* a few too many times? Like that."

She looked between us and lowered her voice a little. "I think something shifted. She didn't say anything bad about him, not exactly, but I got the feeling things had changed a little between them. She seemed unsettled. Like she was walking on eggshells or something."

Yikes. The bestie had just given a checkmark on the con side of Abbott's innocence.

"Can you remember anything specific she said?" Bishop asked.

She ran her thumb along the eyeliner cap. "She mentioned a few things here and there. Last week, we were walking through Avalon, just window shopping, and she said something about missing the days when she could go wherever she wanted without checking in. I thought she meant work, but she followed it up with this weird joke, like, 'Ray gets anxious when he can't find me.' It didn't sound funny."

She finally looked at Bishop. "Another time, I complimented her top. It was cute, but not her usual. She said Ray didn't like when she wore low-cut things anymore. Then she laughed it off and said she didn't mind keeping the peace. But I don't believe her. She'd always dressed a little less conservative when she wasn't working. We all do."

Her gaze dropped to the table again. "I guess I didn't realize I was collecting red flags until now."

We pushed for more, but she'd given us all she had. It was enough, though, to return to Abbott and grill him like a filet.

Ray Abbott sat on his couch, bouncing his leg like Michels had before. "What did they say?"

"Your wife appears to have followed her normal routine," Bishop said, "but there are some red flags we'd like to address."

"Like what?" He chewed on his pointer finger's nail.

"Like maybe things weren't as good between you as you said."

He flinched again. "What? Who said that?"

"Your wife has alluded to your being anxious and territorial when she's out," I said. "Maybe even suspicious. Do you know why?"

His jaw tightened. "I told you everything is fine."

"Then why would she say those things?"

"Marissa told you that, didn't she? I should have told you when I gave you her name. She hates me. Jen's always put up with it. She thinks Marissa's jealous because we're solid."

"That could be," Bishop said. "But that doesn't mean your wife didn't say those things to her."

"Yeah, sure. I've been a little anxious about things lately. She travels a lot. Who wouldn't be?"

"Someone who trusts his wife," I said.

His eyes narrowed. "I trust my wife. It's men I don't trust. They think women traveling with them are fair game, even the married ones."

He had a point, but that didn't justify paranoia or even anything close. "Did you want her to quit her job?"

"I make enough for the both of us, yeah, but I would never suggest that. She loves working. She'd lose her mind if she had to stay home. Contrary to what Marissa thinks, I don't and wouldn't force my wife to do something she didn't want. And I didn't kill her."

"Kill?" I blanched. "Who accused you of that?"

"I know what the cops think. I've watched the news."

"We've got people checking your whereabouts since you last spoke to your wife," Bishop said. "If it aligns with what you've told us, then you should be okay. If not, we'll let you know."

"Please do," he said.

I checked my watch and pushed myself off the table in the pit's kitchen. "It's 7:30. I'm going home."

Bishop yawned. "I'm with you. We've done all we can. If Abbott could or wanted to be found, it would have happened by now."

"I hate this," Michels said. "We can't help this guy find his wife. I can imagine how that feels. If something happened to Ashley, I'd lose my freaking mind."

"You mean like the time a serial killer abducted and tried to kill her?"

"Yeah, something like that." He shook his head. "I try not to think about it."

"As you should."

My cell rang. "It's Lenny," I said. I answered the call.

"Sweetheart," he said. "What kind of trouble are you in now?"

"What makes you think I'm in any kind of trouble?"

"I got a copy of the photo. Took it to the department, but we can't find anything to pin it to. Looks like whoever you pissed off this time is from Georgia."

"Wouldn't be the first time," I said.

"Department's going to send a few possibles over, but don't expect they'll go anywhere."

"I get it."

"I'll keep you updated if something comes up. In the meantime, take care of yourself and stay safe. I don't want to lose another kid."

"I'll do my best," I said.

I grew up next to Lenny in a duplex in Irving Park. His daughter, Jenny, had been my best friend since about birth, until a drunk driver rammed into her vehicle, killing her instantly on Lake Shore Drive, what Chicagoans called the LSD. Tommy handled the accident, then handled me for the next year while I mourned the loss of my best friend. Lenny had always been a father figure to me, but losing Jenny cemented our bond. We filled a void for each other. For him, the need to be a dad, and for me, my need for someone to be the father my father never could.

Whenever I thought about making a stupid move, Lenny's face appeared in my head. Sometimes, it worked.

The team split up in the parking lot and headed home.

Kyle met me just inside the garage door. I handed him my bag. "It's been a day."

"No luck finding the missing woman?"

"None. She's disappeared completely. The question is whether or not it's by choice."

"What happens next?"

I cleared my weapon and removed the magazine. "We're waiting on bank and cell info, and Bubba's checking other means of communication like What's App. Tomorrow we'll look at additional footage and analyze the bank and cell info and see where that takes us."

"What's your feel on it?"

"Nothing good." My cell phone rang. "It's Bishop." I clicked accept. "Get lost on your way home?" I asked.

"I found Jennifer Abbott."

My eyes widened. "How? Where?"

"Someone stuffed her body in a suitcase and left it on my front porch."

7

———————

Blue and red lights stuttered against the rows of suburban homes as I turned onto Bishop's street. The chaos of uniforms, reflective tape, floodlights, and loud engines had shattered the usual quiet of his Hamby cul-de-sac. His place matched every other in that part of town. Two-story brick, white trim, a porch swing nobody ever used, and a yard just tidy enough to avoid complaints. But that night it looked like the staging ground for war.

One we had to win.

I pulled to the curb without bothering to straighten the wheel. My stomach turned before I even opened the door. Kyle, who had parked behind me, rushed to my vehicle to walk me to the scene. Diesel fumes, latex and the coppery bite of something too familiar filled the air.

Blood.

Bishop met us on the walk. His face showed little, but his eyes spoke volumes. He'd locked his shoulders and crossed his arms.

"Are you sure it's her?" I asked.

"Yes."

My throat tightened. "Does the husband know?"

"Not yet. Thought we'd send Michels and Levy to get him once she's at the morgue."

"Good idea."

I'd barely processed it. Jennifer Abbott. Gone for days and left zipped into a suitcase like last season's wardrobe.

The driveway had become a triage of law enforcement. EMTs stood back, useless. Patrol officers combed the yard and moved like shadows under the portable floodlights. Jimmy, Levy, and Michels each pulled up behind Kyle, all climbing out with urgency in their step, with grit in their jaws. Nikki's department van followed. She hit the ground before the engine finished cycling down.

"Gear up," she called to her interns. "Nobody touches a damn thing without gloves. And get me a second camera on the scene."

The suitcase sat dead center under the porch light. Gray, weather-worn, and surprisingly big enough to fit a body. Which it did. A note flapped against it in the humid breeze, scotch-taped to the side.

Rachel's next.

I read it again.

Rachel's next.

The words, stark and chilling, were a direct challenge, one implied like it had been written in an invisible ink only I could read. Whoever left that note knew exactly what they were doing. Testing me. Calling me to action and waiting for me to make a move. I clenched my fists, unsettled by how readily my mind began plotting my power move.

Jimmy ran his hand over the top of his head. "Son of a bitch. This isn't how we needed it to go. Damn it."

"Chief," Michels said. "You okay?"

"No, Michels. I'm not okay. I've got a dead woman stuffed into a suitcase."

Michels held up his hands. "Got it."

Jimmy exhaled. "I'm sorry, Detective. It's been a long few days for all of us."

"That it has," I said. I grabbed Michels's arm. "Let's get out of his hair."

"Sounds like a plan," he said.

Kyle stood off to the side as we reviewed the scene. He kept his arms folded and his teeth clenched. A few minutes later, he walked over and said, "This is enough. You need to step away, Rachel. This isn't worth your life. Jimmy, come on. Pull her off. Let her rest."

Jimmy looked my way.

"Don't even think about it," I said.

Kyle didn't back down. "We'll go to Mexico. God knows we both have vacation time."

"Kyle, I'm not leaving." I swallowed hard. "And I'm not stepping down just because some psycho thinks he can scare me. We couldn't keep Jennifer Abbott safe, but we're sure as hell going to find her killer."

His mouth tightened, but he stepped back and stayed silent.

Mike Barron, our county medical examiner, limped up the driveway. Loose khakis, polo stretched over a gut that might have grown over the past few weeks. He carried a clipboard in one hand, a permanent scowl on his face.

"I had just finished meatloaf and sat down to watch a Hallmark movie with the wife. Thirty seconds into a snowball fight, and my pager goes off. I didn't hate it, but those movies do give me indigestion. Too much sugar, not enough substance."

Bishop grunted. "Sorry to interrupt your rom-com."

He sighed. "It is what it is," he said, and crouched near the suitcase.

Nikki joined him, gloves already on, face tight and professional.

"Let's see what kind of sick we're dealing with," he said.

"I'm guessing it's top level, Doc," she said. She carefully lifted the blanket covering the body. The smell that followed turned stomachs. Death had a scent no one ever forgot, one that lingered long after the body's removal and locked into our nasal passages without a key to remove it.

Jennifer Abbott lay inside, not stuffed, but bent to fit. Her body folded like origami. Hands crossed over her chest, eyes closed, as if someone had posed her deliberately. She wore a white hotel robe.

The connection suddenly became obvious. Dear God.

I swallowed hard. "Same type of robe as in the photo, but I doubt it's the same one."

Bishop nodded once. "That's what I'm afraid of, which means we still don't know who that woman is."

Jimmy leaned over and studied the woman. "The good news is we know Jennifer Abbott and the mystery woman are connected."

"I'd say that's the bad news." Nikki's voice dropped as she examined the tag inside the robe. "Standard issue from the Echelon Hotel. Same embroidery pattern as the one in the picture."

Barron sighed as he checked her skin, hands, and hairline. "No obvious wounds. No ligature marks I can see right off. Other than the obvious throat slit."

"Precision with a knife," Nikki said. "I wonder if the killer's a chef?"

Jimmy placed his hands on his hips. "Happens like that in Savannah's girlie mysteries all the time."

"That's fiction for you," Barron said. "There could be some internal trauma with this one. Hard to tell given the pose. I'll know more when I get her opened up."

Kyle studied the body. "There are no signs of a struggle. In my experience with high-level drug operations, when a scene is this clean, it often means the victim was incapacitated or unable to resist before the kill."

"Are you saying someone drugged her first?" Jimmy asked.

"Most females would try to fight back," Kyle said. "Unless they're somehow incapacitated."

"That's a valid point," I said.

"I'll obviously test for drugs," Barron added.

"We wouldn't expect otherwise. Any clues about the time of death?" I asked.

"Rough guess? Twelve to eighteen hours. Still some core heat. They didn't dump her right after."

Bishop shook his head. "Sick son of a bitch."

"It's a game," I said. "And we're losing."

"Not for long," Jimmy said.

"I'm not sure about that." Michels circled around to the back. "No blood trail, which means her murder happened long before he stuffed her in that suitcase."

He looked to Barron. "Is that even possible after rigor mortis?"

"In the early stages of postmortem," Barron said. "After six hours, body manipulation can be difficult."

"Difficult but possible," Bishop said.

"Yes." Barron studied the body carefully. "We'd likely see ligament or tendon tears, joint dislocations, and more than likely, bone fractures. Again,

I'll know more after the autopsy, but I'm fairly confident none of those are present."

"I'd say he either killed her, put her in the suitcase and stuck her in a refrigerated space," Levy said. "Or held her captive beforehand since she's been missing for days."

Kyle crossed his arms as his gaze swept over the pristine body. "This kind of clinical cleanliness," he mused, "takes dedication. It's not a passion kill. We all can see it's too precise. It suggests a killer focused on absolute control, even of the aftermath. It's almost like an audition, where the method is as important as the act itself, designed to leave minimal traces as a signature of efficiency."

Michels added, "And then he delivered her to Bishop's door so we'd get the message."

He was right. "He's showing that he's smarter than us," I said. "So I'm sure he's watching our every move."

"No," Kyle said.

I cocked my head to the side. "He left a note with my name on it. I'd bet my badge he stuck around to watch."

He barked out a laugh, though not as a reaction to something funny. "He's watching you."

Nikki's interns photographed the suitcase, the note, Jennifer's robe, her skin, her hair, anything and everything. One girl gagged behind her mask, turned green, and ducked behind the bushes.

Nikki didn't look up. "Dr. Barron, are you ready to move her?"

"Soon as the scene techs finish. We'll bag the note, suitcase, and robe separately. Everything else gets logged in under Nikki's team."

Bishop stood at the porch edge with his arms wrapped tight across his chest, eyes locked on the suitcase. "Cathy left this morning on a girl's trip with her sister. I don't know what she would have done if she'd opened that thing."

"She didn't," I said. "We deal with what's in front of us."

Jimmy turned toward the road. "Canvass the entire street. Someone's doorbell camera caught something. I want every angle from every house within a hundred yards. Drones up by dawn."

Nikki turned toward me. "This guy's not improvising. This guy structured it. He calculated every move. He's playing a game, and he's setting the rules."

I looked down at Jennifer. She had painted nails, and a faint trace of gloss covered her lips. "He dressed her. Cleaned her up. Made her look presentable. Like a doll. Like a prize." The chilling precision of it suggested not just control, but a depraved reverence for his work.

"Like a doll on display," Bishop said quietly. "We've been down this road before."

I thought back to the numbered murders, and how the killer had stumped us for months, others for years, until he'd finally lost. "A similar one."

Kyle exhaled. "The note said he's coming for you, Rach." He eyed Jimmy. "Take her off the investigation, Jim. Please."

"Don't even think about it," I said to the chief. "Because I'm still here, and now I know what he wants. Attention. Fear. And the satisfaction of thinking he's in control."

"He left her for us to find," Michels said. "Like a calling card."

I shook my head. "Not a calling card. A challenge."

Nikki and her team finished with the body and surrounding area. Barron sealed the body bag slowly.

The weight of the scene had dulled his usual sarcastic lilt. "If this is his opening act, we're in trouble," he muttered.

The suitcase zipped shut, and for a second, everything went still. No one moved. No one spoke. Even the sirens in the distance faded beneath the intensity of what lay ahead of us.

I stared at the note again.

Rachel's next.

No.

Not on my watch.

Kyle exhaled sharply but didn't argue further. Just shook his head and walked off toward the end of the driveway, not because he couldn't look at the suitcase anymore. Because he couldn't look at me.

Barron adjusted his crotch as if we weren't paying attention. "You'd better catch this one quick. Hallmark's doing a Christmas in July marathon, and I already promised my wife I'd be home for the next one." His attempt to lighten the mood failed and no one even grinned.

The hotel robe had given us something. A pattern. A connection. But it also gave the killer something, too.

A signature.

And signatures meant confidence.

Confidence meant that he was just getting started.

8

———

"You can't be serious." Kyle's cowboy boots would burn a hole in our carpet if he continued pacing. "The guy's coming for you, Rach, and you're just letting him."

"That's not at all what I'm doing."

"Then what the hell do you call it?"

I hated to admit it, but my mind was already two moves ahead, mapping out what the killer might do next and how I'd counter it. Sometimes, the karma of worrying about the man I loved doing his job hit like a pitch from Aroldis Chapman. "What would you do if the note had said Kyle's next?"

He sucked in a breath and then said, "Don't do that. Don't turn the tables. We are not the same."

"No, we're not. I'm a detective who's been threatened and attacked multiple times. This is where my expertise lies. Yours is with drug addicts."

"Are you discounting what I do because I don't catch killers?"

I walked to him and placed my hands on his hips. "I would never discount what you do. You save lives. Millions of them at a time. I catch the people who take lives. We might be on the same side of the law, but our jobs are very different. The thing is, Kyle, we're not different. We both do what has to be done, and that includes taking risks we shouldn't and putting ourselves in dangerous situations."

"This is different."

I would have said the same thing, but it wasn't. "It's who we are. We knew that coming in. We can't change the rules now."

A steely edge of professional assessment replaced the usual warmth in Kyle's voice. "Give me a little credit, Rachel. Like you, I'm trained to understand calculated, organized threats. I analyze what's going on, and I can see things clearly right now, probably more than you. This isn't some desperate thug playing games. When someone goes to these lengths, they're orchestrating a psychological operation."

I opened my mouth to argue, but he stopped me.

"Let me finish, please."

"Go ahead."

"The killer delivered the photo directly to you, then dropped Jennifer Abbott's body on Bishop's porch like a calling card. You're so exposed, so personally involved, and that makes you a predictable piece on his board. He wants you to chase and react. And while your stubbornness is usually your strength, here it's a vulnerability he's already exploited to pull you deeper into his game."

"You're probably right, but I won't let him manipulate me. I'm smarter than that, Kyle, and I have to do this. It's the only way we'll catch this guy."

He ran his hand over the top of his head and cursed. "Jesus, Rach. This is your life we're talking about." He shook his head. "I can't do this right now." He grabbed his phone and keys from the dining room table and left.

I yelled, "Are you serious right now?" as he disappeared.

He hadn't looked back. Just walked away with a permanence I hadn't felt from him before. I walked over to Louie, my beta fish, and dropped some pellets into his castle. He swam to one, sucked it down in one gulp, then hurried back to hide under his favorite rock.

He hadn't looked back either.

Maybe he was right. Maybe the killer was exploiting me, but it didn't matter. I had to do what I had to do, and Kyle should have known that. He should have expected it.

I envied how easily Louie could hide knowing I couldn't. I had instantly, without considering the consequences, entrenched myself in the killer's game, thinking in terms of moves and countermoves without even meaning to. The realization made me shiver.

I sat in the investigation room staring at the wall. Normally, we'd all arrive at about the same time, but I'd barely slept. I had convinced myself Kyle would show up a few hours after he walked out, but he hadn't. I'd called him three times and sent four texts, but he never answered or responded. Finally, I gave up, took a shower, and climbed into bed.

I had slept briefly, until the nightmares flooded my subconscious.

Tommy, lying on the ground beside our car, shot in the head, and me, lying there beside him with a matching bullet. The scene shifted to Kyle standing above us, sheer panic in his eyes.

I told you to walk away, Rach. I told you to walk away.

The next nightmare shifted the scene to me standing above Tommy and Kyle, and Kyle was the one with the matching bullet hole.

I shivered at the thought. Knowing exactly how Kyle felt but still believing I had to do what needed to be done. Knowing he would as well.

Bishop walked in. "Why didn't you answer your phone?"

I didn't bother turning around. "I knew you'd be here soon enough."

He set a coffee in front of me. "Everything okay?"

"Kyle's gone."

"On another sting op?"

"If by sting op you mean he walked out on me, then yes."

He pulled out the chair beside me and sat. "How long have you been here?"

"What time is it?"

"Seven ten."

"Then almost three hours."

He tapped his finger on the table. "You didn't get any sleep."

"I couldn't sleep if I tried."

"He's not gone, Rachel. He's worried about you and needs to breathe. Kyle wouldn't act that way if he didn't love you."

"I know, but it doesn't make it any easier. I've got some psycho planning to take me out, and Kyle's pissed at me about it."

"Is that what you think?"

I collected my thoughts and then said, "No, of course not, but I can't afford this kind of distraction."

"Do you want me to call him?"

"And say what? Rachel needs you here so she isn't off her game?"

"I was thinking more like, if you stay gone, who's going to take care of Louie if this guy offs Rachel?"

I laughed. "He loves Louie more than he loves me."

"Everyone does."

I whacked his arm and smiled. "Valiant effort, partner. I appreciate it."

Jimmy walked in and motioned for us to follow him. "Nikki got a print off the suitcase."

No matter how much I respected and valued Nikki's work, I could admit I hated the forensic lab. I'd even pick a night in the morgue over that place. Dead bodies I understood, but forensic technology intimidated me.

The forensic lab sat in the police department's basement, directly beneath City Hall. Nikki had requested an update a while back, arguing that technology in the field changed and the updated systems would improve our chances of solving crimes.

She presented the project to city council and received approval across the board. I hadn't been inside the lab since the remodel.

It was the same space, but updates were obvious. Harsh fluorescent lights still revealed every detail of the room, including the stainless-steel counters, evidence lockers, and fingerprint kits that replaced the old ones. New computers lined one wall, each connected to databases for DNA, toxicology, and ballistic reports. A shiny, brand new central worktable held a microscope, sealed bags of clothing, and trays for trace materials. She had insisted on new refrigerators against the back wall to store biological samples—of what, I wasn't sure—and got them.

The space felt tight but efficient, with every item in its place, every surface scrubbed and ready.

Nikki blinked when she saw us all walk in. "Oh, crap. I should have been clearer, Chief. Sorry. I got a print. It's partial, and not enough to get a match."

I leaned against the metal countertop in her lab, arms folded, and watched with more focus than I expected as she adjusted the magnification of her microscope. She didn't rush. She never did, but she seemed even more deliberate than usual. Bishop stood slightly behind me, and Levy beside him, with her arms crossed and her lips pressed tight. Michels positioned himself near the wall, tapping a finger against his notepad, while Jimmy held court in the middle, hands on hips, impatient yet expectant. He needed a win. I hoped Nikki had one for us.

"Alright," she began. She spoke in a clinical tone, which told me it wasn't good news. She straightened, tugged the hem of her lab coat, and adjusted her glasses. "I've processed a partial fingerprint recovered from the victim's robe. It's not much, and unfortunately, the results are suboptimal, but I'll detail my process for clarity."

A collective sigh filled the lab. Jimmy wasn't the only one who needed the win. Finding Jennifer Abbott stuffed in a suitcase, wearing the exact robe the woman in the photo wore, meant we had a high probability of there being more than one victim.

What we didn't know was how many more. I just knew I wouldn't be one of them, not if I had anything to say about it. But a far colder, more disturbing truth settled in. He wasn't merely killing to kill. He wanted to build something, and I was a player in his game. The thought alone made me draw in a slow breath. I pressed my fingers into my temples. The fact I pictured his game so clearly sent a skitter of unease through me.

She moved to a mounted digital monitor and activated it with a remote. A gray-scale image, blurred and fragmented, filled the screen. "This." She gestured with a slender pointer. "Is our partial latent print. As you can see, it lacks significant ridge detail and clarity. I've assessed the quality and concluded it provides us approximately four identifiable minutiae points."

Jimmy frowned. "Four? That's not good."

Nikki turned her head slowly and shook it. "Not at all. We all understand that minutiae points are the distinctive features of a fingerprint. The ridge endings, bifurcations, dots, and things that can distinguish one unique print from another." She spoke in such detail for the intern working in the lab. "To reliably match a print, forensic standards typically require at least twelve clear points. However, our sample has degraded considerably, resulting in only four distinguishable points. This severely reduces its specificity."

"Then it's useless," Levy said with a hint of frustration creeping into her voice.

"Not entirely. Even a low-quality print has value, but it is contextually limited. Allow me to show you."

She activated another window on the monitor, revealing an enlarged image overlaid with colored dots and intersecting lines. "Here are the four identifiable minutiae I referenced. Two ridge endings and two bifurcations." Her pointer hovered carefully over each marked feature. "These specifics are entered into AFIS, which will then search for matches over available databases."

Michels switched his weight from one leg to the other. "You wouldn't call us here if you hadn't already done that."

"Correct." Nikki's lips tightened slightly before she continued. "AFIS returned several thousand potential matches. To put it precisely, 4,386 individuals nationwide share this fragment of a print."

With over eight billion people on the planet, even four thousand was too broad and too overwhelming.

Jimmy's eyebrows shot upward. "Four thousand? You've got to be kidding me."

"I assure you, Chief, I am not." Nikki maintained her neutral, professional cadence. "Because the partial print lacked detailed ridge patterns, it was too generalized to conclusively identify or significantly narrow down potential suspects. It essentially tells us nothing concrete in its current form."

"So, we're nowhere?" Bishop asked quietly, his frustration clear beneath his controlled tone.

"Not entirely." Nikki tapped the remote again and pulled up another screen filled with graphs and data points. "I ran a secondary search limiting the parameters geographically. It's not great news, but it's better than nothing. Interestingly, not one of these 4,386 partial matches lives in either Georgia or Illinois."

Jimmy exhaled sharply. "That's something, I suppose. But it's a big country."

"Precisely," Nikki confirmed. "The absence of matches in these states might suggest our suspect traveled from outside these areas. However, it remains purely speculative without additional corroborative evidence."

"And we have a population of residents without registered fingerprints," I said. "So, it doesn't guarantee the perp lives out of state."

"Not at all," she said.

The intern, who had lingered quietly in the corner, suddenly turned, reaching for a set of petri dishes stacked on a metal tray beside her. Her elbow caught on the edge of the microscope stand. The world slowed momentarily as a glass beaker wobbled precariously before plunging to the tile floor, then shattered loudly. Her eyes widened, her mouth froze mid-apology, and her face brightened to a deep crimson.

I watched the cords in Nikki's neck tighten.

A brief silence settled before Michels broke it. "I suppose that's one way to reduce the tension." Michels chuckled dryly. "If only broken glass solved crimes."

The intern scrambled and stammered her apologies while desperately retrieving fragments of glass scattered like confetti across the sterile lab floor.

"Leave it," Nikki instructed calmly, briefly interrupting her methodical presentation. "We'll handle it after." She returned her attention back to us. "At least you can use this evidence as an investigative lead. I know it's not concrete proof usable in court, especially without a match, but it's something."

I rubbed a thumb along my jawline. "Any chance of technology improving in the next forty-eight hours?" I kidded, but only a touch.

Nikki inclined her head slightly and smiled. "Essentially, it's always developing. But in forty-eight hours is a big ask. Future technological advancements could allow us to re-analyze this partial print with greater specificity, though it could be years. For now, we document it, preserve it, and move forward cautiously. I've looked for DNA, fiber analysis, shoe impressions, any supportive forensic material that could strengthen our position significantly, but there just wasn't any. I don't know what to tell you. Either we get another body, or we start over."

"Then that's our focus," Jimmy said. "We start over. Bishop, Ryder, circle back and ensure we didn't overlook anything at the scene. Levy and Michels, you two check with patrol about recent travelers or visitors from outside Georgia and Illinois. We need a starting point."

"Chief," Nikki said. "There's more."

He stopped in his tracks. "I hope this is good."

"I guess it depends on what you mean by good." Nikki stood at the end of the table, slipped her hand into a fresh latex-glove and hovered it above another evidence bag. "I found this inside the suitcase." She held up a black pawn in a sealed container, tiny and innocuous, almost laughable if not for the corpse it had accompanied. "I found it tucked into the lining of the suitcase, wrapped in a corner of the sheet under the body, not visible unless you were looking for something that didn't belong."

"Did you look for any matches to known cases?"

"Bubba is working on it. He's running it through VICAP and local databases, and he's checking with Interpol just in case, but he hasn't reached out to me about any of it yet."

"A pawn," I said.

Bishop studied it from afar. "Why a pawn?"

"It's clearly some kind of message," I said.

"Obviously," Bishop said, "but what message?"

"A pawn's not just symbolic," Michels said. "It's strategic. It's the piece used first in the game and it's the least powerful."

"You play chess?" I asked.

"My grandfather taught me. I was chess club master in middle school but haven't played much since."

The room fell silent for a moment, then Bishop said, "I didn't see that on my Bingo card this morning."

I laughed. "None of us did."

"Does anyone else play?" Levy asked. "I don't, but I think he's right. It means something. He wants us to work to figure it out."

Jimmy and I shook our heads. He and Bishop both said they played, but not well or often.

"Same," Nikki said.

"Excuse me," her intern said. "I don't mean to interrupt, but I've played chess since I was three, and I have some thoughts I'd like to share."

"Go for it," Jimmy said.

"Detective Michels is correct. Every game starts with a pawn. It's sacrificed to advance a strategy. That's the message. Not personal, just necessary. And replaceable. I think your killer is telling you he's got a plan, and he's just begun the game."

We stood there even quieter than during Michels's announcement.

"In chess, pawns clear the way for bigger moves," she continued. "Maybe her death opens the path to whoever he really wants."

Everyone, including the intern, looked at me.

"Rachel," Levy said.

Finally, Jimmy asked, "When's your internship over?"

"It's two weeks," Nikki said. "So, three days."

He nodded and looked at the girl. "What's your name?"

"Reagan."

"Reagan, would you like to stay longer? We'll pay you."

"Yes, Chief. I'd love that."

"Good. Answer this for me, please. If this was his opening move, we need to think two moves ahead. What's our counterplay before he strikes again?"

"Do you mean as detectives? I'm not really qualified to answer that."

"No, I mean in chess."

"Right. Okay, in chess, if you want to stay ahead, you take the center of the board early."

"That means we stop reacting and start forcing him to respond to us." Bishop said. He scratched his chin. "Look at the timing and the details. For starters, the photo didn't go to the department. It came for Rachel. But he left the body at my home. My personal space. Is he inviting me to play or is this specifically about Rachel?"

"I think he's already positioning his pieces to limit your options. You'll have to change your positioning to avoid getting cornered."

Bishop cleared his throat. "Are you saying I'm a pawn in his game now?"

"I'm majoring in forensics, not psychology, sir, but I do know chess, and I don't think you're a pawn, at least for now."

He shook his head. "I should have played chess more."

"Also," Reagan said, "there are multiple pawns, so it's possible the victim wasn't the first. Maybe she's what makes the rest of the game possible. When playing the game, you have to meet certain conditions before you can castle. Maybe her murder is the condition?"

"Jesus," Michels muttered. "This is well above my skill level."

"I pick the best interns," Nikki said with a smile.

Reagan said, "In some variations, pawns trap queens as bait."

Everyone looked at me again.

"Well," I said, forcing a dry laugh. "It's nice that someone finally thinks I'm a queen."

Michels jotted down notes quickly, nodding as he followed Jimmy toward the door. Levy lingered momentarily, eyes narrowed in thought, before joining them.

"I have an idea." Bishop touched my shoulder briefly. "Let's get on this."

"Wait," Michels said before they left. "Who's telling the husband?"

"You two," Jimmy said. He pointed to Reagan and said, "Nice work, intern," and left.

It hit me then: we'd fallen into the trap. Instead of investigating a murder on our terms, following our specialized training, we had begun to play the killer's game. We had talked of moves, sacrifices, and targets on a board. Unwittingly, we'd stepped onto the chessboard he'd set for us.

9

Bishop called Cathy on the way to his house. He had to, though it took a forceful convincing on my part. I promised him I'd make the call if he didn't. She'd eventually find out, and as a woman, I knew it would be better if she heard it from him, not a friend or the news.

He finally agreed. To be safe, he put the call on speaker. I smiled. Partners were backup for more than official calls.

Cathy's tone turned from happy to disbelief. "You found what?"

I spoke in Bishop's place, trying to divert her attention away from where the killer left the body to what else mattered. "Cathy, it's Rachel. The killer also left a note saying I'm next."

"Rachel," she said with a panicked tone. "I'm coming home. It's not right for me to be on the beach when y'all are dealing with this."

"No," I said. "It's better if you keep your distance. Bishop's my partner. I don't want you to be in the wrong place at the wrong time."

"She's right, sweetheart," Bishop said. "Don't come home. I'll pay for the additional days at the condo. Let your friends know."

"They'll love that," she said. "But I think I should be there for you."

"No," he said. "It's too close to home. I didn't marry you to put you in harm's way."

I chuckled because, of course, he didn't marry her for that. It just came with the job.

He finished convincing her to stay at the rental as he pulled into Providence Park. Last year, the senior center had pushed for metal picnic tables in the open space near the fishing pond. Their regulars wanted a serene environment to play chess instead of inside the stuffy building. The City Council approved it with a unanimous vote, and a month later, the competition began.

Patrol had been called out multiple times for disagreements between players. One time, it was because of Mr. Haggarty, a grumpy older man who had a habit of dining and whining, as the staff at Duke's said. Based on his chess complaints, the whining extended beyond just dining.

I pointed to the four tables of players. "You don't really think one of these guys murdered and stuffed Jennifer Abbott into a suitcase, do you?"

"Anything's possible, but we're not here to question them. We're here to interview them."

"And the difference is?"

He smiled and said, "Technique," then walked over to Mr. Haggarty. "Hey, Stan." He eyed the chessboard. "You winning this one today?"

"Detective Bishop," Mr. Haggarty said, "all I did was tell him to stick the king where the sun doesn't shine, or I'd do it for him. It wasn't a threat."

Technically, it was, but we didn't go there.

"Not at all," Bishop said with a grin. "We're here to ask a few questions about the people who come here. We've received a report of some unusual sightings and wanted to see if anyone here had anything to share."

"You talkin' about that heavy-set guy with the binoculars that watches the women doing those yoga exercises?" He looked at me. "Don't know how they can contort themselves into those positions. Can you hike your ankle behind your head?"

"I do it every morning after I wake up." I didn't think that was a real yoga pose, but what did I know?

"Strange," he said. "If you ask me, it looks like one of those funny sex positions, but I don't know how any of them keep their balance. Especially with all that pushing and moving around."

It took every ounce of self-control I had not to laugh my ass off.

"Can you describe the man?" Bishop asked.

"Like I said, heavy-set and carryin' binoculars."

"When do the women come for class?" I asked.

"They were here about thirty minutes ago. They'll be back tomorrow. Come every morning like clockwork."

I couldn't wait for that. I figured there was more than one peeper, though without the binoculars.

Mr. Haggarty pointed out where the man usually stood. Bishop took a few photos with his cell phone, but we didn't explore the shrubs too much. I checked for evidence but found nothing. Nikki would perform a detailed search.

"Well," I said as we climbed back into his vehicle. "That was interesting. I don't feel like our guy is heavy set. What about you?"

"What makes you feel like he isn't?"

"The crime speaks to someone with a little muscle as the perp, not a heavy-set guy that breathes hard climbing up a flight of stairs."

"Remember the real Hannibal Lecter? He wasn't small."

"There isn't a real Hannibal Lecter," I said. "Are you talking about Joe Methany?"

"That's the one, and no, he wasn't the inspiration for the movies, but he confessed to killing multiple women and claimed to have butchered and sold their remains as meat sandwiches from a roadside stand. He was close to five hundred pounds."

"An exception to the rule."

Bishop pulled out of the parking lot. "Which is my point exactly. His size made his crimes particularly shocking because people didn't expect him to be so physically capable of such brutality."

"Okay, I'll give you that, but I still don't think the peeper's our guy. It's too easy. Besides, he's there to watch women twist themselves into border-line Kama Sutra positions to get off, not watch wrinkly old men play chess."

"I'll give you that," he said. "We can send another officer to check it out tomorrow. If it looks like it's connected, we'll go with it."

"If not," I said. "It'll be an easy bust for a peeping Tom."

He laughed while I looked at my phone.

"He'll be home tonight, Rachel. Try not to worry. He wouldn't want you distracted, especially now."

I stuffed my phone back into my bag. "I guess."

Bishop turned into the Union restaurant parking lot. "Listen, I don't want to upset you, but I think Kyle's right. Staying on this case isn't safe."

"I know that, but if I'm not involved, who's going to draw out the killer? The note said I'm next. If that's correct, then aren't I better off being with you and surrounded by the department than staying in some boring safe house binge-watching Dexter on Netflix?" I smirked. "Though I've already watched it."

"That's a valid point, but have you considered the fact that it makes everyone else's job harder? We're worried about you, and that's distracting. Let's be honest, partner. Sometimes you break the rules, and if you do that in this investigation, you could put more than just your life on the line."

"Then I won't break any rules."

He laughed. "And I'm a saint."

Levy and Michels met us at the restaurant for lunch. I ordered the Aunt Jo's Sloppy Sandwich, a deliciously borderline-unhealthy ground beef, Velveeta cheese concoction with extra pickles. Levy ordered the same, while Bishop ordered the salmon BLT, and Michels, a salmon quinoa bowl.

Bishop stuck out his bottom lip when he saw our tasty treats. "My arteries are clogging just from looking at those."

"Don't be jealous," Levy said. "We're younger, so we don't have to worry about that yet."

"Your day will come," he said.

"But it hasn't yet." I lifted my sandwich and took a big bite, purposefully letting the sauce cover my mouth. "Gah, this is amazing."

My cell phone vibrated in my pocket. I set down the sloppy joe, wiped my hands, and then pulled it out. The text read, *Sometimes the bishop guards the queen. Sometimes he doesn't.*

I glanced at Bishop.

I didn't tell him it wasn't Kyle. I tapped back a response. *I'm coming for you, asshole. You won't get away with this.*

The response was quick. *Screw you, River. You cheated on me. The tires are the least of what I'll do to you.*

That made no sense. I excused myself and called Bubba.

"Hey Ryder, what's up?"

I explained what had happened. "Is this the killer messing with me?"

"I mean, yeah, it could be, but I doubt it. It's probably spoofing."

"Spoofing?" I tipped my head back and groaned. "I feel like Bishop. Can you explain using old people's words?"

He laughed. "The person who sent you the message used someone else's phone number, but not through their phone. Your response went to the actual owner, who is likely some chick this River cheated on."

"Is it hard to do?"

"Not even a little. Just takes a smartphone and an app."

I blew out a breath. "Which app?"

"I'm not sure. Maybe SpoofCard or Hushed. It could be TextMe, Dington, or even Burner. It's easy to do, but there are other ways too."

"Such as?"

"If it's been done with a burner app, a virtual private network, a dark web tool, or a public Wi-Fi connection, I'm not sure I can find the real number."

"Break it down for me in a way Bishop could understand."

"Spoofing apps hide everything. It's like sending a letter with someone else's return address and dropping it in a mailbox two towns over. The only way to find the sender is to pull records from the app, and that's if they didn't cover their tracks with the VPN or the other stuff I mentioned."

"So, there's no way to trace it."

"If it's a spoofing app, I'll need a subpoena and a warrant for the app's records, but it's still a long shot because I'll have to figure out which app, and that's unlikely."

"But we could get subpoenas for each of them, right?"

"Sure. Want me to call Nowak?"

"Not yet. And Bubba? Let's keep this between us for now, okay?"

"I don't like the sound of that."

"Just give me some time, okay? I'll take care of it. I promise."

I returned to the table and was immediately hit with questions from the team.

"Is he coming home?" Levy asked.

Michels smiled before asking, "Or did you piss him off enough for him to leave for good?"

"Is everything okay?" Bishop asked.

"It wasn't Kyle," I said. "Just a text from someone I needed to talk to."

Bishop raised an eyebrow and looked me in the eyes. I had to look away because I didn't want him to catch me in the lie. At least not then.

"Levy," I asked, changing the subject. "How did Abbott handle the news?"

"Not well," she said. "But we checked the list of places he said he'd gone before we found the body, and verified he was there."

Bishop watched me carefully. "And during the estimated time of death?" Bishop asked.

"He claims he was at his house waiting for his wife to call."

"Can anyone verify that?"

Michels said, "Nope. Convenient, huh?"

"We need to interview their friends, his work associates, the neighbors, anyone that might have heard or seen something," I said. "I want you two on that, and I'd like to interview him."

"We've done that," Michels said.

"I know, but I'm not part of that we."

"We'll go there now," Bishop said. "If he's innocent, then he'll be more willing to talk because it's all raw. If he's guilty, hopefully we'll catch him in a lie."

"No," I said. "I need you to go deeper into the Abbotts' finances. We checked for activity, but not any purchasing or spending patterns. We also need a thorough analysis of her cell phone. Levy said it before. We haven't confirmed whether she had any accounts Ray didn't know about. I want a full sweep of her personal emails and financial records, for work as well, or anything hidden or under a different name. Same for Ray. We're looking for unusual transactions, transfers, prep for a disappearance, even though we found her body. And I need those results yesterday. Same with her phone and email records. Get on that with Bubba."

"We've already got that in the works," Bishop said.

"Dig deeper, please. Oh, I also want the two of you to expand the search of both Jennifer and Ray Abbott's online presence, including less common social media sites, forums, or online communities that might reveal hidden interests, connections, or conflicts."

"Bubba already did that," Levy said.

I had forgotten. All that mattered was my getting to Abbott's place to interview him and letting the killer see me alone. "Right. My bad."

Bishop narrowed his eyes at me. The last thing he wanted was to separate, and he knew why I wanted it. Because I wanted the killer to consider me vulnerable, even though I wasn't.

If Levy and Michels saw the fight brewing in Bishop's eyes, they didn't say a thing.

He had asked two officers to check print shops, including UPS stores, for anyone printing unusual photos of scenes like the photo we received. They called with an update.

"Detective Bishop, this is Officer Jeffers with an update on the print shops. Officer Maynor and I have contacted multiple locations in a one-hundred-mile radius, and none of them reported any inappropriate pictures that coordinate with your investigation. We did, however, find a shop that had considered reporting a customer for photos of children and are moving forward with an investigation along with the Georgia Bureau of Investigation."

Bishop nodded. "Good work, Jeffers. Please tell Officer Maynor the same."

"Will do, sir. Thank you."

Bishop ended the call. "So, our perp is printing from home."

"Or work," I said, "which would be risky, but that only decreases our chance of finding the printer."

"Correct." He pulled into the department's employee lot. "Are you sure you want to separate?"

"Yes."

"It's not a good idea."

"We have a potential serial killer on our hands. We need everyone on assignments right now. The chief made me lead, and that's what I'm doing."

He laughed, but not one that meant I was funny. One that made it clear he thought I was an idiot. "I'd like it on record that I oppose this strategy one hundred percent."

"Noted." I opened his vehicle door. "We'll meet back here when we're done."

"Ryder," he said as I climbed out.

I turned around. "I'll be careful. Promise."

10

Friends had gathered at the Abbott home, which, as law enforcement, frustrated me. Kicking them out looked bad, but I needed Abbott alone. Having his friends there to defend him muddied the waters.

The front door stood wide open. Not in welcome, but chaos. News of Abbott's death had traveled fast, though I would have expected nothing different.

Jennifer Abbott's friends, family, and neighbors packed the living room. I vaguely recognized someone from the hardware store, and a woman in fleece pajama pants clutching a coffee mug, who—if I was right—had once been a regular at Duke's.

Ray Abbott stood by the fireplace, one hand in his pocket, the other wrapped around a half-full rocks glass. The amber liquid barely moved. He wasn't drinking it, just holding it. His grip looked deliberate, controlled, as if the glass gave him a reason not to wring his hands or punch a wall. Some people responded to the death of a loved one with anger, but something felt off about Abbott's response.

His posture stayed too upright for a grieving husband. His shoulders were square, and his chin lifted slightly as if he observed and judged, not mourned.

There were no bags under his eyes, no swelling, no trace of redness. His face remained composed, untouched by grief or fatigue. Which seemed the opposite of how he had acted prior to learning of her death. His skin looked rested, his expression unmarked from tension in the jaw or tightness around the eyes. His eyes didn't shine with held-back tears or brim with the exhaustion that came from crying. They scanned the room like a man checking for exits.

I didn't sense mourning from him. I sensed anger, and I understood it, having reacted that way after Tommy's murder. Even so, something struck me wrong with Abbott.

I watched him and the people there for almost thirty minutes to note reactions. He nodded at people without warmth and said thank you when someone offered condolences, but he never touched anyone's arm or leaned into a hug. He didn't fidget. He didn't tremble. He didn't even blink too often. He just watched. Detached. Controlled. Measured.

If he was in mourning, he hid it well.

I had seen enough. I needed to get down to business. I held up my badge and whistled. "Hamby PD. I need everyone who doesn't live here to exit through the front door now, please."

Nobody moved.

I made another kind effort, but it would be my last. "I wasn't kidding, people. I need you out now. Take your casserole and your commentary and go."

That did it. Some shuffled toward the door while muttering under their breath. I didn't care. It wasn't a memorial. It was a murder investigation.

Abbott stepped forward. "Detective Ryder, they're just trying to support me."

"I understand, but we're investigating your wife's murder, Mr. Abbott. You need resolution and justice more than support right now, and I need answers to my questions to find her killer."

He didn't argue; instead, he waved an arm and repeated the order with less force than I'd used. The rest filed out like a herd of cattle. One man slapped Ray's shoulder on the way out and whispered something. Ray nodded. I made a mental note of him just in case.

I took a long look at the room when the door finally clicked shut. I saw nothing obviously disturbed. Noted the few photo frames on the mantel, though none of them appeared recent. I also noticed most didn't include them as a couple.

Ray hovered near the couch. He'd set down his drink and stuffed his hands in his pockets. He offered me no invitation to sit, but I didn't need one.

His jaw clenched. "Do we really have to do this now? I've already told the officers everything I know."

"We do," I said, taking out my recorder and setting it on the coffee table. "We're doing everything we can to find your wife's killer, Mr. Abbott, but to do that, we need our questions answered."

"You think I did it."

"As I believe we mentioned before, we have to look at the spouse first, and with a trained eye. Too many murders are committed by a spouse or close family member."

"So, this is a guilty until proven innocent thing." He snickered. "I thought it was supposed to be the other way around."

"It's my job to find and catch a killer, not to make you feel warm and fuzzy."

"I didn't kill my wife."

"Good to know. Now, let's start from the top." I flipped open my notebook. "Some of these questions will be repeats from before, but it's necessary."

He finally sat. "Do I need a lawyer?"

"This is an interview, Mr. Abbott. You're not being charged with any crime."

"That doesn't answer my question."

"Getting an attorney is entirely up to you, Mr. Abbott. You're not under arrest, and we're at your home. I didn't request for you to come to the station, nor am I taking you there. This is just an interview to gather information. But if you're unsure, you have every right to speak to an attorney."

He spoke through tightened lips. "I'll hold off for now."

"Understood. Okay, when was the last time you saw your wife? Be specific. What time, what she was wearing, what she said. Walk me through it."

"As I said before, she had been missing for two days when I contacted you. She had the conference in Atlanta," he said as his eyes fixed over me toward the front door. "Around seven-thirty."

"What was she wearing?"

"I don't remember every detail."

I snapped my eyes to his. "Your wife leaves for a conference and then disappears, and you don't remember what she wore?"

"A blazer? Pants, I think? She always dressed nicely. Clothing isn't something men notice. I think that's more of a woman thing."

Convenient. I let it hang.

"You said she was heading to a conference," I said. "Did she give you any information? Location, company sponsoring it, hotel?"

"Do you think my answers are going to change?"

"It's important to ask them again, Mr. Abbott, and we may do it multiple times."

"Her company sent her. She said it was downtown. I didn't ask more."

"You didn't ask where she'd be staying?"

He shook his head. "I trust my wife, but we share our locations. I didn't need her to tell me."

"So she could come and go as she pleased, without you worrying about where she went?"

He nodded. "Again, I trust my wife."

"That's funny," I said. "Her friends say you didn't like it when she went out. That you got anxious if you couldn't get in touch with her."

His gaze twitched. "I just worry, that's all. The world isn't safe, and I think her death proves it."

"Right. But not knowing which hotel she was in didn't bother you?"

"I didn't want to be overbearing."

I nodded slowly. "You reported her missing after how long?"

"Two days."

I still couldn't understand why he had waited so long. "Her phone was off. She wasn't answering. Why did you wait that long?"

He looked me in the eye. "Contrary to what her friends said, I don't obsess about my wife or track her every move. I'm not that kind of husband."

"Had she ever done that before?"

"Done what?"

"Turned off her phone and not contacted you."

"If she had, I didn't notice." He swallowed. "I didn't think I would have to explain myself for trying not to jump to conclusions."

"Actually, you do." I paused. "Let's go over your whereabouts during that time. From the morning she left until you filed the report. Walk me through it, hour by hour."

His voice dropped into something he probably thought sounded steady. "I already provided this information to the other detectives."

"Understood, but I wasn't there, and I'm the lead on this, so I'd appreciate you repeating them for me."

"I went to the gym that morning. After that, I walked the dog. I showered. Had three Zoom meetings. I went to Chick-fil-A for lunch and ran a few errands while eating it."

"What errands?"

"Got my oil changed and dropped off my dry cleaning. I came home and didn't go out again. The next morning, I went for a run with the dog and worked from home again. My work associates confirmed that I had multiple Zoom calls."

"What are the names of the places?"

"Hamby Athletic Club. Mavis. I'm not sure about the dry cleaners. It just says cleaners on the sign."

"What about during the timeframe of her murder?"

"I'm not exactly sure when that was, but I had been out searching the area, which your team can verify, and then I stayed home at their urging in case she or someone else called."

"Did anyone stay with you?"

"No. I wanted to be alone."

"Got it," I said. I tried not to sound judgmental, but in my experience, those who gave home-alone alibis were usually hiding something.

He must have sensed my BS meter going off because his nostrils flared.

"Let's talk about your marriage. You told officers you two don't fight, and that everything was good."

"It was."

"Yet Jennifer's friends tell a different story."

"Her friends never liked me."

"Marissa said Jennifer felt like she had to walk on eggshells. Said she looked tired. Started canceling plans. Wore what you liked to avoid conflict."

"I would never hurt her," he said. "She wanted our marriage to be transparent. She did things that made me happy, and I did the same for her. People, especially her friends, didn't understand that. She told me that all the time. I wrote it off as jealousy, which made them not like me."

"Did she ever say she wanted to leave?"

"No."

"Did you?"

His mouth opened, then shut. "No."

I took out the photo of the woman in the hotel robe, throat slashed, posed like a goddamn message.

"We showed you this before. You said it wasn't Jennifer."

"It's not."

"Do you know the woman?"

"Her face is blurred. How can I say if I know her?"

"Is there anyone from your past or your wife's who had issues with either of you?"

"I don't know anyone, but that doesn't mean there aren't people like that."

"Do you play chess?"

"What? Why would you ask that?"

"Please, just answer the question, Mr. Abbott."

"Yeah, I mean, I have. A little."

"Then you know a pawn's role. Can you explain it to me?"

"What does that have to do with Jennifer's murder?"

"Can you answer the question?"

"It's meant to protect the king, to die for him." His eyes stayed fixed on the coffee table. "I don't understand why you're asking me these questions." Finally, his eyes reddened. "I didn't kill her. I didn't kill my wife."

"It's funny that you keep saying that even though I've never asked." I let that sink in. Then I shifted gears. "Jennifer had a work laptop, a personal laptop, her phone, and a tablet. We'll need them."

"I don't know where her work laptop is."

"You're sure it's not in the house?"

"I haven't seen it."

"And her passwords?"

"I don't know those."

I checked my notes again. "Jennifer had her own bank accounts?"

"We have several accounts together. She has credit cards I'm not on, as I do with her."

"Any individual bank accounts?"

"I don't have any without her, but she might have some. I'm not sure."

"You weren't sure about her hotel. You're not sure about her finances. You didn't know where she was. But you're certain you didn't kill her."

He stared me down.

I flipped to the last page in my notebook. "We're going to need you to take a polygraph sooner rather than later."

His jaw twitched. "I thought those weren't admissible."

"They're still useful. Unless you're worried about how you'll do."

He hesitated. "I'm not refusing."

"Good. Because right now, your timeline doesn't hold, your alibi doesn't exist, and your wife's last weeks paint a picture of someone afraid to come home."

"I loved her."

"Then help me find who didn't. Let us prove it wasn't you."

———

I pulled out of Abbott's driveway and turned toward Hawthorne Ridge, the old two-lane that cut through Hamby's quiet backcountry. My Jeep's tires crunched along the gravel edge before I eased onto the worn blacktop. I kept the radio low, though that didn't quiet the thoughts rolling through my head. Abbott's voice still hung in the air, calm to the point of wrong. For a man whose wife had just been zipped into a body bag, his voice was too measured and too controlled.

Trees lined both sides of the road, mostly with thick trunks but all pressed close to the shoulder. I loved the area and took the specific route for a reason. If the killer had told the truth, if I was next, I wouldn't be alone.

Bishop must have only partially believed the note with the body.

Rachel's next.

Because if he had, he would have glued himself to me with the strongest stuff available. Though it was possible he had followed me as well. My partner could have won a stalker of the year award for his following-without-detection skills. I glanced in my rearview mirror, but I was alone on the road.

I reached the four-way near Fox Run. The light blinked yellow, so I tapped the brakes. A glance in the rearview mirror again froze my fingers on the steering wheel.

A black car sat two lengths behind me. No movement. No flash of a turn signal. Tinted windows. Glossy finish. New. Maybe an Audi, maybe something higher end. It could've belonged to anyone, but it didn't. I knew that deep in my soul.

"Game on, buddy," I said. "Make your move."

The light changed. I rolled forward. So did the car. I turned left, and I took the long way to the department. I passed Hartman's feed store and the closed peach stand. The car trailed behind. Not tailgating. Not pushing. Just back there. Too smooth. Too deliberate. "That's three turns now." I looked in the mirror again. "You lost, buddy, or are you going to play your piece?"

I passed Cedar Hollow, then dropped onto Watson Hill Road and admired the ranches, thinking back to Sean's murder and how things had changed so much for his sister, selling the ranch, selling her animals, and moving out of state. Sean's murder changed Hamby for her, and even though we had caught his killer, she couldn't stay.

I understood. I had left Chicago partly for the same reason.

I checked in the mirror again. The car kept its distance but made no move to hide from me. He wanted me to know. Wanted me to see him. He wanted to deliver a message, that he was watching me.

The road dipped into a curve. I took it without touching the brakes, then swung onto Willow Trace. A buck darted across the road ahead, but I didn't flinch. The car behind me slowed. Never stopped. Never turned.

I tightened my grip on the wheel.

"Okay," I muttered, low. "You wanna dance, let's go."

I crossed into a cul-de-sac, spun a quick loop, and waited just long enough for the tires to squeal before pointing back toward the main road. The black car didn't follow. For a second, I thought I'd been wrong, but then it eased around the corner behind me.

I took my time. Speeding showed fear, or guilt, or panic. I turned again, then again.

The road narrowed. I swung right onto Crawford Lane because it was barely wide enough for two cars. Ditches filled with water and mud ran on either side. If he wanted to pass me or try to run me off the road, he'd end up stuck in the mud.

The car never lost its place behind me. No swerving. No mistakes. I gritted my teeth.

I pressed harder on the gas and headed back to the station, finally turning onto Municipal Drive. I thought I'd lose him, but he kept on me.

I slowed and turned into the employee lot and waited. "Your move, big guy."

The car reached the entrance and then drifted past without hesitation.

"Chicken."

Jimmy barreled through the investigation room door. "Update me." He sat at the head of the table. "I need to brief the mayor in fifteen minutes."

Michels and Levy spoke first.

"We interviewed the Abbotts' neighbors," Levy said. "They don't live in one of the mini-mansion communities, so no one has security cameras, but they have doorbell cameras."

"Which got us nothing," Michels added. "None are next to or across from the Abbott home."

"No one's seen any abnormal behavior from either of them. No loud fighting or scenes in the yard," Levy continued. "Jennifer played Bunco for a while but stopped about six months ago."

"Why?" I asked.

"She didn't give a reason, just stopped showing up."

"We talked to Marissa Leverton. Her story stands. The wife hasn't been happy for a while. Said Abbott's controlling and jealous."

Jimmy tapped his pencil eraser on the table. "Does she think Mrs. Abbott was having an affair?"

"She does not," Levy said. "Work associates say the same thing."

Michels leaned back in his chair and clasped his hands behind his head. "Looks like the perfect relationship the husband thinks they have ain't so perfect after all."

Bishop nodded. "They never are."

"Everything's clear on my end," Bishop said. "Though I wasn't necessary for the job. Bubba worked his magic and found nothing unusual."

Susan carefully opened the door. "Chief Abernathy, do you have a minute?"

"Not really, Susan. What's up?"

"An envelope just arrived for Detective Ryder."

The room fell silent. She moved to hand it to me. "Give it to Jimmy," I said.

He opened it, studied what was inside, and said, "Damn it. We're getting another one."

"Chief," Susan said, "I believe we already have. There's a suitcase at Fowler Park."

"What's in the photo?" Michels asked.

As if we didn't already know.

"A man. Same setup."

My stomach clenched as an icy knot formed deep within my gut. Fowler Park. A public space. My mind immediately connected the location to the previous photo, Jennifer Abbott, and the chilling note that landed on Bishop's porch: *Rachel's next*. This felt like a direct response to my press conference, to my challenge, to my audacity in believing I could dictate the terms. He wanted to prove his control.

"Well," I said in an obviously sarcastic tone. "Told you I wasn't in danger."

Jimmy narrowed his eyes at me. "Not funny, Detective."

He passed the photo to Bishop, who then passed it to me. We all studied it carefully.

"Any idea what's in the suitcase?" Bishop asked, though I suspected he already knew the answer. Bad news always arrived with a specific, clipped tone, and a lack of extraneous detail, and Susan had nailed the delivery.

"The kids didn't open it," she said. "Thank God for emergency training for active shooters, though I hate having to say that. They knew to leave it and told their parents, who saw the red liquid on the ground and called it in."

"Blood?" Levy wasn't asking. It was more of a surprise. The killer cleaned Jennifer Abbott. We found no blood at her crime scene.

Susan shook her head. "The officer on scene says it's paint."

"Let's go," I said. "I'm taking my Jeep."

"I'll go with you," Bishop said.

"No. If we're going to catch this asshole, we need me to be the bait. We can't afford another body. He wants me. Let's give him what he wants." I stormed out before anyone could push back, hurried to the parking lot, and jumped into the Jeep. I slammed my hand on the steering wheel as I pressed the button to start the engine. The sharp impact jarred my palm, but I didn't care. I cut a hard turn to back out of the parking spot. The Jeep's engine whined in protest as it strained against the abrupt maneuver, but I pushed it. *Not another one.* The killer played games, and Hamby was his board. He had already announced the next move, and it felt like his definitive declaration.

11

Fowler Park erupted in a chaotic ballet of flashing lights that oddly lit up the afternoon sky. It always happened that way as a response to the negative energy, where the sun would hide behind the clouds in some spiritual mourning process. Blue and red pulsed against the darkening trees, painting the landscape in urgent hues as if things weren't already tragic enough. Uniformed officers had cordoned off a wide perimeter with yellow tape. Their grim expressions reflected the severity of the situation. We all knew it would get worse before it got better. It always happened that way.

Civilians and reporters huddled at the edges of the tape, their curiosity warring with morbid fascination. How did they get there so fast?

"We just got the call ten minutes ago," I said. "How is it this crowded already?" I pulled the Jeep to the curb and threw it into park. I climbed out and strapped on my belt, then walked over to Bishop who had just exited his patrol unit.

The air tasted like fumes from idling patrol cars.

"This is going to be bad," he said.

"It already is."

We met Jimmy near the yellow tape. "The town's going ballistic." He ran a hand over his head. "The bastard sent a letter to the paper. God knows how many people have already corrupted the scene."

Bishop's face reddened. "Son of a bitch."

Jimmy already had the letter bagged and tagged. He called for the officer he had given it to. The officer handed it to him.

Jimmy read it out loud.

To My Dearest Opponent: The first move was only to get your attention. This second proves the game has begun. You cannot stop what is already in motion. Each piece falls where I place it, and each body will remind you that control is mine. Watch closely. The next one you will not be able to ignore. Fowler Park. Look for a gray, weathered suitcase.

"Perfect." I pinched the bridge of my nose. "Now the whole damn town gets a front-row seat. Exactly what he wanted."

Bishop scanned the area. "He wanted the media eating out of his hand and they are."

Michels and Levy stood on his other side, their shoulders set and their expressions mirroring ours.

"Thank God," Jimmy said as Nikki's department van squealed to a stop just behind Bishop's patrol unit. She exited the vehicle, her ponytail swinging with an abrupt movement like a flurry of controlled energy. "Gear up!" she yelled at her interns. Her voice, usually calm and precise, held a sharp, urgent edge. She understood the seriousness of the discovery. It was not just a body; it was a message.

I moved to Jimmy's side, my gaze fixed on the center of the secured area, bypassing the clusters of officers and the general chaos. A large gray suitcase rested on the damp grass with its lid gaping open. The color and size mirrored the one left on Bishop's porch, like a chilling and identical reproduction. The same brand suitcase. Same color, same size, same intent. The killer had a signature, and that was it. "He's escalating." My voice fell flat, and the words felt heavy on my tongue. "No note this time. Just the body."

"He didn't need a note," Jimmy said through a clenched jaw. His eyes narrowed. "He already informed the media."

"He wants notoriety," Michels said.

He did, and we would give it to him. There were two ways to catch a killer. Mess with him and piss him off so he makes a mistake or make him look invincible, so he'll try to brag. We would make him look invincible.

Nikki and her interns, all fully gloved and gowned in their protective white suits, approached the suitcase. The lead intern held a camera and had already been snapping shots with practiced efficiency. They moved with silent, almost ritualistic precision, documenting every detail of the scene. Nikki had trained them well, taking every single movement seriously.

She crouched beside the suitcase with her head tilted, observing its contents with a professional detachment that belied the horror of the situation. I couldn't. I needed to get it together, but all I could do was imagine what it took to position the body, and that image in my head featured me.

Bishop gently knocked me with his shoulder. "You okay?"

I nodded. When I finally spoke, I said, "We need to bring this son of a bitch down. No one's getting stuffed into another suitcase."

"Especially you."

"Male victim," Nikki said, her voice low, barely a rough rasp. "Same white robe. Slit throat. It's all the same other than the sex."

My breath hitched. An icy dread seeped into my bones with the connection solidified, as if I hadn't known what we'd find.

First the woman, Jennifer Abbott, and then the man, John Doe. The killer replicated his method, flaunted his confidence, his meticulous, disturbing artistry. It wasn't just a murder; it was a taunt.

Nikki gave a soft command to her intern to lean in. She did as instructed and snapped close-up photos. I watched, my eyes tracing the details I already knew existed, but saw now in stark reality. The folds of the white robe, pristine and unblemished, contrasted against the internal lining of the suitcase. The careful placement of the body, posed almost reverently. The clean surgical slit across the throat, a precise, clinical line that almost defied the violence it represented. No blood stained the robe, no messy splatters marred the suitcase. The killer cleaned his victims, showing us, with no bragging, his chilling display of control.

"He cleans them," I muttered, mostly to myself, the words barely audible above the noise of the scene. "Like a trophy."

Michels ran a hand through his hair. "Sick bastard."

Nikki straightened slightly, her voice cutting through the quiet muttering of the lights and distant sirens with professional clarity. "Chief, Detective. We found it."

"A black pawn?" I asked.

"No. This time it's white."

My gaze snapped to her. A white pawn. Jennifer Abbott, the previous victim, had the black pawn.. The killer's game continued as he shifted the pieces on his board. What did the white pawn mean? The team's past comments about pawns being strategic, sacrificial first pieces, ran through my mind. Reagan, the intern, called them bait for queens. A cold ripple traced my spine. *Bait for queens.*

Me. I was the queen. The killer targeted me. The previous note, *Rachel's next*, proved it. The absence of a note on the current suitcase simply meant he believed the message had already been delivered.

"Document its exact location before you touch it," I said. "Please. And photograph it from every angle."

She nodded, already directing her intern, who carefully moved around the innocuous piece of plastic nestled beside the victim. The camera clicked, capturing the tiny piece in a deadly game.

Barron arrived, his usual grumpy demeanor in full force. He limped up the driveway, a clipboard clutched in one hand. "We need to catch this one pronto," he grumbled, though his eyes, dark and sharp, took in the scene with professional focus. Nikki moved to give him room as he crouched beside the suitcase.

He began his preliminary on-scene examination. His gloved hands moved with a delicate precision that belied his gruff exterior. He checked for obvious wounds beyond the throat slit, for ligature marks, for any signs of struggle. "No obvious trauma," he announced, his voice muffled by the circumstances. "Clean cut. And he's posed like the other. Body folded like origami, hands crossed over his chest, eyes closed."

The description sent a fresh shiver through me. As he said, Abbott's body was also folded like origami, with her hands crossed and eyes closed. This killer possessed a meticulous, disturbing artistry.

"Time of death, Doc?" Bishop asked, his voice tight.

Barron checked for remaining core heat, for rigor mortis, for lividity, with a methodical touch. "Rough guess? At least twelve to eighteen hours. Still some core heat. The killer didn't dump him immediately after death. Killed elsewhere, then moved." He paused, as if completing his thought before speaking. "As I've said, manipulating a body after rigor mortis sets in is difficult. Possible, but difficult. It requires force and usually leaves signs like ligament tears or bone fractures. I'm confident none of those are present. We'll know more at autopsy, but a clean body, posed like this, suggests a controlled environment. Not a struggle."

"He killed him, then refrigerated him," Levy deduced, her brow furrowed. "Or held him captive beforehand."

"Or moved him after rigor mortis set in, then cleaned him," Michels added. "Difficult, but possible."

Nikki's team worked with impressive focus around the suitcase. They prepared to bag the body, the white robe, and the suitcase separately. Each item would undergo further forensic analysis at the lab. "We'll search for trace evidence," she said, though her tone held little hope. "Fibers, hairs, pollen. But like before, and given how clean the scene is, I don't expect much. He wore nitrile-based latex gloves, I'm sure." She had found traces of them on the envelope for the first photo.

"The precision of the throat slit," I mused, the thought forming in my mind. "Nikki, you suggested with Abbott that the killer might be a chef. Does this cut look similar?"

"A surgeon's precision," she confirmed, a professional assessment replacing any personal revulsion. "Same clean line, so our perp could be a chef or a surgeon."

My mind spun as it tried to grasp the killer's full message. He was not improvising. He calculated every move. He played a game, and he set the rules. It was a challenge, a calling card. His signature. And that signature reeked of confidence.

"The white pawn," Levy reiterated, turning the piece over in her mind. "Michels, if the black pawn started the game, what does this one signify?"

"The same as the other," he said. "It's a strategical sacrifice, just by the other player."

"And Reagan said they clear the way for bigger moves. Or are bait for queens," I said.

The thought hung in the air, thick with unspoken implications we all understood as veiled threats. *Bait for queens.*

"He's taunting us," Bishop said, his voice rough. "Taunting you."

My jaw tightened. "He wants attention. Fear. The satisfaction of thinking he's in control."

The black car from the previous night flashed in my mind. The tinted windows, the matte finish, no license plate. He had been watching me, had likely followed me to Bishop's house. He had been watching again today, a dark silhouette against the waning light. He knew my habits. He knew I would chase.

"Bubba needs to run the pawn through VICAP and local databases again," I instructed, pulling out my phone. "And Interpol. Same as the first one."

"Bubba also needs to identify this victim," Jimmy said. His voice regained some of its usual authority and cut through the morbid silence. "Facial recognition, DMV, passport databases, social media scraping. Everything."

"He'll prioritize it," I promised.

Barron finished his on-scene assessment. "Ready for transport when you are, Nikki."

Nikki's interns moved swiftly, preparing the gurney and the body carefully for transport. As usual, a young woman from Nikki's team gagged behind her mask and ran off to throw up behind a tree.

She secured the body bag. The sound of the zipper sliced through the evening air, and for a second, everything went still.

Levy crossed her arms. "This is psychological warfare. He's doing this to mess with us, with Rachel."

"He's confident," Michels added. "Too confident."

I stared at the closed suitcase, the male victim removed and covered on the gurney. He was not Jennifer Abbott. He was a shift in the game, a change in the killer's strategy. A male. A white pawn. The rules changed, but the game continued.

Barron cleared his throat and said, "Y'all need to catch this bastard."

"We're on it," Michels said.

The hunt was on. And we would not lose. We couldn't afford to.

12

I called Kyle, but it went straight to voice mail. Annoyed, I tossed my phone onto the locker room bench. "What are we? Fifteen?"

Levy tied her boot. "Still haven't heard from him?"

"It makes no sense. You should talk when you don't agree on something. If he's not capable, then we have no future." God, I hated being a girl. I didn't need the distraction of emotions.

"Maybe he's busy."

I pulled my hair back and smoothed the sides with the palms of my hands to keep the fly-aways in place. "I'm in the middle of a murder investigation where the killer wants me dead. You'd think he'd be worried."

"He is, Rachel. You've struggled with his work. Is it any different for him to struggle with yours?"

I dropped onto the bench. "This emotional outburst isn't looking for rational reasoning, Levy."

She laughed. "It never is."

I sent him a text. *If you haven't heard, we have another victim, and it's not me. Don't be like this.*

"He's processing. Just give him—"

A knock on the locker room door interrupted her.

"It's open," I said. "And we're dressed."

Bishop opened the door and peeked inside. "Ryder, you're needed in your office."

I exhaled. "I'll be right there."

It had been a long day. Prior to Jennifer Abbott's murder, I had made plans for a girl's only dinner with Savannah, Nikki, Ashley, and Levy, or Lauren, as I referred to her by her first name off hours. Savannah needed those nights as much as the rest of us, if not more. Kids exhausted moms, even the most adorable ones. I figured she'd brought dinner to us, but she hadn't asked for Levy, so I wasn't sure.

I carried my notes from the second crime scene and reviewed them as I walked into my office and bumped straight into Kyle. It hadn't even been twenty-four hours, but I threw myself at him and wrapped my arms around him. "You're an asshole."

"I am, and I love you too."

I broke loose and let his presence sink in. After staring at him for a good two minutes, I finally said, "What the hell kind of middle school behavior was that?"

He glanced at my pocket, where I kept my cell. "It wasn't middle-school behavior. Check your phone."

"I've checked it multiple times. You should have called."

"Rachel, pull up your voicemail and look at it."

I realized he knew something I didn't, and that I would likely be the one wrong about things. I checked my voicemail and saw a few unknown numbers, but nothing from him. I shoved my phone at him. "See? Nothing." He snatched my phone from me and tapped the screen. His voice came through the phone. "Rach, it's me. I came to work and dropped my phone into the toilet. Call me back at this number. I'm sorry. I love you, and I'm an idiot."

I bit my bottom lip, said, "Oh," then shook my head. "It's been a day. You had plenty of time to get a new phone, or you could have come to the office or texted me."

"I didn't think a text message was appropriate given this was basically our first fight, and I couldn't get to Verizon because we had a Hansen Jenks sighting, and we needed to move on it. This is the first chance I've had to do anything, and I came straight here."

Well, hell. I had a hundred responses, all of which showed a mushy, emotional side of me that, if they had been there, would send my team into a laughing fit. Instead, I simply asked, "Did you get him?"

He nodded, then took two steps toward me and pulled me into his arms for a long kiss, which was quickly interrupted by Jimmy clearing his throat at my door.

"Ryder, we need you in the investigation room." He smiled at Kyle. "Don't let her get hurt," Kyle said.

Jimmy nodded. "I'll do my best, my friend."

I smiled up at Kyle. "Get a phone."

"Going now then heading back to work. I'll be late tonight, but I want updates, and don't do anything dangerous." He shook his head and walked out before I could argue that.

I practically skipped into the investigation room but caught myself and realized I looked like a complete idiot.

Bishop smiled. "Feel better?"

"I do."

"That's too bad. You're so much more efficient when you're freaking out about something you can't control."

I punched him lightly on the shoulder. "You're such a jerk."

"But I'm right."

***

The phantom scent of death in the room clung to us like cheap perfume. The reality of the situation had settled in, cold and hard, just like the smell. Murder investigations, though different each time, had that in common.

Jimmy looked as if someone had pushed him off a ledge. His sharp eyes carried a deep, unshakeable weariness, one created by a serial killer and the fear of an insane mayor waiting to bring in a new chief. He slammed the investigation room door shut. "Alright, everyone, update me. I'm going for we-have-the-killer vibe, if you need a push." He walked to the head of the table and stayed upright with hands braced on the polished steel.

Michels spoke first. "Fowler Park's secured, Chief. Nikki's team bagged and tagged everything we could find."

"I know all this. I was there, remember?" The stress in his voice came out as anger. "We've got a male victim, approximate age thirty to forty, white. Found him stuffed in a suitcase, the same gray, weather-worn model as the first one." He ran his hand over his head. "Tell me what I don't know."

"We've confirmed the robe has the same embroidery pattern as the Echelon Hotel robe found on Jennifer Abbott," Bishop said. "As we expected, the throat slit is identical. Surgical precision. Again, the killer did not leave any blood at the scene; this implies he killed the victim elsewhere, cleaned the body, and then transported it."

Levy, who had been typing on her tablet, looked up. "The pawn is white, but you know that too."

A collective sigh filled the room. Reagan's earlier words, *pawns clear the way for bigger moves*' and *'bait for queens,'* rang in my ears. The connection between the two victims wasn't a copycat. We had given no specific details to the press, so the murder solidified into a cold, hard fact. My stomach clenched. The killer wasn't just taunting us; he was escalating.

Susan walked in without knocking. "Barron's on the line. He's got the preliminary autopsy results for Jennifer Abbott."

Jimmy nodded. "Thanks, Susan." He clicked on line one on the landline and put it on speaker. "We're all here, Doc. Lay it on us."

Barron grunted. "Right. I estimate the time of death to be somewhere between eighteen and twenty-four hours before they found her on Bishop's porch. Rigor was setting in, but manipulation wasn't impossible without significant damage. Minimal internal trauma. But here's the kicker: the cause of death isn't the throat slit. The killer performed that after she died. Clean cut, though, as you observed. No hesitation marks, no struggle."

A collective intake of breath rippled through the room. My mind raced as it tried to process this new information. Dead *before* the cut?

"Then how did she die?" Michels asked.

"A fentanyl overdose. Likely administered quickly, based on the small needle prick between her hallux and digitus secundus pedis."

"Her what?" Bishop asked.

"Between the first two toes. Though we have also located blistering on the inside of her cheek which points to some type of lozenge or lollipop.

We are running more tests, and Nikki will have more information on that once we've completed our procedure."

"But you've already found fentanyl?" I asked.

"Yes. Labs confirmed traces throughout her system. It incapacitated her, then shut down her organs. If administered through a needle, it would react quickly, but we would see the same, if not a stronger reaction from a lozenge or lollipop."

"I don't think he wants a medal, Doc."

The room erupted in a chorus of muttered expletives.

"Fentanyl," Bishop repeated. His brow furrowed. "So, he drugs them first? Then cuts their throats?"

"Afraid so. At least that's my provisional conclusion for Abbott," Barron confirmed. "The cut was purely symbolic, a flourish. No blood trail, no messy spatter, obviously because her heart wasn't pumping. He wanted to display her, and he did. He posed her, cleaned her, and then slit her throat."

Jimmy slammed his palm onto the table. "And the man from Fowler Park is the same."

"Based on preliminary observations, yes, but we've not yet confirmed or completed the autopsy. But from my preliminary examination, I can say that, as with the first victim, this was a clean cut, no struggle, body posed. I'd bet my last dollar on fentanyl for him too. Just waiting on tox reports to confirm."

"So, the 'surgeon' theory is out," I mused aloud, a new profile of the killer forming in my mind. "He's not a surgeon. He's a poisoner. Someone with access to highly controlled substances, or the knowledge to acquire them."

"And someone who knows how to administer them," Nikki added, stepping forward into the light. She had arrived quietly, dressed in her lab coat, her presence a calming, professional anchor in the chaos. "The precision of the fentanyl dose, the method of administration all point to this not being amateur hour. It suggests someone with medical or pharmaceutical knowledge, or someone who's done their homework."

"I agree with Nikki," Barron said.

"So, our killer isn't a chef *or* a surgeon, in the traditional sense," Jimmy summed up, pacing the room. "He's a performance artist with a flair for the macabre, and a pharmacist's touch."

"Or a vet," Michels chimed in. "They deal with controlled substances, too."

"Or someone who just got out of prison after learning how to make illicit fentanyl," Bishop added. "Or knows a guy who can get it."

"Good point," Jimmy said, acknowledging the grim reality. "Alright, Barron, thanks for the update. Get those tox reports expedited for the male victim. We need confirmation of the fentanyl for him, and any other anomalies you find."

"Will do, Chief. Keep me posted on your end. I'm hoping to get some uninterrupted Hallmark time in tonight." Barron's voice crackled, then the line went dead.

"Everything he does is controlled," I said. "The environment, the cleaning of the bodies, the absence of blood."

Jimmy turned to us, his eyes hardened. "He's playing games with us. He kills them with fentanyl, performs the throat slit as a ritual, cleans them, poses them, and then deposits them with a pawn. This is a detailed operation aimed to confuse us." His gaze fixed on me. "And it's aimed specifically at you, Ryder."

Bishop crossed his arms and tightened his jaw. "He's doing all of this for an audience, isn't he? Not just for the kill, but for the recognition, the validation of how clever he thinks he is. He wants us to acknowledge his twisted genius."

My jaw tightened. "Which means we lean into it. He wants to play? We play. But we set the rules now. He wants attention? We give it to him, but on our terms."

"And we include the DEA," Bishop said. "Kyle's knowledge of the illegal drug world will help."

"Agreed," Jimmy said. His eyes scanned the room. "Alright, this is still our top priority. Everything else takes a backseat. More than before. We're operating under the assumption that this killer is watching, calculating, and waiting for our next move. Our priority is to identify our John Doe.

Bubba, you need to dedicate every available resource to this. Facial recognition, DMV, passport databases, social media scraping—the works. But expand your search beyond just those. Check national missing persons databases, cross-reference with all open cases. Look for any unique identifiers Barron might find."

Nikki interrupted with, "Old injuries, unique dental work, tattoos if he has any, even surgical scars or medical implants that might be registered."

"Already on it, Chief." Bubba cleared his throat. "And you, Nikki."

"Nikki," Jimmy continued, turning to our crime scene tech, "I need a comprehensive forensic profile on both victims and their suitcases. Re-examine Jennifer Abbott's body, the suitcase, and the black pawn, specifically for any trace of fentanyl residue. I want to confirm the method of death with absolute certainty for her, and then cross-reference with our new victim once his tox results are in. For our John Doe, I need everything you can get from that suitcase—the white pawn, the robe, the paint. Fibers, hairs, pollen, latent prints—even if they're partials like the last time, you document every single one. Analyze the red paint—type, brand, any unique chemical composition that could trace it back to a specific source or region. And confirm the latex gloves are still present. This killer is meticulous, but even the most careful leave something."

Nikki nodded, though her expression showed doubt. "Consider it done, Chief. My team will pull an all-nighter if necessary."

"Michels, Levy, you're on victimology and canvassing for both victims. For Jennifer Abbott, revisit everything. Her friends, family, coworkers, neighbors. Now that we know she was likely drugged with fentanyl and dead before the throat slit, we need to ask different questions. Who had access to her? Who might have had access to fentanyl? Any strange encounters, any new people in her life, any medical history that might explain drug use, even recreational? Dive into her financial records again, beyond just looking for unusual transactions. Look for anything that could suggest a secret life, a hidden addiction, or any connection to someone who deals in drugs."

We'd done that already, but our job included a repeat button we hit on the daily. Sometimes on the hour.

"For our John Doe, start from scratch," Jimmy instructed. "Once Bubba gets us an ID, use the same deep dive. Friends, family, work, habits, hangouts. And for both victims, I want comprehensive canvassing of the areas where the suitcases were found, Bishop's cul-de-sac and Fowler Park. Every house, every business, every doorbell camera, every security camera. We need to establish ingress and egress routes for the killer."

"We've done that, Chief," Michels said.

"Do it again."

"We've got patrol officers deployed already," Levy confirmed, "but we'll expand the radius for cameras. And we'll revisit the Abbotts' place with the new information, especially the fentanyl. His reactions before seemed off to me, too composed for a grieving husband."

"Right," Jimmy agreed. "And Bishop, Ryder, your focus, beyond managing the overall investigation, is on the killer's message and motivation. He's leaving us chess pieces. He left a note saying 'Rachel's next' for the first victim, yet he lied. He's toying with us. He's taunting you, Rachel. We need to figure out what game he's playing, why he chose you as his target, and what the pawns signify beyond just being sacrificial pieces."

"Michels has some chess background, and Reagan, Nikki's intern, she's a chess prodigy," I offered, already forming a plan in my mind. "They had some insights earlier about pawns being strategic, sacrificial, and clearing the way for bigger moves. Reagan even suggested they could be bait for queens."

Jimmy's eyes narrowed. "If she's got insights, I want them. We'll put her on a task force dedicated to the chess theme. Michels, you work with her. Research every chess strategy, every historical game, every known variation where pawns play a critical, symbolic role."

Michels looked surprised but nodded. "Yes, Chief."

My jaw tightened. "Jimmy, I'm not going to be a damsel in distress. If he wants me, I'm not hiding. I'm bait. Let's use it." I thought of the black Audi from the previous night, the car that trailed me. Clearly too deliberate, too knowing. I knew he was watching. I wanted him to see me out, active, a visible challenge.

"That's a valid point," Bishop conceded, looking between me and Jimmy. "He wants to play chess, then he needs an opponent on the board. A queen."

"He wants to play chess? Fine." I straightened my shoulders and flexed, then unflexed my fingers. "I'll act as his opposing queen and draw him out." Despite my resolve, a faint unease curled in my stomach at how ready I was to engage on his terms. Was I prepared for it?

Jimmy exhaled. "Alright, but you move with extreme caution. Bishop, you're glued to her. If she goes for coffee, you're ordering the same damn latte. If she drives, you're the shadow she can't see but knows is there."

"Understood, Chief," Bishop said, as a grim smile touched his lips. "Consider me her personal, slightly grumpy, guardian angel."

"And what about the killer's profile beyond the medical/pharmaceutical connection?" I asked, pushing the conversation forward. "The luxury hotel robe, the staging, the clean-up. This suggests someone with means, access, and a bizarre sense of artistry. Not just a common drug dealer or street thug."

"Could be a disgruntled former hotel employee," Levy suggested. "Or someone who travels frequently for work and stays in high-end places. Someone who could blend in."

"Bubba, check for any past incidents involving fentanyl overdose deaths that were initially deemed accidental or suicides, but later had suspicious elements," Jimmy added, his mind seemingly already racing ahead. "Especially in high-end hotels, or where the killer cleaned or posed the body."

"We'll cross-reference traffic camera footage from Hardscrabble to Red Barn, and around Fowler Park for any suspicious vehicles," Jimmy confirmed. "Bubba, you're on that too. Look for patterns, recurring sightings."

Bubba and I made eye contact. We had checked that location before, but for different times and different reasons.

"He's digitally savvy," I added. "He knows how to obscure his tracks. Bubba, you'll need to explore advanced methods for tracing burner apps, VPNs, dark web tools, and public Wi-Fi connections used for communication. It's a long shot, but we need to try."

"I'm also interested in the motive," Bishop stated. "Why Rachel? He's clearly studied her, but why?"

"We've already dug into her old cases, and Tommy's," Jimmy said. "We couldn't find any obvious connections, but now that we know the killer's method, it suggests a new type of enemy. Someone polished. Someone with resources and control."

"And the timing," Levy reminded us. "What triggered this *now*?"

"That's a critical question," Jimmy agreed. "Bubba, once you have an ID for the male victim, check his digital footprint for any connection to Rachel, or to anyone in law enforcement, or anyone from Jennifer Abbott's life that might have been overlooked."

"And we need to brief the mayor again." Jimmy sighed while rubbing his temples. "We need to control the narrative. Ryder, your press conference was good, vague enough for the media but clear enough for the killer. We continue with that approach."

"We make him look invincible, so he'll try to brag," I said. "That's how we'll catch him."

Jimmy gave a sharp nod. "I agree. It's basic serial killer ego targeting. We give him his notoriety. Let him think he's in control. Let him think he's winning. And then we corner him." He looked directly at Bishop, though I didn't understand why. "This is a game, and he thinks he's the master, but we're about to show him that Hamby PD plays for keeps. Everyone stay focused. We find the killer. We do not lose. We can't. Our community depends on us. From now on, no more reacting. Let's make a move he doesn't expect."

We just needed to figure out a move to make.

13

The old oak doors at the Georgia Tech Chess Club dragged against their hinges when Bishop shoved them open. "Damn, these are solid."

"Or maybe you're weakening in your old age?"

He flipped me the bird, his usual way to show me he cared.

Dust motes spun through slivers of sunlight slicing in from the tall, arched windows. Boards covered the tables, each one mid-game, pieces locked in place as if the players had just stepped away to think, though there were only three of us there.

The calm hit differently. No chatter. No coffee-stained notes. No slammed doors or barked orders. Just silence layered over strategy. A strategy that didn't demand quick answers like ours.

Bubba had researched who to contact for a more detailed analysis of the game related to our investigation and found criminal psychiatrist and chess expert Anya Sharma at Georgia Tech.

I wondered if she would be our golden ticket to understanding our killer.

A woman seated at a grandmaster's table in the center of the room looked up from a chessboard abandoned mid-game. "Good afternoon. Detectives Bishop and Ryder, yes?"

Bishop nodded. "Dr. Anya Sharma. I'm Detective Bishop, and this is my partner, Detective Ryder."

Dr. Sharma radiated a different authority, one born from countless hours of education and experience, and clearly spent in the silent crucible of the game.

She was older, perhaps late sixties, with a neat silver bun and eyes that held the sharp, unwavering focus of a predator. They darted over us, assessing, dismissing, then settling on my face with an unnerving intensity that made me feel like an open book she was already halfway through.

I hadn't felt that uncomfortable since my first department required therapy after Tommy's murder.

"It's a pleasure to meet you despite the circumstances." Her voice was low and gravelly, yet surprisingly clear. She gestured to the two chairs opposite her, not quite inviting us, but more like commanding our presence.

"Thank you for meeting with us," Bishop said. "And so quickly."

"Of course. This presents the exact psychological complexity I specialize in."

"That's good to know," he said. "We'll get right to the point as we understand your time is limited."

I pulled up photos of Jennifer Abbott, then the unidentified male John Doe on my phone and showed them to her.

"We have two victims so far," Bishop said. He cleared his throat and paused. I knew he wanted to choose his words carefully.

"Detective Bishop, I sense you're searching for the polite way to discuss a serial killer's actions, but there is nothing polite about this. Please spare me the softened version. I need the facts as they are to properly assist you."

"Understood," he said. "Both victims were posed in suitcases, their bodies cleaned, and throats slit post-mortem. The cause of death for Mrs. Abbott was fentanyl overdose. We're awaiting confirmation for the male victim, but preliminary observations suggest the same."

He explained the luxury hotel robes from the Echelon Hotel.

"Your colleague mentioned a connection to chess?"

"Yes, ma'am. The killer left a chess pawn with each victim. Black with the female and white with the male victim." He then mentioned the note found at his house.

"What did the note say?" she asked.

"Rachel's next."

Dr. Sharma listened without interruption. Her gaze remained focused, though occasionally flicking to the images on the screen. She didn't flinch at the gruesome details.

Bishop laid out the context of the taunts, the press conference, and the chilling appearance of the second victim after my public statements. "We believe this killer is highly intelligent, meticulous, and playing a game with us, targeting Detective Ryder specifically."

She nodded slowly as her fingers idly traced the lines on the chessboard before her. "Indeed. Chess is not merely a game of pieces, Detectives. It is a language, a reflection of the player's mind, their philosophy, and in this situation, it's unfortunate, but their very soul." She paused. Her eyes finally left the board to fix on mine. "And in your killer's case, it speaks volumes."

She picked up a black pawn. "They are the soul of the game, the foot soldiers, the most numerous, yet seemingly weakest. Their primary role is sacrifice, as your colleague stated in our brief conversation. They open lines, they guard, and they are expended to gain tactical advantage or space."

She placed the pawn back down. "Your killer used the black pawn with their first victim, Ms. Abbott. This is a symbol meaning the game has begun. He or she used it to mark his territory and declare the intent. A challenge, aimed directly at you, Detective Ryder." She looked at Bishop. "The note at your home was merely an address, a declaration of where the message was to be received. But it was for her. It's location, in my professional opinion, holds more meaning, but I'll get to that in a moment."

A chill washed over me as she dissected the killer's intent with such cold precision. "And the white pawn with the male victim?" I asked.

"Ah, the counter-move," she said. "In chess, white always moves first. But sometimes, black dictates the pace, thus forcing white to respond. It's a sign that this killer believes they hold the initiative. The black pawn was the opening gambit. A statement, if you will. The white pawn, then, is his response to your move." She tapped the table. "You spoke to the press, Detective. You made a statement which, to the killer, is effectively your first move. His, and I said that to make this conversation simple, not because I believe the killer to be male, white pawn is his retort, a demonstration that he remains in control, that he dictates the terms. Not you."

"It also reinforces the idea of pawns as expendable, doesn't it?" Bishop asked. "Player plays and notes pawns as being sacrificial and clearing the way for bigger moves."

"Precisely," she confirmed. "They are fodder, the cost of doing business on his board. But pawns also have a unique potential. Promotion. If a pawn reaches the opposite end of the board, it can become a queen, a rook, a knight, or a bishop. It suggests that even his disposable pieces serve a higher purpose in his grand design, perhaps transforming into something more significant in his twisted narrative."

"I'm not sure I understand," I said.

"Do you play, Detective Ryder?"

"Not enough to understand the game."

She smiled. "The murders are not merely acts of violence, but calculated steps designed to advance the killer's twisted narrative and escalate his control over the game. The choice of two initial victims, represented by both black and white pawns, signifies the formal commencement of this game, where their deaths are foundational to the killer's ability to promote his strategy or himself, perhaps in his mind, into a more dominant role. This escalation of his game is directly tied to his ultimate target," she looked me in the eye. "You, whom the team believes he views as the Queen. The sacrifice of these pawns could be the condition for the killer to unleash his full capabilities or achieve his larger, more significant goals within his diligently planned psychological operation."

I would have to review that multiple times to understand as it sounded like what Reagan had said, just with extra words.

"Next is the Rook." She slid the castle-shaped piece across the board. "Solid, powerful, moving in straight lines, both horizontally and vertically. Rooks symbolize strength, control, and territory. They often protect the king and can castle with him, a unique move that secures the king's position." She glanced up from the board. "The luxury hotel robes, the expertly cleaned and posed bodies, the absence of blood at the scene—these are signs of the Rook's influence."

"He killed them elsewhere, in a controlled environment, then transported them," I said. "Does that fit with the symbolism of a rook?"

"Yes. His castle is his sanctuary, his killing ground. It's a place of absolute control, where he can carry out his macabre artistry without interruption or mess. The hotel robe is not merely a prop. It's a symbol of his domain, his chosen environment where he reigns supreme and unimpeded. Though it doesn't mean the killings happen at a hotel. He cleans and poses the bodies like trophies, a performance artist's flourish in his own personal fortress."

What happened to basic murder? I didn't support any murder, but it was easier to define and made more sense to do a drive-by shooting.

"Then we have the knight," she said as she moved the horse-shaped piece with its distinctive L-shaped leap. "The knight is the trickster of the board, and you've experienced him already, though you might not realize it. It's the only piece that can jump over others, making its movements unpredictable, sudden, and difficult to anticipate. Knights are often used for surprise attacks, to fork multiple pieces, or to infiltrate enemy lines."

"Are you saying he's the knight? I thought he would be the king to my queen."

"That's a very insightful question, Detective Ryder, and it truly gets to the heart of the killer's current methodology and mindset." She glanced at my phone. "I suggest you record this, as I'm going to go into very specific detail."

Bishop had already been recording and pointed to his phone to show her.

"Thank you," she said. "You see, a king in chess is the ultimate prize, the piece everyone protects, but its movements are actually quite limited—only one square at a time. This killer, however, is not limited; he's unpredictable, sudden, and difficult to anticipate—exactly like a Knight. He isn't looking to be the centerpiece yet; he's actively engaged in disrupting and setting the stage."

She gestured as if demonstrating a knight's leap. "Consider his actions, and how they perfectly align with the knight's role on the board." She must have noticed my confused look. "I'll explain. Your colleague and I discussed specific details of the killer's actions. The manipulated photo you received initially was a profound trick, wasn't it? He used a fake tattoo, photoshopped a real woman into a staged scene, and made it look like the victim died from a throat slash when that wasn't the case. This deception, designed to mislead and disorient us, is a classic trickster move. His use of generic, untraceable supplies for his prints and communications, like consumer-grade HP inkjets and stock paper, and phone spoofing, further reinforces his trickster nature by making him elusive and hard to trace.

"So far, the killer has acted as a knight. Jennifer Abbott's body suddenly appearing on Bishop's porch, zipped into a suitcase, was a surprise attack, designed to shock and bypass expected investigative channels. The same applies to the male victim found in Fowler Park, a public space, complete with red paint resembling blood. These weren't expected. They bypassed our usual defenses and appeared in places we wouldn't anticipate a body to be, literally jumping into our lives. Even the act of delivering the first photo directly to you, Detective Ryder, rather than the department, was an act of jumping into your personal space and drawing you into his game. He's launching surprise attacks against our sense of security and control.

"He is forking multiple pieces and targeting you, Rachel, as the queen, but he's also affecting Bishop by leaving a body on his porch, your team by creating a high-profile, complex case, and the entire community with his public displays and psychological warfare, evidenced by the note to the paper. He's creating multiple simultaneous problems for your team to handle. And he is infiltrating enemy lines by sending the photo directly to you, delivering the first body to Bishop's home, and the second to a public park, making his presence known within our perceived safe zones.

"So, while preserving the king is the ultimate goal, and perhaps what he aspires to be in his twisted narrative of being in control, his current actions —his deceptions, his sudden strikes, his strategic disruption of your team and your life—are all hallmarks of a knight's play."

"Just to make sure I understand," I said, "you're saying he plans every move to hit where we're not looking, to make us question what we see, what we think, and who we can protect."

"That is correct."

All that to say he liked the element of surprise.

"Unfortunately, there is much more to the game, and I suspect he will play each move." She picked up another piece. "The bishop moves diagonally, always on the same color squares, but with a longer reach. They are often used to control long diagonals, creating pins or skewers that limit the opponent's options. Bishops, like rooks, can be powerful in open positions, but their strength lies in their ability to restrict and confine."

I immediately thought of Bishop, my partner, sitting beside me. "And how does that relate to us or to the killer?" A shiver ran down my spine. The way Sharma spoke, the analytical way she connected the piece to control and confinement, made me think of Rob. It was a fleeting, unsettling thought, one I quickly dismissed. It couldn't be a coincidence. Or could it?

She focused on Bishop. "Detective Bishop, your name itself holds resonance here. The killer left the first body at your home, a deliberate act to involve you directly, not just as law enforcement, but as a named piece on his board."

She paused for a moment, presumably to let that sink in. "Bishops operate on specific diagonals. They can limit escape routes, force decisions. This killer is trying to limit your options, to funnel your investigation, to control your responses. He is creating a confined game space where he sets the rules of engagement. He wants you both focused on the board he has laid out."

Finally, she brought her hand to the queen. "And here we have the queen. The most powerful piece on the board, combining the moves of the rook and the bishop. She is the heart of an offense and the bulwark of a defense. In chess, the queen is the piece most often targeted by an opponent, because her capture dramatically weakens the opposing side. She is the bait, yes, but she is also the ultimate prize, the piece whose presence defines the strategic landscape."

Her eyes locked on mine. "Detective Ryder, as I've said, you are the queen. The note was not merely a threat, but a declaration of your pivotal role in his game. You are the reason for his actions. He is trying to get to you."

I swallowed. I knew that, but I didn't know why. "Why me?" I asked, my voice barely a whisper. "Why now?"

"Because he sees you as his ultimate challenge, his most worthy opponent," she said without a hint of flattery. "You lead the investigation, you speak to the media, you are the visible face of Hamby PD's pursuit. He wants to prove his superiority, his intellectual dominance, by challenging the strongest piece on your side. He wants to control you, to instill fear, and ultimately, to show his invincible control by making you his next victim, thus eliminating the queen and ensuring his perceived victory."

"How is killing strangers eliminating me?" I asked.

"He's putting you in a position of weakness. Exhausting you, if you will. The harder you work to stop him, the more easily controlled you become. Let me ask you this. Have you ever lost someone you love?"

I swallowed back the instant lump in my throat. "Why does that matter?"

"Because loss matters. We don't have to know the person to experience the loss, and that's especially true for people in your field and mine. So, if pawns are sacrificed, if pieces are removed from the board, does that make the queen weaker, or does it, perhaps, change her power?"

"It makes her weaker," Bishop said.

"One might think that." Dr. Sharma observed my reaction, then continued. "Many might believe a depleted board weakens the queen. But it does the opposite when in the hands of a true master or when facing an opponent who believes they are. When the initial skirmishes have stripped away the clutter, when the pawns have cleared the lines, the queen's inherent mobility and devastating reach are amplified. She becomes the undisputed, dominant force. Her path is clearer, her targets more defined. She is no longer just a piece among many. She is the singular engine of attack and defense. Her vulnerability may appear to increase, as she is more exposed, but her capacity for decisive, game-ending moves becomes absolute. She is a sharp blade in an open field, capable of striking anywhere, often when the opponent believes they have gained an advantage by removing her protectors."

I exhaled. "I'm not sure I understand."

"He believes you've somehow been stripped down by these murders and made into a viable, worthy opponent, one he believes he must beat."

"And he needs an audience to witness his masterpiece," Bishop added. "That's why he needs a queen."

"Precisely," she confirmed. "He thrives on notoriety, on the attention his macabre artistry garners. His goal is not just to kill, but to orchestrate a narrative, to perform a psychological operation where he is the mastermind and law enforcement. And you, Detective Ryder, are merely his next grand performance."

"Last, the king," she said as she picked up the tallest piece. "The king is paradoxically the weakest yet most important piece. He moves slowly, one square at a time, but his survival dictates the game. The entire aim of chess is to checkmate the opponent's king." She looked at us, her gaze encompassing the entire room. "Your killer's king is his ego, his absolute control, his twisted sense of ultimate victory. He is playing to show his power over life and death, over the law, and most importantly, over you, Detective Ryder. He believes he cannot lose. He is confident, meticulous, calculating."

"So, what's our next move?" I asked.

"In chess, the queen, though powerful, must always be protected. But she is also the most effective piece for launching an attack. He has invited you to play. The question is, how will you move your queen?"

Bishop glanced at me. I noted the grim, determined look on his face. He knew. We were pieces on his board and neither of us had a clue how to handle that, but we started to understand the game. We had our assignments from Jimmy to focus on the killer's message and motivation, to lean into the taunt, to make him look invincible so he'd brag, and to bring in the DEA for their expertise in the drug world. Armed with a deeper understanding of the killer's twisted game, we had a clearer picture of his strategy and, perhaps, the opening to make our own calculated moves.

The killer wanted to play. And thanks to Dr. Sharma, we could. The killer had presented the challenge. And I, the queen, was ready to make my move.

Bishop made it to his vehicle without a word, but once inside, he said, "You always have to be a challenge, don't you?"

"Yep." I stared out the window. "Lenny tried to teach me chess back in the day."

"I take it he was unsuccessful?"

"Let's just say I consider it a slightly more complicated checkers."

"It's so much more than that."

"I know that now. I guess I should have paid more attention."

"Not the first or last time you'll say that."

14

The stale scent of cold coffee and lingering barbecue from the previous night's frantic session filled the investigation room, proving our aggressive, if exhausting, pursuit of a meticulous killer. Maps plastered with red pins marked Bishop's cul-de-sac and Fowler Park, scribbled timelines, motives, and the unsettling symbolism of chess pieces covered the whiteboards. Jimmy stood at the head of the long table, arms crossed, his gaze fixed on the door. He stood so still I wanted to poke him and make sure he was real, but he didn't give off the vibe of finding anything funny at that moment.

I leaned against the credenza clutching a mug of nasty cop coffee. We'd upgraded to Keurig coffee years ago, but somehow it still tasted like stale motor oil from the department vehicles.

Bishop sat across the table, running a hand through his hair and staring at his notes.

"They won't change, Bishop. No matter how long you stare at them."

"That's the problem. There's nothing that even hints at the killer's identity. Hamby's not a small town anymore. We went from under 5,000 when I started with the department to over 41,000 now. It's like finding a needle in a haystack."

Levy chuckled. "Have you been talking to my father again?"

I busted out laughing but stopped when Bishop gave me his death stare. "My bad."

Just as the silence threatened to stretch into discomfort, the door burst open and Bubba strode in, a whirlwind of nervous energy from copious amounts of Red Bull. It didn't give Bubba wings, but it gave him a double shot of chaos. The man talked like he was buffering at triple speed.

He hugged his tablet like a lifeline, and from the looks of him, he needed it. His hair, a disheveled mess, suggested he hadn't left his multiple laptops, desktop, and printer since our last update. His usual bounce was slightly more pronounced. My heart beat faster because I knew that to be a telltale sign of a breakthrough.

"I've got something." He dropped the tablet on the table as a faint grin broke through his focus. He walked straight to the large monitor on the wall and wirelessly connected his tablet. "You wanted an ID for our John Doe? Well, Chief, I've got one."

A collective sigh of relief rippled through the room. Jimmy straightened. "Thank God."

Bubba tapped a few keys, and a clear, high-resolution photo of a man around forty popped up on the screen, followed by a driver's license photo and what appeared to be a professional headshot. "Meet our victim. His name is Gary Kinder, a forty-two-year-old resident of Alpharetta. No prior criminal record, no outstanding warrants. Until his death, he was a regional sales director for a medical supply company."

A familiar surge of adrenaline rushed through me. "Dang, Bubba, how did you get him so fast?"

"It was all luck."

Bishop called his bluff on that.

"Okay, so a little of it was luck. I went all in and dedicated every available resource just like the Chief ordered. I started with facial recognition. Blew up the image, cleaned it as much as possible, and ran it through all the usual channels first: DMV databases, passport databases. It's a hazy image from the original, but the quality was decent enough to get some preliminary hits. Thankfully, it was nothing like the first victim's blurred face in the photo.

"Once I had the name, I thoroughly analyzed social media and looked for an online presence or connections, or you know, anything that might pop up. That's actually where I got the clearest hit. His LinkedIn profile had a professional headshot. So, I cross-referenced that with a few public photos, and boom—solid match."

"You're da bomb, Bubba," Bishop said.

Bubba stared at him as if he'd just spoken in Latin. "Is that good?"

"What the ancient guy means is great work," Michels said.

Bishop flipped him off. I thought that was our love language, but whatever.

Levy scribbled furiously on her notepad. "So, he's not connected to Jennifer Abbott through social media, then? Any shared friends, groups, anything?"

"That was my next step after the initial ID," Bubba said. "I checked Jennifer Abbott's socials again, thinking maybe she knew Gary Kinder, but I couldn't find anything that suggested she might. No mutual connections, no shared interests online, no events they both attended."

"What about unique identifiers?" Jimmy pressed. "Barron mentioned old injuries, dental work, tattoos, surgical scars, medical implants. Did anything come back on those?"

Bubba nodded as he navigated his tablet with practiced ease. "That's where it got interesting, and honestly, lucky. Barron's preliminary notes from his initial examination were a huge help. Gary Kinder had a very distinctive surgical scar on his McBurney's Point from a childhood appendectomy. It was noted in his medical records, which under HIPAA Barron is allowed access to for deceased person's identification. He would have eventually made the ID. I just did it in his place."

"Good work," Jimmy said.

"Thanks, Chief. The victim has no registered medical implants or unique dental work that stood out in Barron's initial scan, but the scar was a solid, unique identifier, and it matched our guy's records."

"Was he listed as missing?" Michels asked.

"No. I cross-referenced his details with the national missing persons database's open cases, but he wasn't on it, likely because he was a frequent business traveler, and it might have taken a few days for his company or family to notice his absence, especially since he'd just left for a supposed conference."

"You said medical supply company sales, right?" I asked. "Is that pharmaceuticals?"

"Yes, and that's the exact thought that crossed my mind. His company deals with a range of pharmaceuticals, including those that could be precursors or even the substances themselves for fentanyl. This definitely fits with our new profile of the killer being someone with medical or pharmaceutical knowledge, or access to controlled substances. I've already flagged this for the DEA liaison."

"So, it's possible the killer knew this victim," Bishop said. "We'll need to find out if that's the same for Jennifer Abbott."

"Yes, sir," Bubba said.

"Excellent work, Bubba," Jimmy said. A rare, genuine smile graced his lips. "This is exactly what we needed. A name. It'll move things along quicker. We'll need a death notification." He eyed Levy. "You and Michels can take that."

"Yes, sir," she said.

"Now we dive deep into Gary Kinder's life. Friends, family, work, habits, hangouts. And we look for his connections to fentanyl, or to anyone who might have access to it. We need to find out if he had any links to Jennifer Abbott, no matter how obscure."

"The killer could be a disgruntled former employee from his company, or a competitor, or someone he met through his work," Levy said.

"Bubba, you're on it," Jimmy said. "Dive into Gary Kinder's digital footprint. Look for any conflicts, any unusual interactions, anything that might connect him to Rachel, to Jennifer Abbott, or to anyone in law enforcement who might have been overlooked. And cross-reference his network with Jennifer Abbott's again, relentlessly."

"Consider it done, Chief," Bubba said as he tapped away at his tablet.

Jimmy nodded. "I've got Kyle and his team on call. I'll get them here to work with you." He scanned the room. "Who's next?"

"Chief," Nikki said, "I've re-examined Jennifer Abbott's body, with the permission of Dr. Barron, of course, the suitcase, and the black pawn for fentanyl residue, but there's nothing, not even a speck of the stuff anywhere. Our killer left no trace, which means we're dealing with someone who's experienced in drug handling."

"God," Bishop said. "That opens the door to hundreds of jobs. Everyone in the pharmaceutical business, including pharmacies."

Nikki folded her arms. "Exactly. Fentanyl *can* come from a pharmacy, but only with a legitimate prescription. Patches such as Duragesic are commonly prescribed for chronic pain and for people diagnosed with late-stage terminal cancer. These release it slowly through the skin over a few days, which wouldn't be helpful for our killer unless he used multiple patches at a time. But we now know from Abbott's autopsy that's not what happened."

"Because of the needle marking between the toes?" Levy asked.

"That and the blistering on the inside of the cheek. Dr. Barron mentioned it before. I followed up and it was a lozenge. As you already know, fentanyl levels spiked fast with those, and though it originally pointed to the shot, a lozenge or lollipop overdose from Actiq would spike it even higher faster. Based on the blisters, Barron confirmed both were used, or the needle prick was just meant to distract us."

"And do you think he'll find that in the second victim's blood as well?" I asked.

"I suspect he already has, but we'll cross-reference findings with the new male victim once his toxicology results are in. In the meantime, we have to consider he might use alternative forms of the drug like the patches and, of course, pills, for other victims."

"Let's hope there are no other victims," Jimmy said.

"Unfortunately," I said, "there will be."

"She's right," Bishop added. "Each player has sixteen pieces in total. That includes eight pawns, two rooks, two knights, two bishops, one queen, and one king. So far, the killer's only used two pawns."

"Shit." Michels's eyes widened. "That means we've got a potential for thirty-four murders."

We played the recording of our interview with Dr. Sharma which, when finished, caused the entire team to deflate.

"We're not going to close this one," Levy said. "This guy's a genius. I'm lucky if I don't get my ass kicked in Go Fish."

"I'm no game player, but I know how to read a crime scene and analyze it." Nikki popped a pod into the Keurig. "I went through everything in Gary's suitcase, and just like we expected, it all matches Abbott's. I checked for fibers, hairs, pollen, and found nothing, though I found a partial latent print, but it's unusable. Every single thing matches what we pulled from Abbott's scene. Same robe fiber blend, same latex glove residue, Not that we're thinking this, but it wasn't a copycat. It's the same killer."

15

Michels scratched the back of his neck as he spoke, locking his eyes on the map pinpointing the two crime scenes. "We assigned four officers to complete a comprehensive canvass of the areas where the suitcases were found. They checked every house, business, doorbell, and security camera to establish ingress and egress routes for the killer."

He looked exhausted. So did Levy, who picked up where he had left off. "Obviously, the footage hasn't changed. No unfamiliar vehicles. No suspicious foot traffic. No surprises."

I fixed my eyes on the timeline taped to the wall beside the board. "Did you extend the timeframe?"

"By twelve hours in both directions," Michels said. "Still nothing that couldn't be verified. Either the killer knew where the cameras were, or he wasn't anywhere near one to begin with."

Levy sighed. "We had the officers look for alternate routes through backyards, service roads, and even hiking trails near Fowler. No prints, no tire marks, no sign of someone passing through. Nothing stood out. No debris, no broken branches. It's like he dropped them from the sky."

"That's not good enough," Jimmy said, his voice low but sharp. "Have four more officers do it again."

Levy opened her mouth, probably to argue, but thought better of it. "Understood," she said instead.

Michels's eyes focused on Jimmy. "We've got three officers scrubbing through background movement in the footage now. They'll flag anything that doesn't track with the usual patterns."

"Thanks. We know more about our guy because of you, Michels," I said. "He knew exactly where to stand, how long he had, and what would and wouldn't be seen."

"And he didn't rush," Levy added quietly. "That's what bothers me. He was deliberate."

Kyle leaned over the edge of the conference table, one palm pressed flat to a scatter of case files, the other gripping a cup of black coffee that steamed like his temper. His jaw clenched. Every movement radiated tension, a controlled, deliberate, and lethal when needed tension. We'd just reconnected an hour before, but that Kyle, the one whose eyes flashed passion and love, took a backseat to the drug-hunting hulk standing in front of me.

I liked them both equally.

"Whoever did this," he said, "knew exactly what they were handling."

Michels sat with a pen frozen mid-tap. Levy's brows narrowed. Bishop leaned back but didn't relax. No one dared interrupt. We knew the professional in the room, and we weren't about to challenge him.

He flicked his wrist and tossed the photo we all had seen onto the table. Jennifer Abbott. Dead eyes. Clean skin. No visible trauma.

"She didn't take a street product," he said, "which you already know. Based on the autopsy information, it's clinical. Prescription only. Schedule II. Nikki nailed it. You don't just pick that up on the corner from some dealer with a backpack."

Bishop leaned forward and spoke first. "You can confirm it came from a pharmacy, then?"

"I can't confirm it with verifiable evidence yet, but I'm an expert in this field, and I can say with confidence it's either from a pharmacy or a pharmaceutical supply chain. And not through proper channels. Either stolen, forged, or funneled through someone who knows how to game the system. This is the type of precision you see with medical professionals. Or someone who's spent a long time pretending to be one."

Bubba tapped his keyboard. "It could be a veterinarian, right? They have access to fentanyl for animal surgeries."

Kyle nodded. "Or someone with a revoked license who kept his black book. Or a guy fresh out of prison who learned how to cut fentanyl from powdered precursors and thinks he's a chemist now, or—and this is what I suspect—a physician who works for the cartel."

He pointed to the second victim, Gary Kinder. "This one's our in."

"Because he worked in medical supply?" I asked.

"More than that. He repped a region for a company that distributes surgical kits and high-schedule drugs, fentanyl among them. If you're trying to steal Actiq or patch fentanyl, that's your guy. His badge gets him through the doors. Warehouses. Clinics. Even transport hubs."

"Are we thinking he sold it?" Levy asked.

"Maybe," Kyle said. "But I'm leaning toward unintentional access. Someone used him. Or killed him to shut him up."

I scribbled the word "intermediary" in my notes.

"And the lozenge delivery system?" Michels asked. "Nikki said that's a quick way to get it into the blood, which honestly doesn't make a lot of sense because fentanyl enters the system fairly quickly anyway. But Barron never confirmed if the needle mark between the toes was officially involved or not."

"We can find out the answer to that with one call," I said. I dialed Barron's number on the landline and put it on speaker.

After a quick run through of our questions, he confirmed what we needed to know.

"The presence of both buccal blistering and an injection site, combined with fentanyl levels in the bloodstream, confirms administration by more than one route. However, the sequence of delivery cannot be determined with certainty."

After ending the call, Kyle added, "Given the appearance of the victims, I would say they were given the drugs before understanding who they were dealing with."

"So maybe a trusted friend," Levy said. "Or someone they felt comfortable with."

"Exactly. Which tells me this wasn't someone experimenting. We're dealing with a rehearsed, deliberate act. Calculated to avoid detection. And it worked at first. Jennifer Abbott's tox screen lit up like Vegas, and the lack of physical trauma bought the killer time."

"Unless they didn't need time," Bishop said. "Unless this was the message."

Kyle nodded. "Right now, my agents are running serials and batch numbers on any missing Actiq shipments. We're cross-referencing DEA registrants for the last three years. Every pharmacy tech, clinic nurse, hospice distributor, or vet assistant who got fired for theft—we're digging into all of them."

Bubba lifted a hand. "What about black-market synthesis? You know, bootleg labs, backyard chemists?"

"Possible," Kyle said. "But again, the dosage was perfect. Lethal, fast-acting, but not messy. No vomit. No seizures. No foam. That's a pro. Your average basement cook doesn't hit that mark without killing themselves."

"And here's the bigger piece," Kyle continued. "We've seen this before. Not here. But cases where high-schedule drugs got used in non-standard murders. New York two years ago. Phoenix last fall. We're seeing a pattern."

I blinked. "You're saying this could be part of something bigger?"

"I'm saying we need to ask if this is the first time they've killed like this, or just the first time it's landed in your lap."

I stiffened at that. Kyle saw it. He softened his tone, but not his stance.

"Rach, you weren't chosen by accident. Someone sent you that photo for a reason. If it's the same killer, they're elevating. Getting bolder. But they also want to rattle you. Throw you off."

"Mission partially accomplished," I muttered.

"Right. Which leads me to believe you've been involved in something with this person before. Could be something as simple as a speeding ticket, but this person knows you."

I exhaled. My book of citations topped the mileage from California to New York.

Kyle stepped around the table and dropped into the seat beside me. His thigh brushed mine. "We'll find the connection. But I'm telling you now, I don't think this is just a murder. I think it's a controlled event and obviously a message."

"Using fentanyl as a signature," Bishop said.

"Exactly. Clean. Lethal. Untraceable unless you know what to look for. And now we do."

I stood and circled the table with my hands on hips. "So, what do we do to catch this POS?"

"I'll loop in my team. You get warrants for Gary Kinder's company. Employee rosters, warehouse inventory, client lists. We'll run every name against DEA watchlists, theft reports, and known diversion rings. Meanwhile, someone needs to dig into Jennifer Abbott's background again for any whispers of drug history. Addiction. Medical scripts. Even rumors."

"I'm on it," Levy said.

"And if we're lucky," Kyle added, "Kinder left a footprint. A login. A contact. Anything that puts this in motion."

Kyle drained the last of his coffee. "One more thing. These don't feel like just kills. They feel like auditions. The killer wanted to prove they could do it quietly. Efficiently. And now they want you to chase them. I don't see a drug connection to chess just yet, but if there is one, we'll figure it out." His eyes landed on Jimmy. "She's not going anywhere without a follow, right?"

Jimmy nodded. "Right." He folded his arms and cleared his throat before continuing. "We're already pulling pharmacy records, checking known associates, anyone with a habit or history."

Kyle nodded. "That's good. But as I said, this is a pattern. New York and Phoenix might not be the only places other than us, and I'll bet our perp's got a beef with cops in those areas as well."

"This is going to end up a federal case if we're not careful," Bishop said.

"The hell it will. This is ours. We own it. Let's just forget about them now," I said. "We have more important things to worry about."

Bubba turned in his chair with a half-eaten protein bar clenched between two fingers, and crumbs clinging to his hoodie. "Right. Let's move on. I'm way ahead of you, Kyle. I already ran a scan of local OD cases tagged as accidental or suicide but flagged unusual in the coroner notes.

Cross-checked for fentanyl, especially Actiq-grade or anything delivered non-traditionally."

"And?" I asked.

He dropped the wrapper on the desk, wiped his hands on his jeans, and spun to face the screen. "Got three possibles. One in Alpharetta. A woman was found in a boutique hotel, lozenge still in her mouth. No history, no prescription, and tox levels were off the charts but clean otherwise. Barron called it a bad choice at a party, which is highly possible."

Levy muttered, "Sure. Fancy hotel, no witnesses, perfectly placed lozenge sounds like a rager."

"Second one was a guy in Buckhead. Same thing. No visible trauma, same delivery method, but his was halfway dissolved. Whoever gave it to him didn't even wait for the full hit. And the weird part is the hotel room was spotless. Like, turn-down-service clean."

"That sounds familiar," I said.

Bubba nodded. "Last one happened in a public restroom near the convention center downtown. Guy worked in tech sales. He was visiting from Charlotte, North Carolina. Also mid-forties. Found with a blister pack in his pocket. Lozenge was missing. The patch on his neck didn't match any prior medical history. ME called it suicide."

Kyle frowned. "Damn. Are all of those within the past two years? Why didn't the DEA know about them?"

"Eighteen months," Bubba said, tapping on his keyboard rapidly. "But they were in different counties with different MEs. No red flags on their own."

"But together they look like prep at least for Georgia," I whispered. "Dry runs. Clean kills, low profile."

Bubba pointed a finger at me, then turned back to the keyboard. "That's why I'm expanding the search. I'll scrape records from NY and Phoenix next, cross-referencing hotel-based deaths with fentanyl delivery methods. I'll look for boutique settings, soft staging, minimal blood, digital silence, and see if more than those two Kyle mentioned come up."

Bishop raised an eyebrow. "You can do that manually?"

"I wrote a few filters last year during a security conference. Built for

OSINT scraping and DEA mortality dump comparisons. I'll run 'em overnight."

Kyle gave a half-laugh. "You moonlight as a hacker?"

"No," Bubba said without looking up. "I daylight as one."

I exchanged a glance with Michels, who mouthed, *weird little genius,* then smiled.

Bubba leaned into his desk again. "If there's more like this, I'll find them. If not, well, then our guy's just getting started here." His voice didn't change, but the chill in the room deepened, anyway.

"Alright, everyone," Jimmy said. His gaze swept across the team and appeared sharpened by the new information from Bubba. "This changes everything. Abbott wasn't our killer's first. He had others he likely used to hone his craft. These dry runs Bubba found in Alpharetta, Buckhead, and downtown are critically important. They show his methodology evolving, his deliberate practice." He cleared his throat, then paused for a moment, I assumed, to plot our next moves. I was right. "Michels, Levy, your victimology now expands beyond Abbott and Kinder. I want you to pull the full original case files for the Alpharetta, Buckhead, and Downtown/Convention Center overdose victims. That means every police report, ME report, witness statement, and piece of collected evidence. Once you have those, I want you to re-interview the original medical examiners, the police officers who worked those cases, and any witnesses or family members. Go in armed with everything we now know. The fentanyl overdoses as the *true* cause of death, post-mortem throat slitting, clean scenes, and the specific lozenge/patch delivery method. Ask if any new information or suspicious elements were overlooked or dismissed as accidental."

"Got it, Chief," Levy said.

"Nikki, the general forensic re-examination of Abbott and Kinder already applies. Now, I need you to secure any physical evidence that was kept from these three earlier Georgia cases. Clothing, drug containers, anything. Re-examine them specifically for fentanyl residue, any robe fibers that match the Echelon Hotel pattern, or traces of nitrile-based latex gloves. We need to confirm whether a signature was present, even subtly, from the beginning."

"We'll get it done as quickly as possible, Chief."

"We need it sooner than that. We can't let this psycho kill again." He looked at Bubba. "Your existing search for past fentanyl overdoses in hotels is vital. Now, for these identified dry run victims in Georgia, I need you to perform the same exhaustive digital footprint analysis as you did for Jennifer Abbott and Gary Kinder. Look for any shared direct or indirect connections to anyone. This includes expanding the search for any hidden conflicts, unusual online interests, or communities that might link them back to our guy."

"Yes, sir, boss."

"Alright, Jimmy," Kyle began, "This has patterns, so I'll have my team reach out to police departments and coroners' offices across Georgia, New York, and Phoenix. We'll share the killer's profile, his confirmed fentanyl overdose method using lozenges, and the chess-themed M.O. There might be more out there that fit this pattern, especially those where high-schedule drugs were used in non-standard murders."

Jimmy looked at me, then back at Kyle. "Good. We need to hit him from every angle."

Kyle and Bishop met with Jimmy privately while Levy and I made coffee in the pit's kitchen.

She poured caramel creamer into her cup. "You know they want you out of this."

"And you know that ain't happening."

"They care about you, Rach. They only want to keep you safe."

"This is a job, not a group of friends worried about their other friend. I appreciate the concern, but they need to let it go. If I'm in this perp's head, then I'm in danger whether I work the investigation or not. Jimmy said it himself, I should be the bait. Didn't we already decide that?"

"That was before Kyle got involved."

I closed my eyes and sipped my coffee, imagining it was an espresso from Italy, not the sludge from the department. "I'm not a naïve college girl who thinks ride sharing is safe. I can handle myself."

"Of course you can. That's not their issue. They're worried you'll intentionally put yourself at risk. Which we both know you will."

16

Bubba dimmed the lights with one elbow while the other hand flew across his keyboard. "Alright, pulling all camera feeds between Hardscrabble and Fowler Park," he said. "Every set of working traffic cams, business feeds, even a couple doorbell cameras. Don't ask how I got those."

I raised an eyebrow. "You always say that like we'll stop asking."

He smirked without looking up. "Because I live in hope."

The footage blinked to life on the main monitor at the end of the investigation room wall. Grainy at first, it started with an overhead view from a traffic camera outside a pharmacy on Hardscrabble Road. Bubba tapped a few more keys and overlaid time stamps.

"Okay, this is four hours before the killer dumped Gary Kinder's body. If the killer scouted routes or staged the suitcase ahead of time, we might catch a vehicle in both zones. That is if he used the same vehicle."

Bishop braced his arms on the table. "Let's hope he used the same vehicle each time."

"It's a long shot," I said. "Vehicle make, tag patterns, timing, or anything that shouldn't be there is expected from an amateur, but someone who plays chess well enough to relate it to his crimes is above average intelligence."

He nodded. "Agreed."

We sat in silence as the video sped along at double speed. Cars rolled through intersections, headlights flicked across lenses. Normal traffic. Normal people. Normal life just being lived while two victims died quietly.

"Nothing yet," Bubba murmured.

We watched another stretch of feed with a parking lot exit to the Red Barn off Hardscrabble. Then a grainy clip from outside a gas station near Fowler Park.

"Pause," Bishop said, pointing. "Back up four seconds."

Bubba reversed. "There?"

"Yeah, that black vehicle. Pause on the tag."

We squinted. The image blurred into blocks, resolution fighting against distance.

Bubba zoomed, then shrugged. "Can't enhance it cleanly. I can guess at two digits, maybe a letter."

I studied the vehicle. Black. No decals. No plate frame. Tinted windows. My stomach turned.

I thought I had seen it before, driving behind me, but I didn't say a word.

"Same one showed up at Abbott's drop site too," Bubba said. "Not the same timestamp, but within twenty minutes."

Bishop leaned in. "And that's not normal traffic?"

"Not in that part of town. Especially not lingering. Watch. This one slows before it exits the lot. Look at the brake pattern."

The vehicle crawled through the edge of a parking lot, then paused near a trash enclosure. No one got out. No one moved.

"Could be stalling to check sightlines," I said. "See who's around. If it's clear."

"Or waiting for someone to finish dumping the body," Bishop added.

"I don't know," I said. "I can't see our perp being so obvious without intention."

Bubba brought up another video. "Here's where it gets fun. Same vehicle, or one nearly identical, was picked up on a camera half a mile from Fowler Park three hours after the second suitcase was found. Driving casual. Headlights dimmed. Might've been doing a pass."

My blood chilled. I kept my expression neutral. "Can we get a make?"

"Working on it," Bubba said. "No plate from this angle either. But the taillight pattern's consistent with something late-model. Blackout trim. No chrome."

"That narrows it down," Bishop muttered. "To half the country."

"Still," I said, "if it shows up at multiple scenes, we treat it."

"Already ran through ALPR matches," Bubba added. "Closest I've got is a partial tag match near the old fire station. Vehicle came up clean. Registered to a landscaping business, but the description's off. That one's silver."

"So either stolen tags or burner plates," Bishop said.

"Or the real tag never showed at all."

We all watched as the footage played again. That vehicle moved intentionally. Not fast. Not flashy. Measured. Intentional.

"Let's map it," I said. "Plot every confirmed appearance on a map overlay. Locations, time stamps, direction of travel."

"Already doing it," Bubba said. He snapped a new window open, dropping pins onto a digital grid. One near Hardscrabble. Another outside Red Barn. Two more flanked Fowler Park. The path curved in a soft loop, nearly full circle.

"See that?" he said, tapping the screen. "That's not someone who's lost. That's someone rehearsing a drop."

My eyes drifted back to the paused frame. A dark vehicle halfway out of the lot, driver shielded behind pitch-black tint. I knew that angle. I remembered checking my mirror and seeing the same hood line creeping into view. "What about vehicles near Abbott's workplace?" I asked. "Anything similar?"

Bubba typed, then shook his head. "Still pulling cameras from that sector. Half of 'em are older than me and twice as blind. But I'll flag any match."

"Do it," Bishop said. "Tag every black car that lingers over thirty seconds. We'll build a pattern if there is one."

"I'll run a query too," Bubba added. "See if any stolen vehicles of that type were reported within a month of each death." He dimmed the screen. "I'll run facial rec next. See if we catch a driver stepping out anywhere. I doubt it, but worth the Hail Mary."

"Do it," I said. "This vehicle might be our thread."

He looked at me and then at Bishop. I knew he wanted to acknowledge the vehicle from before. I knew if I didn't bring it up, he would, and Jimmy would pull me from the investigation.

"I think it's one of the vehicles I've seen following me."

I felt Bishop's eyes drill into my skin. "Followed you?"

Bubba pushed his chair back and stood. "I'm out of this convo. Hopefully, both of you will survive." He flicked his eyes to me. "Good luck."

After Bubba left, Bishop shot me a look. He didn't say a word—but I confessed, anyway. "Okay, yes. I need to tell you something."

He laughed. "That's an understatement. When?" he asked, not bothering to wait for me to start.

"Twice. The first time was the night after I got the photo of Jennifer Abbott."

"Jesus, Rachel."

"I knew you'd freak out. That's why I didn't say anything."

"The second?"

"The second was after I left Abbott's place. The night we confirmed Jennifer was missing."

He pushed out of his chair and paced behind it. "Someone followed you, and you didn't think your *partner* should know?"

I stood too, not to challenge him, but because sitting made me feel smaller. "I didn't tell you because you would have told Jimmy, and he would've benched me. You know that."

"You don't think maybe there was a reason for that?"

"I *am* the reason," I said, my voice sharp. "The photo came to me. I'm the target. If I stepped back, we'd be guessing instead of tracking."

He turned toward the wall and placed his hands on his hips. "You're supposed to tell me when something like this happens. We've built our work on trust, and you just—what? Decided to cut me out?"

"No. I decided to stay in it."

He pivoted back to me. "So you brought Bubba in and swore him to secrecy?"

"I asked him to pull traffic cam footage. That's it. He didn't ask questions."

"You didn't have to. He knows you as well as the rest of us. You put him in a compromised position, Rach. What if Jimmy found out? What if something had happened to you? You think Bubba wouldn't take the fall for not reporting it?"

I swallowed the guilt rising in my throat. "I didn't think it through."

He dragged his hands down the sides of his face. "You rarely think through anything. That's what makes you dangerous."

"I thought about the victim. About the fact that whoever sent that photo knew where I'd be, what I'd do. I couldn't afford to be sidelined by an overprotective department, Rob. You would have done the same."

"If you think that, you clearly don't know me that well."

"I don't want to be dropped from the case, Bishop."

He crossed his arms again as the lines on his face deepened further. "Describe the car."

"First time, it was a late-model Malibu. Matte finish. No plates. Tinted windows. It matched my speed, stayed with me through every curve on Birmingham Highway, then darted off into a bend like it knew the road better than I did."

"And the second?"

"Near Fox Run. Glossy black car. Possibly an Audi. Newer. Kept its distance but didn't hide. It wanted me to know it was there."

"Jesus Christ, Rachel."

"I'm sorry, but at least I didn't panic."

"That's not the point." He stepped closer and lowered his voice. "You're a senior investigator. A high-profile detective who just got handed a case by the killer himself. You're being hunted, and you think keeping that a secret helps us?"

"It helped me stay in it."

His jaw tightened, but he didn't fire back right away. Instead, he dropped into the chair again and rubbed his hands together. "You could've been run off the road. Shot. Snatched. We'd have no idea why. You think Jimmy would've shrugged and moved on? You think I would've?"

"I made a call."

"Yes. The wrong one."

He let the silence sit between us. It hurt more than if he'd yelled.

After a moment, he asked, "Why Bubba?"

"He's the only one with access to the traffic cams without raising flags. He owed me."

"You pulled a favor from him, knowing it would drag him into your lie?"

"It wasn't a lie."

"It was a *withholding*. And you're better than that."

I leaned against the table and let the metal press into my palms. "I didn't plan it this way. But once I saw the footage, once I knew the car was real, it was too late to go backward. If I'd said something then, I'd have been pulled off everything. And I'm not letting psycho use me like a chess piece."

Bishop stared at me for a long time. "You don't get to decide that alone."

"I do when I'm the target."

"No. You don't." His voice dropped. "You let the team decide how to protect you. Not the other way around. That's how this works. That's how we keep each other alive."

I opened my mouth to respond, but nothing came out.

"You're lucky nothing happened. And Bubba's lucky Jimmy hasn't sniffed this out yet. But from now on? I'm in. No more secrets."

I nodded. "Okay."

"I mean it, Rachel."

"I know. You're right."

His eyes locked on mine for a moment before walking to the door. "Drop the hero complex, partner, or find someone else to work with." He opened the door, walked out, and slammed it shut behind him.

I pounded my fist on the table. "Damn it!"

"All I'm saying is I need a little time without a tail." I dropped onto my leather couch and groaned. "Like thirty minutes. Is that really too much to ask?"

Kyle sat beside me. "You know most drunk driving accidents happen within a mile from home."

I looked at him and burst out laughing. "Seriously? That's what you're going with?"

"The theory is the same. The risk is big wherever you are, but even more so at night in or around our home."

"So does that mean you're going into the bathroom with me?"

"Depends. Are you taking a shower?"

"Nope."

He grinned. "I'll wait outside the door then."

"Tomorrow's the Red, White, and You parade."

"I know. To honor the city of Hamby and our patriotic contributions to America."

"Quite exciting," I said. "I'm actually kind of looking forward to it."

"You're not going."

"I understand you're worried." I tucked my legs under me. "But it's a parade. Our guy isn't interested in public displays. He likes to make his move in private and get the big reveal."

"Maybe, but a crowd of people is an easy target, and you know that."

"I know, but don't worry. The team has too much going on to go to a parade. Jimmy's planning to stack a few extra officers there just in case, but there's no way he'll give us even thirty minutes to enjoy ourselves while this whack job is on the loose."

He yawned. "Parade or no parade, tomorrow will be long. I'm hitting the sack."

"Right behind you. After I talk to Savannah." I sent her a text. *You awake?*

Yes. This is the only time I get by myself. What's up?

I stepped into the garage and called her. "Has Jimmy told you what's going on?"

"As if he could keep anything from me. How're you handling it?"

"I want this guy."

"I know you do, and I know you'll catch him, so why do I hear worry in your voice?"

"I spent several hours today revisiting everything I've done in my career. I have 1269 field notebooks, and I can't find anything to connect to this guy."

"What if he's not connected to your past? What if he's not connected to you at all? You've helped to close multiple investigations. Maybe this psycho thinks you're a challenge? Like they're the one that can beat you."

"Honestly, that's what I think. How did you get so smart?"

"My bestie is a cop."

"And your husband is the chief of police."

She laughed. "Darlin', that man can't keep his thoughts straight around me. Bless his heart."

"Valid point. Are you taking my non-biological niece and nephew to the parade tomorrow?"

"Absolutely. Of course, Jimmy's not happy about it, but I'm not going to let this investigation scare me into locking my kids at home."

"Maybe you should reconsider?"

"Why? Is your intuition pinging again?"

"I just worry about the people I love."

"If there isn't a specific threat, then I'm going. My kids didn't pick a police chief for a father, and I can't let his fear, however accurate it might be, stop us from living our lives. Are you going?"

"Doubtful. Our police chief is a toughie."

"Oh, honey, you have no idea."

———

The investigation room smelled of vinegar, oil, and oregano. Thank God Susan really had gone all-in on the Jersey Mike's order. Half of the table sat covered in sandwich wrappers and crumpled napkins. Bubba dug into a giant club like Michels might snatch it from him if he hesitated. Mayonnaise streaked the corner of his mouth.

"Ever heard of a napkin?" Bishop asked him.

Michels handed Bubba one of Bishop's. "Here. Use his."

I laughed. "Cue psychotic germaphobe reaction in three, two…"

Bishop flipped me off.

"And there it is."

Levy nursed a soda and picked the tomatoes off her turkey, flicking them with the same surgical precision she used on crime scenes. One hit Michels in the eye.

"Come on," he said as he threw it back at her. "You're an adult, partner."

"We're in the middle of a serial killer investigation. Forgive me for wanting to destress." She whipped the tomato slice back at him.

"Enough," Bishop said. "Susan will never bring us lunch again if she has to clean up a food fight."

"Duly noted," Michels said. He plopped the tomato slice in his mouth just to gross us all out. It worked.

Bishop unwrapped his sandwich. "Damn, these are heaven in a wrapper." He groaned as he chewed his first bite.

"You realize you sound like a porn star every time you eat, right?" Levy said. She wiped her hands on a napkin.

Michel laughed. "That's because at his age, a sandwich is better than sex."

I covered my mouth so I wouldn't spit food at anyone while laughing.

Once I gathered my self-control, I said, "Dang, Michels. You're on fire today."

Laughter circled the table. We didn't get many calm moments. When one showed up, we devoured it—literally and figuratively.

"Hey," Michels said, pointing at Bubba. "What's the dipping sauce?"

"It's mint-coriander chutney. I grew up dipping everything into it."

"What's in it?" Levy asked.

Bishop chuckled. "I've got ten bucks on mint and coriander."

Bubba dipped a chip into the dip again. "Pretty much."

"I love you, Bubba, but that sounds gross. In Chicago, we put sport peppers on hot dogs, so I think I know flavor."

Bubba grinned. "You also think ketchup is a sin, so your opinion's invalid."

"Well," Levy smirked. "Look who's spicy today."

Bishop leaned back in his chair and crossed his hands over his full stomach. "I swear to God, I've never been so happy not to be a beat cop. You know they're out there sweating their asses off in polyester while they wrangle toddlers hopped up on bomb pops."

Levy laughed. "And listening to float music on repeat. I've already heard 'Born in the U.S.A.' three times before noon."

"I hate to say this, but I'm glad we've got an investigation going on. Otherwise, we'd be out there in that heat shaking hands and kissing babies." Michels said. "I'd have to quit. Full-on walk out."

"Can you imagine poor Sergeant Mendez trying to manage crowd control?" I asked. "Five-foot-two and barely speaks above a whisper."

"She brought a bullhorn," Levy said. "I saw it this morning."

"Then may God have mercy on all our souls."

Bishop pulled the paper off his second sandwich and sighed like he'd reached nirvana, or, God forbid, something none of us ever needed to hear. "This is it. I die right now, bury me with the number nine."

"No," I said. "We're putting you in the ground with the Italian combo and one of those banana pepper stains on your shirt."

"You act like I'd be mad."

We all laughed again, that easy, shoulder-dropping laughter that only comes when no one's bleeding and the phones stay quiet. For a second, it felt like we could stay there, like maybe the world wouldn't ask anything of us that afternoon.

But who was I kidding?

The department landline rang.

The laughter didn't stop at first. It just dipped enough to let us breathe and hear it ring again.

Bishop reached for it, chewing as he did. "Bishop." A pause. His jaw went still. The sandwich froze inches from his face. "Say again?"

We all stopped. Bubba set his sandwich down, Levy dropped her napkin, and I felt the shift before Bishop even moved.

"Putting you on speaker." He pressed the button and set the handset down. "Say it again," he said.

"This is dispatch," the woman's voice came through, clear and shaking. "We've got a 911 call from the Red, White & You Parade. A white van broke through a side barrier on Elm and plowed into the crowd. Estimates are over thirty people hit. Multiple critical injuries. EMS is en route, but the chief wants all officers on this now."

No one spoke.

She continued. "It drove through the east perimeter and into the crowd. Witnesses say the driver didn't stop. Just kept going down Main Street. Last seen heading toward the west exit. Officers on the scene are requesting immediate backup. It's bad. Real bad."

My chair scraped back.

Bishop stood fast. "Has the van been located?"

"Negative. APS and County have units en route. Closest visual puts him past Maple about thirty seconds ago."

"Shit," I muttered.

Bubba already shoved his laptop closed and grabbed his phone. "I'll tap into city traffic cams and pull footage from Elm to Maple. I'll send anything I get straight to Michels."

"Let's go," Levy said, moving before anyone could speak.

No one gave orders—they just moved. Trained, drilled, practiced into instinct. Michels threw open the cabinet, grabbed the go-bags. Levy returned with the med kit and handed out gloves and tourniquets.

"No time to wait," she said.

"I'm on comms," Bubba called, already typing. "Pushing updates to squad frequencies now."

My phone buzzed. Jimmy. I answered. "You on site?"

"Heading out now."

"Good. We're on our way."

He hung up.

I looked at Bishop. "We go now."

"I'll drive, but we're taking a cruiser."

"Works for me."

We didn't run, but we moved fast, every step tight and loaded. Doors slammed open. Radios lit up. The air in the room had shifted from light to sharp. We kept silent as we headed to a cruiser and into something worse than a crime scene. Something chaotic. Uncontrolled.

Public.

"Shit." I slammed the vehicle door after I climbed inside. "Savannah's there with the kids."

18

Bishop almost hit the barricade at forty-five, but he slammed on the brakes and skidded to a stop.

"Go!"

I killed the siren and jumped out before the cruiser stopped rolling. "Holy shit." The air reeked of burnt sugar, gasoline, and iron. The scene exploded in front of me. I'd seen too much bad in my life, but never something this bad or this up close and personal.

I heard Bishop's breath, fast and clipped, beside me. "Dear God."

I sucked in a breath.

Bodies covered the street.

Not debris. Not costumes. Not abandoned floats.

Bodies.

People sprawled across the pavement, some bleeding, some screaming, others crying, many silent. Some moved. Most didn't. Blood smeared the crosswalk and pooled under a twisted stroller near the cross-street curb. A small shoe sat next to it. Empty.

I grabbed my phone and called Savannah, but she didn't answer. "Let's go," I said. "If you find Savannah or the kids, call me first, and not on the radio."

"Copy that." He took off running.

Heat pressed against my skin as I dropped to the ground beside a teenage girl howling for her parents. "Are you hurt?"

She turned onto her side. "My head hurts. Where are my parents?"

"What's your name?"

"Addison. Addison Minor. Do you see my parents?"

I helped her stand. "I'll look for them, but we need to get you to an ambulance. Can you walk?"

She nodded.

"Good. Do you have a cell on you?"

"Yeah. In my pocket."

I dug into her pocket and grabbed the phone and then sent myself a text. "I sent a text to my cell. I'm Detective Ryder. Let the EMT's take care of you and then get out of here. Do not look for your parents. I'll put the word out that you're looking for them. If something happens, I'll call you, but you've got my number now if you need me. Do you understand?"

She nodded again.

"Good." I handed her off to an EMT with a firm order to keep her out of the crowd.

"Yes, ma'am," he said.

I headed back into the chaos. Adults wailed names I couldn't make out. A man stumbled past with his hand clamped over his eye. A woman chased after him, blood streaked down her arms and leaving a trail behind her.

Officers yelled commands. Some set up barriers, some knelt over victims. A few vomited behind parked cars. Sirens from ambulances, fire, and backup couldn't cover the sounds of fear and tragedy. I counted twelve units already on scene, but more poured in with their lights spinning over shattered glass and upturned folding chairs.

I scanned fast. Triage zone to the west. EMTs worked in a blur. Gloves snapped. Gurneys rolled. Hands moved at rapid speeds. One medic pounded a chest. Another clamped gauze to a gash so deep it exposed bone.

For the first time in my career, I felt the fight drain out of me. Hopelessness washed over me.

Come on, Rachel. Get it together.

I turned in place and locked it all in. Burned the scene into my soul, forcing myself to take in every piece.

Float signs crushed into garbage. Popcorn bags melted into the sidewalk. A man in a flag t-shirt lay face-up, lips purple, eyes wide and unmoving.

A thin wail that sounded broken and desperate cut through the noise. I followed it, slamming my boots onto the pavement as I dodged past a stretcher, a bag of bloody gauze, and a line of civilians herded toward safety.

The sound led me to the curb.

A little girl, not older than five, crouched beside a man sprawled across the pavement. I saw a little of Scarlet in her and nearly lost it. Her hands pressed against his chest. Blood soaked through her fingers. Her face twisted in fear, too young to understand what death meant, but old enough to know something had gone terribly wrong.

I dropped to my knees beside her.

The man was in his early forties, with no visible ID, and bled from too many places to count. His eyes stayed open but didn't move.

Shit.

The girl sobbed harder until her voice shattered in quick gasps. "Daddy, wake up. I'm scared."

Her words cut straight through my soul.

I quickly examined her but noted no obvious injuries, so I reached out, slowly and carefully, trying with every ounce of calm I had not to scare her more. "Sweetheart, my name is Rachel, and I'm going to help you, okay?" I placed my hand gently on her arm. "You're okay now. I've got you."

She looked at me, eyes wide, face streaked with dirt and blood. Then back at him. "He's just sleeping. He said don't let go."

Her hands trembled where they pressed his ribs.

My gut twisted. I swallowed it. *Focus, damn it!* "I won't let go," I said. "You can come with me, and we'll find someone to help your daddy, okay?"

She didn't answer.

Someone screamed behind me. A medic barked orders. Time blurred.

I crouched lower and set my free hand gently on hers. "What's your name?"

She whispered it. Too soft to hear.

"What was that?"

"Evie."

"Evie. That's a beautiful name. Does anything on you hurt?"

She shook her head.

"Good. That's good. Sweetie, I need you to come with me now. There are people who can help you. People who will make sure you're safe."

Her bottom lip quivered. "But Daddy—"

"I know. I know, Evie. We'll take care of him. I promise." I released my hand on her arm and snapped a photo of her with her father's face in view. We could ID him through her, but more importantly, we would know who she belonged to once someone checked his ID. I could have, but I didn't want to do it with her watching. "Let's go now. Okay?"

She nodded.

I scooped her up. She weighed nothing. Her arms wrapped tight around my neck. She buried her face in my shoulder.

I stood and cried as I hurried her to an ambulance.

The street moved around us. EMTs ran. Officers shouted. Metal clanged against metal as the barricades dropped. I carried her straight through the noise.

A medic looked up as I approached triage.

"Got a little," I said. "No visible injuries. Father's down. Confirmed."

The medic nodded and reached for her.

Evie clung tighter. "Where's the kids' section?" I asked. "I'll take her." I kept walking behind the tape into triage.

"We've got a space in back for kids only," she said.

"Take me there, please." I followed her behind the triage tent, where a young officer sat with a toddler on his lap. Another child slept curled on a folded blanket. It felt like an alternate reality, so separate from what happened only feet away.

I knelt beside a chair. Evie loosened her grip.

"This is Evie," I said.

The nurse held out her arms. "Hey there, Evie. You can stay with me until we find someone you know. Is that okay?"

Evie turned to look at her, then at me. "My daddy?"

"We'll get him help," I said. I handed her over to the nurse.

"Do you know her last name?" the nurse asked.

"No. Just her first." I whispered, "Her father's gone. I've got a photo of him with her for ID. What's your cell?"

"Send it to the main line." She gave me the number.

I sent the photo with my name and Evie's name as well.

"We've got volunteers from CPS coming in now. We'll keep her safe."

I nodded once. "Thank you."

I left and didn't look back. I didn't breathe until I hit the edge of the next block.

I looked back once, just long enough to lock the image in.

Then I headed straight for the next scream. Two bodies blocked the curb cut. One bled from the mouth, ribs caved. The other was facedown with her limbs twisted. No one had time to cover them yet. I stepped past and froze when a woman clutched my leg.

"Please—my daughter. I can't find her. She was right here."

"What's her name?"

"Tori. She's six. She's wearing red. Please—"

"Are you hurt?"

"Not really. Just sore."

I pointed to the medic station. "Go there. Tell them. They're organizing survivors."

She didn't move.

I crouched down and grabbed her shoulders. "Look at me. Tori needs you to stay upright. Understand?"

"I'm trying."

"You can do it. Go. They'll help you."

She finally stood and wobbled toward the medic station.

Behind me, a paramedic shouted for morphine. Another called out a pulse rate. Someone screamed for airway clearance. More officers poured in.

Jimmy appeared at my left. "Perimeter's loose. Crowd control's breaking. Main's still open on the south end."

"Where's the block?"

"They're working on it. Have you heard from Savannah?"

"Not yet, but she's okay, Jimmy."

"She'd better be." He jogged away.

A firefighter crouched beside a woman slumped against the base of a traffic barrier. I slowed to see if he needed my help. Her jaw glittered with shards of glass. She lifted her hand toward him, slowly and clumsily. Her fingers curling partway before falling limp. Her eyes stayed open, but they didn't follow movement or lock onto his face. He shouted for a medic as he pressed gauze to her throat. She blinked once, then nothing.

The medic arrived five seconds too late.

I shoved past a vendor cart that had tipped over. Popcorn coated the ground like confetti.

Blood soaked into the kernels. I almost slipped on it, but I adjusted and kept going. A girl sat on the curb holding her ankle, skin torn raw. She shook.

I pulled off my overshirt and handed it to her. "Wrap it tight. Help's coming."

"I can't find my brother," she said.

"We'll find him. Hold tight."

I kept moving.

Levy radioed in. "Two bodies pinned under the float at Main and Locust. One's alive. The other isn't. We need hydraulics."

I cut east toward her. Smoke billowed near the bandstand. I passed a boy no older than twelve trying to push his unconscious dad onto a trash can lid.

I shouted to a medic, "Help this kid!"

She ran past me to him.

Main Street split in two ahead, one side was gridlocked with emergency responders, the other still swarmed with civilians.

"Why aren't they cleared?" I asked the closest officer.

"We can't hold them back. They're trying to find people."

"Set up a cordon. Tape if you've got it. Barricades if you don't."

"Yes, ma'am." He took off.

An elderly man leaned against a fence, hyperventilating.

I grabbed another medic. "He needs oxygen."

"I'm out," she said. "They've got tanks at the second triage tent."

I introduced myself to the man and helped him walk there. Step by slow step. He never let go of my wrist.

"Thank you," he whispered.

"Stay safe."

Someone screamed. I ran toward it. It came from a woman crouched next to a girl laid flat on the concrete. The girl convulsed. Her eyes rolled, and foam leaked from her mouth.

"Seizure!" I yelled.

A medic slid beside me. "Clear space!"

We did. He did his job while I held the mother back.

"She has epilepsy," the woman sobbed. "But not like this."

"Let him work."

"She was on the float. She fell off. She fell off when it hit—"

I heard enough. I looked at the medic. He nodded once.

"She's going to make it," I said to the mother.

The calls over the radio kept coming. Status updates. Officer locations. Ambulance requests. Victim tallies. Witness accounts. A dozen overlapping voices on every channel.

Bubba broke through with a single line.

"Van spotted westbound on River. Traffic cam cut after warehouse alley. Could be a switch."

Jimmy came on next. "Units en route. Set a net."

I tuned it out, needing to stay grounded.

A child wailed from inside the ambulance I just passed. Another medic shouted vitals to a nurse. Someone else called for blankets. I couldn't see where it all ended. I paced the entire perimeter. Each turn brought more pain, more blood, more chaos.

A teenage girl filmed the entire thing on her phone. I took it from her and stuffed it into my pocket, then grabbed an officer and said, "Collect every damn phone that's recording. This isn't entertainment."

"Yes, ma'am."

I pushed through the crowd, shoulder to shoulder with panic and noise. My ears rang from the pressure, from the heat rising off the pavement. I turned a corner and scanned for Savannah when something cracked against the back of my skull.

White-hot pain exploded through my head.

And then—

Nothing.

19

My head throbbed. Each pulse hammered behind my eyes hard enough to make me nauseous. I tried to lift my arms, but they wouldn't move. My wrists burned from a rope tied around them. My shoulders ached from being twisted unnaturally behind me. I couldn't stretch.

Damn it!

The rope around my hands hurt. I wiggled my hands the best I could, but they had been tied too tight. I leaned to the right, and then to the left, and hit my head on something that felt like cement blocks. The small space was too tight for me to move or get anything, including air. Whoever put me there had bent my body to fit. But not well. I couldn't shift. Couldn't breathe without scraping against something cold and hard.

Where the hell was I? How did I get there?

I blinked and realized they'd covered my eyes. Keeping them opened underneath whatever covered them didn't help. No light seeped through. Blackness filled the space.

I screamed. No words. Just a guttural scream from deep inside my soul. I sucked in a breath as my heart pounded in my chest.

Keep calm. Keep calm. I needed air. I calmed my breathing until it came out in slow, natural breaths. *You won't get me, you bastard.*

Bishop and the team had to be looking for me. I needed to figure out how to tell them where I was. But how the hell could I do that when I couldn't move?

How long had I been out? *Shit!*

I stopped struggling. Stopped trying to move. I needed to figure out where I was. I listened carefully, hoping, no, praying I would recognize a sound. Not that it would help, but still.

No traffic sounds. No distant voices. Just thick, stale air pressing against my chest and the dull rhythm of my heartbeat rising in my ears. The profound silence wasn't natural. There was not even the sound of distant power lines, or the faint, almost imperceptible thrum of earth from passing vehicles. Nothing to tell me someone could easily find me. Or find me at all.

I didn't know where I was. I didn't know how I had gotten there.

I took a breath, slow and steady. My ribs protested. My skin stuck to something slick. Sweat. My clothes were damp. I shifted again—just an inch—and slammed my shoulder into metal again. I jerked my knees upward and hit another. My knees scraped against what felt like corrugated metal, then again on a smooth, cold panel. It wasn't a perfect cube, then. It felt more like an irregular shape, possibly pieced together, or perhaps a repurposed industrial container. The cold press of metal hinted at minimal insulation, suggesting either a temporary holding or a calculated disregard for my comfort, a detail I filed away for later.

Close. Cramped. Contained.

A box? A container? Maybe a cellar? Maybe worse.

At least it didn't feel like a coffin. Or maybe it did.

Think, Rachel. Think! God, my head hurt. I needed to focus, to push the pain aside and clear the fog. I had to figure out where I was so I could escape.

I wasn't in an open room. The air made that perfectly clear. Was it a sealed container, or a deeply buried chamber? The very stillness, devoid of any natural draft, suggested an airtight seal, or at least a highly controlled environment.

My captor wasn't a run of the mill criminal. He knew what to do, knew how to keep me from escaping.

Damn it.

My mouth was dry. I tasted copper and filth. Blood. Dust. My jaw ached.

They'd hit me—hard. From behind, I guessed, but I had no memory of it. One second I was walking—no, running. The parade. The explosion of motion. Then—

Darkness.

Someone took me. Someone planned it. Waited until I was distracted, until my back was turned.

Him.

The chess piece killer.

He'd taken me. He'd planned the entire tragedy as a diversion, a knight's leap to infiltrate my safe zone. All those people hurt, bleeding, dead. Because of me. Just pawns sacrificed to clear the board, to make his opening move for the queen. This was his game. A psychological operation designed to break me, but I wouldn't let him win. I'd bleed before I'd beg. I'd bruise before I'd break. I refused to be his checkmate.

Panic tried to climb into my throat, but I swallowed it. Hard. I didn't have time to panic. I needed clarity. I needed a way out.

I tilted my head and pressed my ear to the wall. Nothing. Not even a buzz of electricity. Either I was underground or too far from anything to hear.

The space smelled like oil and mold and something older—something rotten. It wasn't just oil, not as far as I could tell. It carried a faint metallic tang, like an infrequently used engine bay, or perhaps heavy machinery. The mold and rot were not just organic decay, but suggested dampness, a lack of regular human presence, or perhaps even a deliberate concealment of odors, a chilling thought I cataloged. Where was I? A metal box? It couldn't be a garage. The space was too small, but since I had air, maybe I was in a metal box inside a garage?

Think, Rachel. Think.

I twisted my wrists just to test the rope again as if maybe something had changed. It cut into my skin. Coarse. Not new. Not clean. Tied by someone who'd done it before. But not too tight. I still had circulation. Thank you, God. I could work with that.

I focused on the pain just to clarify my injuries. The throb behind my eyes. The fire in my joints. The stiffness crawling through my back. I took inventory. No broken bones. No sharp pain in my ribs. My head was the worst of it. Dull and thick and pounding. A concussion. That would slow me down. But I was still alive. Still thinking. Still dangerous.

I'd had concussions before. I'd been in dangerous situations before. They didn't end me, and I wouldn't let another one take me either.

He'd stripped me of everything—my phone, my badge, my weapon. My watch was gone too. No way to know how long I'd been out.

I shifted again and tried to sit up straighter. My back scraped against the metal. My knees hit the wall again. Not enough room to extend. Not enough air to fill my lungs without effort. It wasn't just confinement. It was designed to disorient. To make me panic.

But it wouldn't work.

Think Rachel. Who saw me last? Bishop? Bubba? I replayed the scene in my head, over and over, hoping for a hint to my abductor. Maybe I saw them out of the corner of my eye?

The crowd. The sirens. The sound of people screaming. I was moving through the chaos—then nothing. No scent. No sound. Just a flash of pain, and then black.

Someone had gotten close. Close enough to knock me out cold. Our killer had a plan. He knew I'd be there. Knew I'd be distracted, and that no one would have eyes on me.

If he had wanted me dead, I'd be dead. If he wanted me scared, he'd be watching. Talking. Showing me his face. But there was nothing. No footsteps. No threats. Just silence.

He wasn't done with me yet. The absolute silence, after the initial chaos of my capture was a calculated psychological pressure. He wasn't absent; he was *waiting*. Waiting for my panic to peak, for my defiance to wane. He wanted me to believe I was alone, utterly helpless, to erode my mental defenses without laying a single hand on me. It was a strategy designed to break, not just to hold.

But I couldn't let him win. I wouldn't.

I braced my feet against the opposite wall and tried to shift my weight.

Nothing. I pushed harder as if I could.

Sweat ran down my temple. My breathing stayed even. I focused on each movement. Each grind of my shoulders against the back wall. Each scrape of the rope across my skin. I'd bleed before I'd beg. I'd bruise before

I'd break. I repeated that again, hoping it would give me the emotional strength I needed.

And when I got out he'd regret leaving me alive.

The pounding in my head intensified, but I didn't stop. I used it. Let it fuel me. Let it burn away the fog. Rage pushed through the pain, sharp and clean.

I would get out of there.

I would find who took me, and I would end them.

The air pressed down on me like wet wool, heavy, clinging, and impossible to escape, and the sharp tang of my sweat filled my nose, adding more torture with each struggling breath. Panic surged inside me before I could stop it. It rose fast as the oxygen thinned and retreated with every shallow inhale until my lungs clawed for relief. My chest tightened. My ribs strained against the pressure, and I knew, with terrifying clarity, that I was suffocating, and there wasn't a damn thing I could do to stop it.

I breathed shallowly, rationing the air, knowing it would quickly run out.

Time had no meaning in the dark. I didn't know how long I'd been in the box, only that my body ached in too many places to count, and my brain kept circling the same question like a vulture: *Where the hell am I, and when will he let me out?*

I shifted slightly and winced. The movement sent a bolt of pain through my shoulder. The ropes. The knots. They all created a pain so intense it weakened my resolve. Whoever he was, he knew exactly what he was doing.

I clamped down on the panic rising in my throat and focused with every ounce of energy I had left to stomp it back down where it belonged. I needed to stay calm, no matter what it took. He'd come for me eventually, and I needed to be ready. To hide the fear engulfing me.

Don't think. Breathe. Assess. Survive.

I focused on what I could feel. The cold press of metal beneath me, the way my breath rebounded off the tight space, the new, but subtle whir of something mechanical just outside the box. Maybe a fan. Maybe something worse. Either way, it told me I wasn't buried. Thank God for that.

Just when I thought I might scream, the box shifted. A low scrape of metal against concrete or asphalt vibrated through the floor. Someone was moving me.

I went still. Every nerve snapped to attention. *Come on, bastard. Open the box.*

The motion stopped as quickly as it started. Maybe. Time didn't work right in the dark. I had no way to reference it.

Then came the sound of a lock clicking. Precise and unhurried.

I would breathe without pain again.

The lid cracked open and let in a rush of air that hit my face like a slap. I sucked in as much as I could handle, then released it slowly.

Then I smelled him.

Not cologne. Not body odor. Something worse. Something clean and clinical, like antiseptic and nitrile gloves. A scent that didn't belong anywhere near me.

It reeked of control.

Gloved fingers pressed against the side of my neck. He checked my pulse like I was a specimen, not a person. He didn't speak. Didn't grunt or sigh. Just touched and waited.

I wanted to bite him. Instead, I went still. I would have my chance, but I needed to measure it carefully. Timing meant everything. One slip up and I'd be done. He wouldn't let me live. Then again, would he anyway?

He slid his arms under me and hauled me out of the box like a sack of laundry. My muscles screamed from the sudden change in position, but I didn't give him the satisfaction of making a sound. I forced my head up, even though the blindfold stole any hint of where we were.

My boots dragged across the floor, first concrete, then something softer, but not much. Carpet, maybe. Each step he took imprinted itself in my memory. Five steps, pause, turn. Two more. A slight incline.

Then a chair.

He dropped me into it without a consideration for my sore body. Not that I thought he would consider anything. That wasn't part of his plan. My wrists hit cold metal armrests before the cuffs clamped down. Waist strap. Ankles. I was locked in place again, but more securely, more permanent.

He adjusted my arms and then lifted my chin. He didn't hesitate, didn't speak, didn't rush. He stood still when he finished and stood close enough for me to feel his breath on my face. I felt the heat, the weight of his attention, bearing down on me.

My voice cracked on the first try, so I swallowed and tried again. "You like playing with your food, or is this just a warm-up?"

He said nothing.

A beat passed, maybe two, then he walked away. No footsteps, but I felt his absence. He vanished so smoothly I wondered if I'd imagined him.

But the smell lingered.

I waited.

Eventually, he returned. The scent hit me first again, like a signature or a calling card. He crouched near me, let his gloved fingers brush my cheek. I flinched, then bit my tongue, hating how much that single gesture got under my skin.

He didn't pull away. Instead, he whispered, low and rough, like wind through broken glass. "Now you know how she felt."

My stomach twisted.

"Who?" I demanded, the word sharp and too loud. *Relax, Rachel.* I knew who. Jennifer Abbott.

He didn't answer. Instead, he repositioned my limbs with the same methodical detachment he'd had before. One arm up. The other at my side. He placed a hand under my jaw and tipped my head like I was part of some grotesque sculpture.

Then the tape came.

He smoothed it across my mouth without hesitation, sealing me in silence. I screamed against it, but it came out muffled and useless.

He leaned in close enough that I felt his breath on my ear. Not warm. Not cold. Just *there.* "Not yet." And then he was gone again. No door. No slam. Just gone.

I sat in the chair, my pulse pounding, my jaw clenched so tight my molars ached. Every part of me wanted to thrash, to fight, to tear the restraints apart. But I couldn't waste energy. Couldn't fall apart.

Not then.

He hadn't killed me. Why? Because it wasn't about my death. Not yet. He wanted to make me a spectacle, and I'd be damned if I gave him the show he wanted.

20

———

A door opened, then footsteps scraped across the floor. I stiffened. He didn't speak. Just unlatched the door and stepped into the room. Each step echoed with deliberate intent. Slow. Heavy. Confident.

Somehow, it sounded familiar. Why? Where had I heard that rhythm before? Was it someone from the department? Someone from Duke's? We'd just been there. Could I have met my captor there?

He cleared his throat. I recognized the sound immediately. Who was he? Where did I know him from? *Damn it, Rachel! Think!*

I flinched when I felt his breath on me.

"Easy," he said. His voice hit like a gut punch.

I didn't breathe. I couldn't.

His fingers gripped my chin. He peeled the tape back just slow enough to make it hurt. My skin burned where it lifted.

I didn't move. I didn't speak. I wouldn't, couldn't make a move. Not until I knew what I was up against.

The blindfold came next. My eyes flinched against the sudden brightness, a cheap LED glare reflecting off steel walls.

And then I saw him.

Lawin.

My doctor.

The man who took my vitals, checked my reflexes, wrote prescriptions when my migraines kicked too hard. The same man who laughed at my jokes, listened to stories I didn't share with anyone else. The man Kyle once teased me about. *Schoolgirl crush.*

My stomach churned.

Dr. Torey Lawin stood inches from me, calm as ever. He wasn't dressed like a doctor. No lab-coat. No stethoscope hanging from his neck. He wore a gray button-down and dark jeans. He looked clean. Polished. Controlled.

A doctor anyone trusted easily. Especially women, drawn to his polished charm and distractingly good looks.

My brain scrambled. I searched his face, hoping for a mask to slip, for any hint to tell me what he wanted. What he intended for me. His posture was too relaxed, almost preening. The faint, barely perceptible tremor in his left hand. A minute tell of suppressed excitement I could have missed before. His eyes, though outwardly calm, held a glint, not of warmth, but of a collector admiring his prize. *Me.*

"Hello, Rachel."

I swallowed and said his name through gritted teeth. "Dr. Lawin."

"Ah, it's nice to know you recognize me in my street clothes. Those scrubs are like Halloween costumes. No one recognizes me without them." He smiled, but the warmth never reached his eyes.

My throat tightened. Words crawled to the edge of my tongue but died before reaching air. Instead, I scanned his face for details I'd missed during appointments. His watch. His cologne. The way he closed the door behind him too quietly. The questions he asked—*How often do you run alone? Do you still carry your firearm when you jog? How's your sleep, really?*

Things a primary care doc might ask.

But not like that.

Not while holding eye contact too long. Not while tilting his head as if dissecting my thoughts.

He'd done it. He'd manipulated me into trusting him in the privacy of his office. Where he'd had me in a compromising position, one I finally understood as intentional. He'd planned it for a long time.

He leaned against the wall with his arms crossed. "You trust me, don't you?"

I locked my jaw. His question wasn't a genuine query but a boast. His tone, too smooth, too practiced, indicated a man confident in his manipulation, a confidence that could be leveraged. Overconfidence was often the undoing of such specifically planned schemes. It bred sloppiness and a desire to prolong the game beyond its logical conclusion. "Not even a little. You're a whack job, Lawin."

"No, Rachel. I have an IQ of 186. That makes me a genius."

I stared at him and forced every memory of our appointments to replay like a movie in my head. Our first appointment. He'd joked about my file being *light reading* but asked if I struggled with trauma-induced fatigue. *From what?* I'd asked. He already knew. Of course, he did.

On one visit he mentioned Kyle by name before I brought him up. He said Kyle seemed like a stabilizing force, but I'd brushed it off. Thinking back, I couldn't recall if I had mentioned him before in another appointment.

He'd asked about Tommy. *You still wear the ring?* Like he wasn't prying. Just curious. Completely harmless.

"You studied me."

He shrugged. "It's my job."

"No. Your job involves healing, not obsessing over some patients and overdosing others with fentanyl. Oh, and how could I forget the stuffing them into suitcases part? You're a sick, twisted son of a bitch, Lawin."

Stay calm, Rachel. He's got the upper hand.

His gaze sharpened. "I did my job the way I saw fit. There's a difference."

The bile in my throat crept higher. "You sent those photos."

He nodded once. "I did because they served a purpose."

"Their purposes aren't yours to decide. You're delusional."

He lifted a shoulder. "I'm a trained physician. I treat people to heal and eliminate pain, Rachel."

"You killed your patients. Why? Did they disagree with a diagnosis? Leave a bad review? Miss an appointment? Why kill them?"

He stepped forward and with a voice still soft, said, "You're asking the wrong questions."

I gritted my teeth. What does he want me to ask? What is he trying to steer me toward? What revelation does he want to control? His dismissal of my questions was a strategic redirection. He wasn't interested in the why of the murders, but the *why me*. He craved an acknowledgement of his intellectual superiority, a validation of his twisted rationale. That desire for validation, that desperate need to be understood, was a potential vulnerability, a lever I might push later to gain information or even control the narrative. "Then why don't you tell me what I should be asking? What are the right questions?"

He leaned toward me. "There is only one question to ask." He paused as if I would figure it out.

I didn't.

"That question, Rachel, is why you?"

My hands fought the binds. I stared past him as my mind sliced through every appointment, every exchange, every damn sentence he ever spoke.

"You never let yourself rest." "You push too hard." "You think surviving makes you invincible."

All delivered like concern. All designed to catalog my weaknesses.

He knew about Tommy's death. About the hesitation. About Kyle, and how hard it had been for me to move on. He knew my guilt lived in my bones.

"You picked me because I didn't see you coming."

He smiled again, and that time, with pride. "Now you're getting it."

I wanted to launch at him. I wanted to claw that smug expression off his face. But I didn't move. Instead, I took measured breaths, hoping to distract him while I committed the room to memory. Every inch of the space embedded into my brain for an escape plan. I had to plan, because he'd planned every detail. But he hadn't planned for my training. And that meant he underestimated me, which would be his biggest mistake.

"Didn't you take an oath to save lives, not take them?"

"Most people don't know the modern version of the Hippocratic Oath by Louis Lasagna. They forget this part. *Most especially must I tread with care in matters of life and death. If it is given me to save a life, all thanks. But it may also be within my power to take a life; this awesome responsibility must be faced with great humbleness and awareness of my own frailty. Above all, I must not play at God."*

"But you are playing God."

He pulled a chair from the corner of the small room and sat across from me. "I am not." His smile sent shivers up my spine. "Though I understand why you might think that. Mrs. Abbott suffered from debilitating migraines. I would have expected Dr. Barron to note that in the autopsy, but clearly, he is not as intelligent as I had assumed."

"You're not as intelligent as you think you are. A doctor can't see that in an autopsy."

"Of course not, but had he waited for her medical records, he would have seen it noted in them."

"And what would that matter? You sliced her throat and stuffed her into a suitcase. What's that got to do with chronic migraines?"

"If I'm being honest, nothing. But you're missing the point again, detective."

"Then explain it to me. Tell me why you murdered Jennifer Abbott and Gary Kinder. Why bring them into this if it's about me?"

"I helped them. I eliminated their pain. Mrs. Abbott has been coming to me for four years now. At first, we managed her migraines through a strict diet and exercise plan as well as reducing her stress levels. Unfortunately, when her marriage struggled, the migraines worsened again. She had a very painful year, and it is my responsibility to eliminate that pain in any way I can."

"Eliminate pain?" I scoffed as I forced the words out past my tightened throat. "With a fentanyl overdose? And how exactly did a respectable doctor like you get his hands on Schedule II Actiq lollipops, Lawin? That's not exactly something you pick up at CVS. Or did you just *eliminate the pain* for Gary Kinder and his company's inventory, too?"

A thin, cold smile played on his lips. "Ah, Detective, ever so direct. And ever so predictable. You're thinking of street fentanyl, aren't you? The messy, imprecise drug used to drag the weak into addiction. But as you've learned, my methods are nothing like that. My victims are curated, my tools, precise. Mr. Kinder, for instance, proved quite *useful* in my acquisition."

My jaw clenched. "Useful how? Did the medical supply rep just hand over a batch of Actiq like a sample? Or did you blackmail him into diverting highly controlled substances for you?" I pushed, trying to pierce his arrogance.

"Let's just say Mr. Kinder had access," Lawin mused. His eyes glittered with a predatory satisfaction. "And certain vulnerabilities. He believed I was helping him find peace—a rather convenient narrative, wouldn't you agree? He understood the efficacy of a buccal delivery; I merely provided the means and the opportunity for him to be part of something bigger. He was so eager to be *useful*. A tragic figure, really. His company's inventory system, while robust, had its blind spots. Easily exploited by someone with a deeper understanding of supply chain management than a mere sales director. It appears his mental issues extended to his professional ethics, didn't they? And the beauty is, Detective, that a few missing units of Actiq, even when initially flagged, could easily be attributed to misplacement or inventory error within a large medical supply operation. Until bodies start turning up, of course."

"Wouldn't a regular dose of fentanyl have worked on Jennifer Abbott? Not the overdose you forced on her? And Gary Kinder as well?"

"I never force anything on my patients. Mrs. Abbott and Mr. Kinder agreed to the doses and happily took them, though one could question Mr. Kinder's decision given his mental issues."

Happily took them? The words curdled in my gut. He twisted their despair, their vulnerabilities, into a perverse form of consent. It wasn't compassion; it was the ultimate betrayal of trust, preying on the sick and desperate. He saw them as broken, but he was the one truly shattered. "What do you mean, mental issues? Was he sick?"

"In a manner of speaking, yes. Bipolar disorder."

"There's medicine to manage that."

"Medicine only works if the patient takes it, which Mr. Kinder didn't."

"So, you killed him because he wouldn't follow your orders?"

He laughed. "Of course not. He wanted to die. He told me so multiple times. I simply helped him reach his goal."

I wanted to throw up, but I refused to show weakness. "And Jennifer Abbott and Gary Kinder were just the pawns you chose for this specific game, weren't they?" I pushed through my nausea. "Because we found your dry runs, Lawin. The other fentanyl overdoses initially ruled accidental or suicide. They were your practice kills, weren't they? Specifically designed to perfect your method, so you could finally make your grand performance here in Hamby."

Lawin's smile widened into a chilling expression of delight. "You understand the concept of a masterpiece, don't you? Every artist has their preliminary sketches, their studies, before the magnum opus. Jennifer and Gary were indeed pawns, as you so aptly observed. Necessary to open the board, to provide phantoms for you to follow, to establish the patterns you so desperately rely on for control. But those earlier accidental deaths, as you so crudely put it, were lessons. Strokes on the canvas, perfecting the masterpiece. Each one refined the rook's strategy. The controlled environment, the cleaning of the bodies, the absence of blood at the scene. Each one honed the knight's play. The deception, the surprise, the untraceable methods like phone spoofing, the fake tattoos, the use of generic supplies. They were crucial rehearsals, ensuring my precision and demonstrating my invincible control. They established my domain, my castle, where I reign supreme. All to expose the weaknesses in your approach, Detective."

"Then why me? I'm not sick. You've given me a clean bill of health." My voice scraped across my throat like it had to crawl out.

Dr. Lawin didn't hesitate. "Because you were predictable."

I glared at him. "Bullshit."

"You were. Not in a simplistic sense, but behaviorally. When threatened, you react. When prodded, you dig. You press forward even when wounded. You call that resilience. I call it a flaw."

"I'd call you a flaming jackass," I muttered, "but that would be giving you too much personality."

He didn't blink. "I knew the exact pattern your mind would follow. First you'd analyze the photo. Then you'd take the lead, build a case around it and assign the photo meaning. You'd search for a pattern because that's what gives you control. I had you by the time you began to question your theories."

"I never questioned my theory. I knew from the start the killer was a psycho."

He smirked. "Then I guess you should have." He folded his arms in a swift, controlled movement. "Because I'm anything but, and I believe you know that."

"Wrong."

"Think as you will, Rachel. It doesn't matter if you know me because I know you. You tell yourself you're a survivor, and you are. But you believe surviving makes you immune to the damage."

"I'm not immune," I snapped. "I'm standing. It's called moving on."

He nodded slowly, almost approvingly. "Yes. And that's precisely what fascinated me. The way you carry your guilt. The way it lives beneath your skin, informing every choice you make. Tommy's death wasn't your fault, Rachel. But you believe it was. That belief is the key to every decision you make."

I clenched my jaw. "You don't get to say his name."

21

___

"I know more about Tommy than anyone else in your life does, Rachel. You told me things you've never spoken aloud to your Detective Bishop, to Kyle, even to Lenny. You brought me your pain in a neat little box and handed it over."

"I didn't do that. You were my doctor. You asked questions and I answered."

"Which makes you my subject. It's quite simple, really."

I wanted to throw something, but I settled for fury. "So what? You decided to conduct some psych experiment on me because I trusted you?"

"No," he said, in a flat voice. "I chose you because you are the perfect Queen. Powerful. Influential, but burdened. You overextend yourself, Rachel. You protect everyone except yourself, and you're blind to your own decline."

I narrowed my eyes. "I was right. You studied me."

"Thoroughly. Completely. Your gait. Your tone. Your tells. You have three different expressions for anger, two for guilt, and none for fear, which is clear now."

"I have no fear *at the moment* because I'm not afraid of you."

"Ah, but you should be, and you will be soon enough. Once you know what I have planned, my queen."

I remained as calm as possible given the threat and my unyielding desire to kick him in the balls. "You're a coward with credentials."

He cocked his head. "That's what makes this beautiful, yes? I don't need to overpower you physically. I dismantled you with information. I opened a door to inside your mind and rearranged the furniture."

"Newsflash, Doc. You picked the wrong woman to psychoanalyze. I've had stronger people than you try to break me, and they're all either dead or in prison."

He smiled thinly and without joy. "But none of them understand you like me. You think this is about killing you. It's not. That would be too final."

I laughed. "You mean too difficult."

"No. Too easy." His voice dipped. "This was about a form of control that lingers. I want to watch you unravel. To show you that the very instincts you rely on could be turned against you."

"So this is what? Your victory lap?"

He walked to a table, picked up a small recorder, and clicked it off. "No. This is a courtesy."

"Oh good. A serial killer with manners."

"I'm not a killer, Rachel. I've explained that. Perhaps we can move forward now?"

"Right. My bad. You helped end her pain. Just like Kinder. Got it."

His eyes flicked over my face. "They were pawns, if you will. Necessary for both them and me. I chose her because she reminded me of you. Weak underneath but with an outward strength that fooled others. You were meant to see yourself in her. That was the point."

"She had a husband. A life."

"You assigned her value. Not me."

"You're insane."

"No. I'm efficient and calculated. You value justice, but justice is subjective. You pursue truth because you fear irrelevance. You fear that without the badge, without the chase, you are nothing."

I stared at him. "You know what I think? I think someone overlooked you. Somewhere in your life, someone decided you weren't important. So you built this pathetic little fantasy where you control everything, where you matter. But newsflash, you scumbag. No one gives a shit about you. And killing people won't make you important to anyone but yourself."

"Wrong," he said, almost bored. "I matter to you and your team. I matter because I see people clearly. I see what they are beneath their posturing. And you, Rachel Ryder, are a masterpiece of repression."

I snorted. "Oh, please."

"You carry Tommy's murder like a sacrament. You relive it. Replay it. That hesitation. That one second pause. You've made it define you."

I looked away. The precision with which he articulated my deepest fears, my guilt about Tommy, sent chills down my spine. He was excavating. He wanted a reaction, but I wouldn't give him what he wanted. Instead, I analyzed the *use* of this information: he wasn't just taunting, he was trying to break my focus, to disarm me psychologically before any physical confrontation. "You think you know me, but you don't. You have no idea what I'm capable of."

He stepped closer and breathed into my face. Mint. His breath smelled like mint. "Yes, Rachel. I do. That guilt is why you never rest. It's the precise reason you are who you are. Why you run harder, fight longer, work later. Because the second you slow down, he's there. Bleeding out. Dying all over again."

I swallowed hard. "You're not going to win, Doc. I will kill you before I let that happen."

A creepy sneer engulfed his face. "Don't be insulted, Rachel. That's not my point. My point is that you've weaponized guilt into purpose. And I admire that. Truly. But it makes you predictable."

"You keep saying that like it's true."

He smiled. "It is true. When I sent the photo, I knew exactly what you'd do. You'd treat it like a case. You'd call Bishop. You'd run digital forensics. You'd dig into it harder than anyone else would have. You took the bait because your pride demands it."

"You baited me. You used a woman's death to get to me."

"She wasn't random. She was curated. She had the same trauma indicators. Guilt. Distress. Dysfunction. The same emotional architecture. She was a mirror. A test case."

I felt bile rise in my throat. "She was a person."

"A person you didn't know. A person whose death changed everything for you just as I'd planned. That's power, and I gave it to you."

"You're twisted."

"No," he said. "I'm precise. I removed the pawn to expose the Queen."

My jaw clenched. "Let me guess. You think this ends with you standing over my body?"

"No," he said softly. "It ends when you understand. When you realize that everything you thought made you strong, your independence, your defiance, your control, is a façade. I stripped it away."

"I'm still here. You won't take any of that from me, and you sure as hell won't take my life."

"We'll see about that."

"You think this makes you smart, don't you?" I asked. "You think exploiting my trauma makes you powerful? All it does is prove what a weak, cowardly little man you are."

"I disagree. I set the board. And now, with one move, I removed your illusion of safety."

I gritted my teeth. "You haven't won anything."

He leaned in, placing his face less than an inch from mine. "But I will."

I narrowed my eyes. "You're so desperate to be the villain, you forgot how stories like this end. You never kill the Queen. She survives. She hunts, and she wins. She always wins."

"Marie Antoinette and Anne Boleyn would disagree."

I rolled my eyes as if I couldn't care less about them. "You think I'll break down? You think you've torn something open in me?" I laughed. "You haven't even scratched the surface, doc."

"I beg to differ, Rachel. I've done more than scratch the surface. I've excavated it. I've exposed you."

"I've been exposed before, yet I'm still standing."

"Not for long."

I laughed. "You think fear will control me? I carry fear like I carry a gun, tucked at my hip, always within reach, never defining me."

"Yet you sit there with no such weapon now. All you have to rely on is yourself."

"Yes, but you've made one mistake."

He tilted his head. "Which was?"

"You let me see you. You should've stayed hidden. Now I know what I'm dealing with, and I promise you, Lawin, you won't win this game."

"Oh, but I already have." He turned to leave.

"Wait."

He paused and turned back. "Yes?"

"One last question," I said. "Why the chess metaphor? What is this to you, really? It's not just a game. Murder is never just a game."

"You think I see you as prey, but I don't. I see you as the only adversary worth engaging. The only mind agile enough to match my own. That's what makes this interesting."

"So you want me to see you."

"And now you do."

I needed to keep him there even if it meant repeating the same things. I had to understand him so I could predict his next move. Letting him leave put others at risk. Bishop. Kyle. The rest of the team. I needed to squash him like a bug before he could get to them.

"You built an entire murder scene just to get my attention?"

"I didn't build a scene, Rachel. I crafted a message."

I sneered. "Well, congrats on the delivery. I got the message. Loud and creepy."

"You missed the meaning." He folded his hands in front of him. "It wasn't the woman that mattered. It was what she represented. You. Like I said."

I shook my head. "No. She wasn't me."

"She could have been, and that's what unsettled you. You saw yourself laid out on that bed, didn't you? Maybe just for a second."

I refused to give him the satisfaction. "I saw a victim. And I made it my job to find her killer. That's what I do." I scanned the room, desperately trying to figure out where I was, what he had stuck me inside.

"And in doing so, you fell directly into the structure I built for you. You were never investigating me, Rachel. You were playing your part."

"I'm not a pawn."

"Of course not. That was never my intent," he said. "You are the Queen. And that's why you have to fall."

"You know what happens when someone tries to take down the Queen, Lawin? The rest of the board burns."

"An emotional response I expected, which is why I pulled Mr. Kinder into our game as well."

"What's that supposed to mean?"

"He represents the bishop. Your Bishop."

"No." I shook my head. "He's a pawn. You left a pawn."

"Confusion and unpredictability are part of the game, Rachel. Consider him practice for my plan for your Bishop." He removed a thermos from his backpack, opened it, and placed it to my lips. "Take a drink. You need to remain hydrated."

I blanched. "I'm not thirsty."

He pressed it to my lips. "It's not a request, Rachel." When I didn't budge, he pressed harder. "Now."

I finally took a sip, and I instantly knew he'd screwed me. The water didn't taste right.

"Bishop will find me. He's smarter than you. You'll never get to him."

"What says I haven't already?"

Please God, not Bishop. Please, let him be screwing with my head. "You think you've won?"

He tilted his head and studied me. "You don't? You're chained. You're isolated. Your team has no idea where you are. Your resources are gone. Your sense of direction compromised. If I had wanted you dead, you'd be gone already."

"Then why aren't I?"

He paused. "Because death is release that would make you a martyr to your own myth."

"You think I care about my legacy?"

"I think you care more than you let on. You built a life out of control, out of justice and order. What happens when I dismantle that? What are you when the structure crumbles?"

I stared him down. "I'm still me. And I'll still come for you."

He gave a small, cold smile. "You say that now. But every hour you spend here, every minute you spend questioning whether you misread the clues, whether you failed to notice something obvious—those are cuts, Rachel. Small and precise. Psychological hemorrhaging."

"I've been tortured before, Lawin. This is nothing."

He gave a small shrug. "Physical torture is amateur. This is erosion. And it's already begun."

"I know what you're doing."

"Of course you do," he said, voice clipped. "You're very smart. That's what made it so exhilarating to design."

"Damn, doc. Take me off that pedestal. I'm in love with someone else. You'll never have me."

He smiled again. "I'm in love with the game, not you. And you're the only opponent worthy of it."

"You keep thinking that. Hey, tell me this. What happens when the department finds me?"

"They won't."

"They already know something's wrong."

"They always know something's wrong. You've trained them to expect you to be difficult. To go off the rails."

"They know me. They know I wouldn't just disappear."

"You're sure of that?"

"Yes."

He stepped closer again. "Are you sure enough to bet your life on it?"

I met his eyes. "Yes."

"Then you're not as smart as I give you credit for."

"And you're not as unreadable as you think."

He quirked an eyebrow. "Oh?"

"This isn't a game. It's a cry for validation."

He didn't move, but the twitch in his jaw said I'd struck a nerve.

"I see exactly who you are. A man with too much time and not enough significance. A man who wanted to feel like he mattered in the life of a woman who barely noticed him."

"You noticed me," he said sharply. "Every time you came into my office."

"Because I thought you were helping me. Not building a psychological case file."

He didn't respond.

"So what now?" I asked. "You keep me here until what? I crack? Beg you for something? Try to understand you?"

"No," he said. "You're already beginning to understand."

"The only thing I understand is that you're a psychopath that needs help."

"I need no one."

"Sure you do. You need me to validate this insanity. You need me to believe that you are somehow clever. You need to prove to yourself that you're in control, but you're not."

"I control everything in this space."

"You control what I let you believe you control," I spat. "But that ends here."

He stepped back, breathed evenly, and studied me for several long seconds. "You'll come around."

"No, I won't."

He nodded once. "That's part of the process."

"You keep saying that. Like I'm supposed to be grateful."

"Not grateful," he said. "Enlightened."

"I've been through worse."

"Perhaps. But not with someone who knew you this well. Who understood what buttons to push. What regrets to invoke. What memories to exploit."

"And you'll die because of all that."

A beat of silence passed. His gaze narrowed. "Is that a threat?"

"It's a promise."

He looked at me for a long moment, then walked to a shelf near the door, selected a folder, opened it, and turned back to me. "Tommy's file," he said.

My heart stopped for just a moment.

"I requested them. I studied them, alongside your psychological profile of course."

I ground my teeth together. "You can't use my husband's death to justify this circus."

"And yet, I have."

I stared at him, breathing heavily, tethered by fury and iron. "You think you've written the ending to my story," I said. "But I'm not done."

"You will be," he replied.

"You don't know how stories work, Lawin. You never kill the queen first. Because when you do, the rest of the board stops playing by the rules."

He covered my mouth and eyes again and left.

22

The silence pressed in first, thick and absolute, until even the sound of my breathing pissed me off.

The blindfold cinched across my eyes and scratched against my temples. I shook my head and rubbed it against my shoulders to shift the blindfold enough to allow me to see a scrap of light or anything.

The more I moved, the more I rubbed it against my shoulder, the more it loosened, but I couldn't get it off. I made progress, enough to see blotches of the peripheral area around me if I moved my head to just the right spot, but my sight was severely limited. I gave up for the time being. I needed to maintain what little energy I had left.

My wrists ached. My legs hurt, and I just wanted to kill Lawin. A primal, guttural urge I wasn't sure I'd fight when he returned. And he would return. He still had moves to make, and I had to be ready. Even bound and gagged, I had to be ready.

I tilted my head and listened, but the room didn't answer me. It was the echo that finally did. A faint bounce of air off a hard surface. No give. A sound the room couldn't absorb, just threw back in waves. Hollow.

The scents settled into my nose next. A carnival of them mixed together, but not intentionally, at least I didn't think. Motor oil. Faint mildew. Dust. Old wood soaked with oil, maybe. Temperature swings. No floral detergent.

No food. Nothing organic beyond the dampness clinging to the walls. Storage. It had to be, but not residential.

The old wood smell hinted at wooden beams, not concrete, and the mildew, maybe a lack of climate control or infrequent air circulation. So, a more personal, less institutional setting. It wasn't a public space; it was private and chosen specifically for its isolation and anonymity.

I shifted and leaned sideways, keeping the motion tight, controlled. I didn't know if he had a camera on me, or if he stood right outside the door.

Door. How had I missed that before? I needed to stay focused. I needed to pay attention.

He'd entered through one. I remembered the sound. The metal knob rattling, the subtle click of a mechanical latch, not the broad rumble of a garage door. He hadn't pulled or lifted anything. No chains. Just a turn and push.

That narrowed it down but didn't stop me from thinking it was some form of storage unit. Whether one in a building or a personal one though, I couldn't tell.

It wasn't some industrial warehouse with a loading dock. Not one of those massive places off the highway with roll-ups and fluorescent lights. This was older. Private. Possibly standalone. Maybe behind a house, or part of a commercial complex that hadn't been updated since the nineties.

I catalogued every sound I could remember from when he'd come in.

His footsteps had echoed sharp against concrete. I remembered the metallic scrape of his boot heel on it from before. The way his breath stayed calm and steady, not like someone hauling weight or hurrying. He wasn't rushed. He had time. Then again, he didn't have to use the space for anything other than me.

Or maybe all his victims.

He'd stood close. I remembered the smell of antiseptic on his skin. Not alcohol. Hospital-grade disinfectant. That acrid, artificial clean layered beneath whatever cologne he wore. Woodsy. Expensive. Sandalwood, maybe? My stomach turned just thinking about it. Something about that scent made my skin crawl.

How long had I been out?

Hours? Days? Weeks?

My tongue was dry, and my mouth tasted like cotton and metal. Had he drugged me? It felt likely. I remembered the crowd, how tragic the situation was, working my way through the crowd and then blackness. It would have been easy to take me then. The chaos. The fear. The people injured, dead, those running around begging for help. The scene too intense to notice an abduction.

And that had been his plan. The sacrifice of lives meant nothing to him. My temple throbbed. I winced as I tried to piece it together. He'd brought me to the storage unit still knocked out, and he could have drugged me while still unconscious. Had he injected me? I scanned my arms for things I wouldn't see and couldn't with the blindfold. Nothing obvious. No sting on the inside of my elbows. No soreness at the shoulder. If he had, he'd done it well. With the precision of a doctor, of course. But why drug me at all if I was already asleep? Because he didn't want me to wake up during transport. Which meant we weren't far from where he took me. Had to be less than an hour. Maybe less than thirty minutes. Because drugging someone for a two-hour ride risked complications. Too much sedation, and I might not wake up at all. And that didn't fit his plan. He wanted me awake, but not right away. So, no. It hadn't been days or weeks. It had been hours. Or, I'd been lucky.

I angled my chin and waited. Sounds carried, and I needed to hear one I could recognize. A beat passed. Then two. And then I heard it.

A truck's diesel engine rumbled past. Not far. Probably within thirty yards. The doppler shift told me it was fast and straight. No turn. That narrowed it. A main road, not a winding residential. I counted ten seconds. Another car. Smaller, its tires squealing faintly as it stopped. Maybe a gas station nearby or a traffic light. I wasn't sure because I couldn't tell. But I knew more than before. The distinct doppler shift of the diesel truck, accelerating and then fading, wasn't just noise; it was an acoustic fingerprint. It told me the road was straight, without immediate intersections or turns that would alter the sound profile. The consistent speed suggested a thoroughfare, not a residential street. It implied an arterial road, perhaps a highway, but one without significant local traffic density, which told me I was near a more rural-industrial fringe, or an area with specific truck routes.

That was something. Something I hoped I could manipulate to my advantage.

I angled my knee and pressed my foot into the ground, using my heel to map out the floor. No insulation. Nothing soft.

It was definitely a utility space. "Storage," I muttered against the tape.

The light had crept in around him. Dim and angled. So not fluorescent ceiling lights. No motion sensor. Maybe a side office or utility closet inside the larger building. Maybe a shed attached to a larger warehouse. Or a rented outbuilding on private land.

Another vehicle passed.

Then a horn blared, long and impatient. A delivery truck? Commercial. Somewhere active. Not fully isolated. Probably just off a major road. So where could we be that was close enough, out of the way, but still near traffic?

North Main? Maybe one of the older warehouse lots behind Crabapple Crossing. That stretch had a few buildings, some empty, some used for contractor storage. Fenced, but not heavily patrolled. Or off Highway 9, where those old landscaper yards sat next to pawn shops and vacant lots.

It could've been Alpharetta, too. He had time. But if he wanted to watch me, wanted to return, he'd keep me close. Closer than Alpharetta. Somewhere he could control. Somewhere near his office in Hamby.

The blindfold itched again. Sweat trickled beneath it and burned a cut on my temple. One I hadn't noticed before. My head rolled sideways. My eyes hurt and my brain had begun to fog. I couldn't stay awake. The son of a bitch had put something in that water. I fought it, but not for long. I simply couldn't.

He pulled the door open, the sound only a whisper against the silence of my confinement, yet it grated across my nerves. I kept my face impassive and my breathing even, refusing to grant him even a flicker of the satisfaction he craved. He stepped inside, his soft footsteps on the slab of concrete. I felt his presence before he fully entered—the subtle shift in the air, the faint, clinical scent of him that clung to the space like a brand.

He stood a few feet away and I intuitively knew he was surveying me with that practiced, assessing gaze I knew from our appointments.

"Still defiant, I see," Lawin said. His voice stayed as calm as a flatline. "Good. The Queen must always retain her spirit, even when cornered."

My jaw clenched. I wanted to unleash a torrent of rage, to demand answers he'd already twisted into his warped logic. But I bit back the impulse. *Don't give him the show he wants*, I reminded myself, the words a silent whip across my own defiance. He was playing a game, and every emotional reaction was a point for him.

He moved, his hand appearing in my peripheral vision briefly. My eyes tracked the movement in the room, but I still couldn't see anything helpful

I stilled, ears straining. A cabinet door opened with a soft thud, followed by the clink of glass against glass. Something metal scraped across a tabletop, then another object dropped with a dull thump. He was choosing things. Arranging them for what? Setting the stage for whatever came next. What fresh piece of his twisted game did he intend to parade before me?

He removed the coverings on my face. Finally.

I immediately said, "I need to use the bathroom. Urgently."

He snickered. "I think you can wait."

"No, Lawin, I can't. Whatever you put in that water is making me sick. You won't like what is coming."

"The diaper will help. It's the best I can do until I administer more medicine, which will be after our talk."

Diaper? He had to be kidding. I shifted slightly in my chair. He wasn't. How had I missed that?

"You need more water. That will help your stomach."

"Screw you, Lawin."

"Manners, Rachel. Manners are always beneficial in these situations, don't you think?"

"You might think that, but I have no experience in being held captive by a psycho doctor."

He placed the thermos to my lips. When I didn't open them, he pressed harder and forced them open.

"What's in it? What are you drugging me with now?"

"Nothing that will hurt you. I wouldn't kill the queen without giving her a chance to win. That would be pointless, don't you think?" He cleared his throat and then smiled. "Now, we spoke of pawns, didn't we?" His fingers dipped into his backpack. "Expendable, yes, but crucial. They pave the way." He removed a chess board and the pieces and began setting up the game. After almost finishing, he retrieved a small, dark object and turned it over in his fingers. "And we established Mr. Kinder's role, didn't we? A trick for you to ponder."

He moved pieces across the board. First white. Then black. Moving pawns and clicking other ones with the pieces in his hand to knock them over and remove them from the game. "There are three pawns eliminated now."

Had he murdered someone else, or was he messing with me? I refused to ask, refused to act as if I cared. The colder I became, the more unsettled he'd become. I hoped.

He played himself again. "It's not a simple game, Rachel. Not just black vs. white, but logic against instinct. Order against chaos.

"The bishop on G5 has been a thorn pinning my knight," he said. "It's mocked him with stillness. Unmoving, but powerful. I needed him gone."

"You're lying. You haven't hurt Bishop. This isn't about him, Lawin. It's about me. Untie me and let me play the game with you."

Lawin chuckled, a low, dry sound that scratched at my resolve. "Are you sure? As I said before, confusion and unpredictability are part of the game, Rachel." His eyes glinted with amusement as he held up the bishop. He smiled up at me and then moved a pawn to knock the bishop off the board, then he placed it deliberately beside it.

"Ah, the Bishop," he began, his voice taking on the cadence of a perverse lecturer. "Long reach, controlling diagonals, creating pins. Limiting options." He tapped the bishop piece. "Gary Kinder was instrumental in creating certain *conditions*. He was the pawn, as you suggest. His death, and the precise circumstances of it, his work in medical supply, his unique access, allowed me to control the narrative. To funnel your investigation. To ensure you focused precisely where I wished."

"On me."

"At times, yes."

My breath caught. He wasn't just talking about Gary Kinder, and he knew I understood that. He meant Rob.

"You see," Lawin continued. His voice dropped slightly. "The pieces are never random. Each has a function, a purpose in the grand strategy." He paused, his gaze fixed on me, and waited for my reaction.

I clamped down, refusing to give him the satisfaction.

"Then, of course, we have the rook." He tapped on the castle-shaped piece, then picked it up and turned it slowly. "Solid, powerful, moving in straight lines. Strength. Control. Territory. My sanctuary." His words echoed Dr. Sharma's analysis. "The cleaned bodies, the absence of blood. That is the Rook's work. My castle is my killing ground, a place of absolute control, where I carry out my macabre artistry. The luxury hotel robe, Rachel. What do you see that as?"

I bit my tongue. I'd begun to feel dizzy. *No, Rachel. Fight it.*

"It's the symbol of my domain. Not that the killings happen *at* a hotel, of course. Just that my fortress is precisely that: a fortress."

My mind raced as I began connecting the dots. He was boasting, wasn't he? Revealing his methods, his artistry. He was telling me that previous victims, perhaps even before Jennifer Abbott and Gary Kinder, had been used to build his castle, to refine his process, to establish his controlled environment. The realization settled in my gut like a stone. *He's done this before, just without the fanfare, without the chess pieces.* And the victims were those who helped him create his untouchable domain.

"And then, the knight." He presented the horse-shaped piece. "Ah, the trickster. Unpredictable. Sudden. Infiltrating enemy lines." He smiled, but not a happy one. A cold, knowing expression instead. "The manipulated photo, the fake tattoo. The phone spoofing. Your sense of security, shattered by a body on your partner's porch. The parade chaos, designed as a diversion for my entrance. And that black car, following you, letting you know I was there without directly engaging. All hallmarks of a knight's play. Those who thought they were simply going about their lives, perhaps with a secret or a vulnerability, easily outmaneuvered by an unseen hand."

He placed the knight next to the bishop.

My stomach sank. I felt like I might be sick. "What did you give me?"

"Relax, my friend. You'll be rested again soon." He exhaled. "Now, as I was saying, these were not merely victims, Rachel. They were lessons. Each one, a stroke on the canvas, perfecting the masterpiece." He gestured to the pieces. "And each stroke designed to expose a weakness, a blind spot, not in them, but in you. To prove how predictable you truly are."

A vein pulsed in my neck. He was reducing human lives, people with their own pain and struggles, to mere *pieces* in his ego game. Anger burned, hot and sharp, inside me, but I forced it down. *Don't. React. Think.*

"There are always more pieces," he said. "Always more moves. And the game, my Queen, has only just begun." He turned his back to me, and walked toward the door, leaving me tethered to the chair, and to the chilling realization that every life he touched, every act of violence, was merely a rehearsal, a step toward his victory over someone he deemed a challenge.

Me.

23

I woke up slowly, groggy from whatever he'd put in the water again. And cold. Not chilled. Cold. No, freezing. Every piece of me ached, both internally and externally. My spine pressed into something hard and sterile, not the damp, musty chair I'd come to expect. The scent of the room had changed. Something clinical, something medical and artificial had taken over.

Like a hospital room.

As my head cleared, I realized the silence had disappeared, replaced by something steady. Something electrical. Ventilation? A refrigerator? No. Not humming. Just air moving with intention.

I sat up. Pain seared through my body.

Wait. Hadn't I already been sitting? I looked down and realized he had laid me on a gurney. That first shock came fast. Then simple slow realizations as the drugs wore off. My mouth, uncovered, my eyes bare. No blindfold. My lashes brushed air, not cotton or tape. For the first time since he took me, since he made me his project, he'd kept the mask and mouth gag off, and that terrified me more than the dark ever had.

I blinked and stared at the walls around me.

Where was I? It wasn't the same place. He'd moved me. It wasn't like the other space. I glanced up at the ceiling. An off-white dry-walled one marked with faint streaks like smoke stains or old water damage. A line of faint discoloration ran along a seam that might've once housed fluorescent panels, but where only static lighting remained. Flat and unforgiving.

A surgical room.

My stomach flipped. I shifted slightly and pain bloomed low in my pelvis. Not cramps, not bruising, but some kind of intrusion. A thick, foreign ache pulsed with the beat of my heart. I'd seen it on victims dragged into ICU beds, from long surgeries, from trauma centers, but I'd never felt it in my own body.

I tried to climb off the bed, but it hurt too much. The rope dug into the same grooves it always had, but he'd loosened the bondage at my shoulders. He hadn't bothered resetting the knots. I glanced at my legs, and that's when I saw it. The clear plastic tube taped to my thigh, trailing down to a half-full drainage bag hooked beside the gurney. A urinary catheter positioned with clinical precision. The tube curved from between my legs. He must have inserted it while I was unconscious.

That motherfucker.

My breath caught in my throat. My bladder felt like nothing. Not full. Not empty. Just absent. Another tube, thinner and affixed along my left flank, snaked beneath the edge of my shirt. The adhesive patch securing it stretched across my hipbone. I shifted my leg. The pull was sharp, unmistakable. Was it a fecal management system? I caught sight of the pouch and realized it was.

The catheter and fecal bag violated me both physically and emotionally, and he knew that. It was a deliberate act of psychological dehumanization. He didn't only incapacitate me, he had reduced me to a specimen. By managing my most basic biological functions to assert absolute control, he could manipulate the outcome to his advantage. Or so he thought. What he didn't know was I had more than the basic medical training every officer learned in the academy. I had opted for more, taken specialty classes when I became a detective because most cases required medical knowledge before the coroner arrived. That medical training kicked in. The devices, while degrading, ensured my survival, preventing critical complications like bladder rupture or sepsis. He wanted me alive and lucid enough to appreciate his artistry. I hadn't believed he wanted to keep me alive before, but the medical equipment proved it, though it couldn't guarantee he wouldn't change his mind.

My stomach heaved. I turned my head, choking back the bile climbing my throat. I twisted from side to side and though it hurt, I didn't feel any intense pain in my abdominal area.

Thank God. At least he hadn't stolen a kidney. That I knew of.

I pulled against the rope again. My wrists burned from the effort. My skin tore from the movement, but I didn't care. I just wanted out. He'd taken away even my most basic needs and replaced them with tubes and bags and surgical tape so I wouldn't move, wouldn't feel, wouldn't know time or place or pressure. I was a body to him. A project. A specimen to be sustained and observed. Nothing more.

Rage took hold before the nausea faded. My teeth clenched so tight my molars ached.

"You son of a bitch," I muttered.

Not that he could hear me. Or maybe he could. Maybe there was a camera somewhere in this sterile hellscape, watching my every twitch, every flutter of recognition. Maybe he recorded it too, the sick psycho.

I jerked my wrists again. Pain radiated down my forearms. The rope hadn't been replaced, but it had been adjusted. Tight enough to hold, loose enough to let circulation return. A gift, I was sure he'd say. A kindness from captor to captive. Medical efficiency. No nerve damage. No ulcerations so far. I licked my dry and cracked lips.

What day was it? I still had no clue. Could've been an hour. Could've been days. The last time he'd spoken to me, his voice had sounded distant, muffled through the fog of whatever he injected. He explained more of his purpose, the same clinical detachment that turned humans into chess pieces. I'd tried to hold on, to anchor my mind to the sound of his footsteps, the rhythm of his breath, but the drug had pulled me under. Again.

But I was awake and clearer than before. No fog. No haze. No mask or tape on my face.

He didn't need to blindfold me anymore. Why? Because he didn't care if I saw, or because there was nothing left to see?

I turned my head slowly. Pain flared in my neck, probably just stiff from immobility. The room was small with no windows. No overhead camera that I could see, but that didn't mean anything. He was too meticulous to leave angles uncovered. A stainless-steel cabinet sat against the far wall. Closed drawers. Handles clean. Wiped. No supplies in sight. The door was solid metal and without windows. It had an industrial latch.

He'd converted a room to a treatment space, maybe in a defunct clinic or a standalone surgical center. No mold. No mildew. Temperature-controlled. Underground? Possibly.

The pressure between my legs made me want to rip the catheter out by hand. But I knew what that would cause. Damage and bleeding, and certainly the risk of infection. And without antibiotics, that would be a death sentence.

No. I had to outlast it. *You can do it, Rachel. You've gotten through worse.*

I shifted again. My feet were no longer bound. Was that a glaring oversight or a deliberate choice? I tested the range of motion, confirmed I could pivot and shift my weight. It was a small, seemingly insignificant detail, but it offered a sliver of leverage, a means to propel myself, to engage a hidden weakness in my restraints. It was my chance. My move. He hadn't forgotten. It was my move.

I turned my head to the side and slowly brought my teeth to the rope at my wrist. The fibers were coarse, frayed at the edge. I bit down. Pulled. Tugged with everything I had. My jaw screamed, but I didn't stop. The rhythm steadied my breath. Bite. Tug. Bite. Tug. The fibers gave slightly. Not much, but enough. No camera hum. No footsteps. No interruption. He wasn't watching. Not then. Or maybe he was waiting. Letting me struggle. Testing how long it would take before I broke. Before I screamed. Before I begged. But I didn't give him that. I wouldn't give him that. Ever.

My teeth tore another fiber. Then another. My wrists ached. Blood trickled down my forearm. I tasted sweat and iron and rope. Didn't stop. He'd made a mistake. His plan would backfire. He'd left me able to see. To plan. And that was enough. If I could get one hand free, I could remove the tubes properly and stop the bleeding. Control the mess. Maybe not escape, but I'd regain something he'd taken. A piece of my own body. I paused to catch my breath. My tongue stuck to the roof of my mouth. I was dehydrated. He'd probably given me some hydration through a slow IV drip while I was unconscious. A calculated balance. Just enough to keep me lucid when he wanted, weak when he didn't.

The catheter throbbed.

Another pull. More fibers snapped. My jaw locked from the tension.

Every sound became sharper. The air vent clicked on. A pipe hissed somewhere behind the wall. Then silence. I worked harder to chew through the rope. Harder than I've ever done anything in my entire life

Footsteps.

"Shit!" My breath caught in my throat. I stopped moving. Every muscle coiled tight.

Footsteps again. Closer. He was coming back.

I angled my head toward the door, still biting down on the fraying rope, fresh blood dripping from my wrists, and my heart slamming against my ribs.

The lock turned with a soft clack and then the door opened.

Lawin stood in front of me with a twisted, sick grin on his face. "Well, I see you've been busy."

I spit blood and smiled after it hit his shirt. I spit to test him, but also to piss him off. I watched his face for any flicker, any break in his composure. He was meticulous and clinical, but even the most controlled psychopath had a trigger. I wanted to find it, to understand what shattered his perfect façade, because I knew that breaking his control was the first step to breaking him.

I didn't look away. I couldn't. The blood on his shirt had darkened into something almost black against the sterile fabric. It felt like an omen, but what it meant, I wasn't sure.

He paused, then lowered his eyes to the stain like it amused him. Then, the psycho smiled. "Well," he said, smooth as ever. "I see you've been busy again." He didn't raise his voice, didn't flinch. Just stepped closer, as the soft click of his shoes whispered across the concrete like a countdown. My pulse thudded louder. He moved past me, toward the chessboard and barely gave my loosened restraints a look.

What? What did that mean? Had he expected me to loosen them somehow? Probably. But was his indifference an act? A plan in motion? Or did he think I wouldn't, couldn't free myself because I wasn't as smart as him?

That indifference to my restraints was the most dangerous game he played. Was it deliberate taunting, an expectation that I would struggle within his pre-planned boundaries? Or was it pure, unadulterated arrogance, an underestimation born of his supreme self-belief? The latter was the more exploitable weakness. He believed his intellect so superior, he couldn't see me outsmarting him, and that was a blind spot I would exploit remorselessly.

Yes, that was likely how the POS thought. He'd already proved that. "The world is full of idiots, doc, but even they know people like you are pathetic losers."

He smirked. "I see you've taken basic psychology. Was that in college or required for your job?"

"I don't need a college class to tell me you're a fake. You probably lock yourself in your house at night and beat off to women's feet pictures."

He looked at me and grinned. "Perhaps you didn't take that class after all."

He picked up a white bishop between his thumb and forefinger, rolled it once, then set it down in a new position in a deliberate move I didn't understand. I chided myself for not knowing the game well enough to understand the move.

"Such predictable defiance, Rachel." His tone dripped admiration and contempt in equal measure. "Even the Queen, when cornered, resorts to the most basic of struggles." His fingers danced across the pieces. Black rook forward. White pawn sacrificed. A knight repositioned like a whisper. Yet during the entire time, he didn't bother to look at me.

"Your tenacity is admirable," he went on, finally turning to acknowledge me again, though with an unrelenting conceit.

I wanted to kick him in the balls again.

"In its own way," he said, "it confirms my calculations. You are nothing if not consistent."

My wrist throbbed beneath the rope. The fibers, once coarse, had softened from saliva and blood. My mouth ached. But I kept still. If he wanted a reaction, he wouldn't get one. And I wasn't about to move any, not even an inch. I couldn't risk him realizing how loose my restraints had become or recall how he'd left my feet free.

A corner of his mouth lifted. "A rather messy move, wouldn't you agree?" He stepped even closer. "Your blood on my shirt." He plucked the fabric between two gloved fingers and inspected it. "A small price, perhaps, for you to confirm the futility of such blunt force."

He crouched beside me, making his face level with mine, and his eyes flicked to the ragged wound along my wrist. "Pawns expend themselves for little gain. Much like this. Don't lower yourself to that level. I picked you because of your strengths, not this desperation. It's unbecoming, Rachel."

I didn't blink. I didn't even move, barely breathing for fear it would somehow show weakness.

His gaze didn't soften. "You're so focused on the superficial. The ropes, the blood, the discomfort. Yet you miss the true artistry. I expected better of you and more from you." His fingers brushed the frayed edge of the rope, not to fix it. Just to feel it. "The confinement. The degradation. Every detail carefully chosen to reveal your deepest vulnerabilities. This—" he flicked the loosened fiber, "—is what I call revelation."

He expected me to accept his narrative as my defeat. But he missed my counter-move. He didn't understand that the queen was gathering strength on a newly cleared board. His belief in his invincibility was the very lever I would use against him at the perfect time. "Lawin, you're the one focused on the superficial. I'm playing the long game too, and I'll make a move you could never predict."

He stood again, calmly adjusted a black knight, and made a sound in his throat, something that sounded like satisfaction. He circled behind me then touched my shoulder.

Not in a rough or kind way. He just touched. "Shall we address the elephant in the room?"

I bit my tongue.

"I hate when you're so quiet. It takes all the fun out of this, especially given how well I know you, and how much I know you want to react."

I glared at him.

"Don't think I don't see the anger in your eyes, Rachel. As a professional, I know what's going on inside you. I see the rise in your blood pressure. The redness in your cheeks. The strain in your neck. I know you're angry. Why not express it verbally? It might help you accept your fate."

He continued babbling on like a psycho when I said nothing. "You've already guessed I haven't resecured your shoulder ties," he murmured. He was right; I had already realized it. "And yet you haven't tested their limits," he noted.

He calmly inspected the frayed rope around my bleeding wrists with a gloved hand in a clinical way, like a doctor examining a specimen, rather than an alarmed captor. "Such a waste, you spending time on your wrists knowing you don't have enough time left to gnaw through them." He tightened the rope making it just a little harder to bite through, but notably not enough to undo my work. "A minor adjustment," he said. His warm breath brushed my ear. "We wouldn't want premature damage to my most prized piece, would we?"

His overconfidence didn't surprise me. He believed the primary wrist and waist restraints, along with the medical devices anchoring me to the space, were entirely sufficient to prevent escape. He acted as if the restraints posed no real threat to my escape. But he underestimated my training and resourcefulness, leaving me able to see. To plan.

I clenched my teeth again. This interaction had deepened my understanding of him, helping me to see the meaning behind his actions in a psychological sense. He reinforced the restraint on my wrists without admitting I had made significant progress, choosing instead to frame it as a precaution for his "game" rather than a direct countermeasure to my moves. He believed he was maintaining control without revealing any perceived weakness, but I knew the truth of my progress and his underestimation. And that was enough. Hope stirred inside me.

"Patience, Rachel," he said. "There are many more moves to play."

I stared at the board. The pieces blurred and sharpened with each blink. I counted them, not because it mattered, but because it helped. It gave me something to hold on to. I stayed alive as long as the queen remained standing.

"Your blood changes nothing, Rachel." He placed a pawn next to the queen and smiled. "As for your other arrangements." He walked around me and lingered near the catheter and poop bag, making me acutely aware of my physical degradation. Each one a symbol of my weakness in his eyes. "These ensure comfort and convenience. Allowing you to focus your considerable intellect on the game. Every physiological need has been anticipated and managed, leaving you free to appreciate the deeper layers of my strategy."

He hadn't been rattled. Of course he hadn't. Every move I made—every bite at those ropes—he'd already accounted for. That room, his twisted version of an operating theater, was his masterpiece. Controlled. Precise. Like I was just another variable in one of his experiments.

He didn't care that I fought. He *wanted* me to. So he could log it, categorize it, twist it into proof that he was right about me all along. My pain, my resistance—they weren't obstacles. They were validations. Evidence that he was always ten steps ahead. That I was exactly who he believed I was. Predictable. Containable. A piece he'd already taken off the board.

And he used it all. Every reaction, every struggle, to tighten his grip. Not physically—psychologically. He wasn't after blood. He was after my will. My breath trembled. *Damn it, Rachel. Police 101! Don't show weakness.*

He paused before me and tilted his head. "You may not speak, but your fear is taking over."

I met his gaze and held it.

"Remaining silent, yes. Perhaps it's your most intelligent move so far." He returned to the board. Moved another pawn. Removed a queen. His. Then he looked at me. "You don't even realize which one you are." He tapped a piece. Not mine. A pawn. "This one thought she was the Queen too."

My stomach coiled. I remembered the black pawn that arrived with the first body. He didn't just kill. He placed. He stepped back and folded his hands in front of him. "You've made one move. I've made many."

He removed his cell phone from his pocket, swiped on the screen, and then held it to my face. A still frame, grainy and washed in gray, appeared. The department parking lot. My Jeep. And me.

He let the silence stretch for a moment, then said, "You think you're chasing shadows, but shadows don't orchestrate. They follow."

He swiped to another photo of my Jeep in another location, then again, and again, and finally, the car that had followed me.

"I could have taken you then," he said. "It most certainly would've been easier, but," he crouched and lifted my chin with one gloved finger. "But easy is rarely satisfying."

"But driving over a parade full of people, including children? That's satisfying?" I spit at him again. "You're sick."

His gaze sharpened for just a flicker, like he wanted more from me. More rage. More panic. A plea, even, but I gave him nothing.

"Well," he said, rising. "You're responding as I expected, but this resolve won't last." He walked to the edge of the room, pressed something on a control panel, and dimmed the lights. A strip of LEDs along the floor glowed faintly, enough to illuminate the board, the blood on his shirt, and a table covered with a white sheet.

He removed the sheet to reveal a steel table where he'd laid out surgical tools that weren't meant to save me when the time came.

When did he put that in the room? And how had I missed it? *Pay attention, Rachel. You're missing things you can't afford to miss.*

"Rest," he said. "Tomorrow, we shift from defense to engagement." He walked to the door and paused before opening it, then turned around. "You're not broken, Rachel. Not yet." He looked over his shoulder. "But that's the most exquisite part."

He opened the door and walked through it, closing the door quietly behind him. I exhaled, then laid back down. The flickering light pulsed across the board below me. I wasn't broken. But I had to start breaking back.

24

My wrists burned, but I didn't stop.

The thick rope, soaked in spit and blood, flooded my mouth with tastes I would never forget, including whatever synthetic coating he'd chosen to season it with. Something medicinal. Poison maybe. My jaw throbbed. My tongue stung. My head pulsed with pressure.

But none of it mattered. I would chew through it. I would escape, and Lawin would pay. One way or another, he would pay. Even if I didn't survive it. I couldn't afford to hesitate; Lawin would exploit any perceived weakness, like he had with my feelings about Tommy's murder. I wouldn't be a second too late again, not for that psycho.

Finally, the frayed end cracked. Fibers split. One by one. I clamped down again, angled my teeth, twisted my neck, yanked, and the last of it snapped.

My immediate thought wasn't just to attack, but to *assess*. Could I reach a binding point on the chair? Could I feel for seams in the walls, for loose bolts? The raw freedom was a weapon, and I would wield it with calculated precision.

My right hand slid free, slick with saliva and blood. My fingers felt rubbery, clumsy. I flexed them once, then twice, ignoring the pins and needles dancing under the skin. I carefully touched my body, the gurney, the bags hanging close by.

Then, with a spite that sent lightning through my soul, I looked up at the ceiling, and though I couldn't see the camera, I knew there was one somewhere in the room. I flipped him off, knowing deep in my soul he was watching.

I dragged my hand to the other wrist and started working at the knot. It was lazy. Sloppy. Probably the only thing in the room he hadn't over-engineered. I clawed at it with numb fingers until the loop loosened until I jerked the rope off like it was a snake wrapped around my bones.

Finally.

I focused on my shoulders next. In some twisted version of a mercy or a taunt, I wasn't sure which, he hadn't resecured the bindings. Either way, the knots fell apart in seconds. I shoved the rope off and rolled my shoulders. My muscles screamed. So did my lungs.

But I was free. Mostly. My stomach flipped. I'd already run through the checklist in my head hours ago. Removing the catheter and the rectal tube without proper technique risked tearing tissue, infection, and even hemorrhage. He counted on that. Counted on me to panic, rip them out, bleed all over his floor like some cornered lab rat. But that wasn't going to happen. I refused to let it.

Good. Let him watch me take it from him.

I spotted the tray across the room. A pair of gloves, sealed wipes, and an empty syringe waited on a sterile cloth next to a metal kidney dish. All the tools a trained individual would use for a clean removal. He hadn't simply left them. He had orchestrated their presence. Did he want me to use them, to prove my resourcefulness while still playing within his predetermined parameters? Or did he think I wouldn't know how? That I would stare at them, hopeful he planned to use them to free me from my captivity? Or maybe, and it seemed more likely, he wanted me to see them as a threat, as the means to finally take my life.

I would kill myself before I let him do that.

I moved slowly. Not knowing how long I'd been held captive meant I didn't know how my body would react to basic movement. And I had been right to move with caution. My knees trembled, ached like I hadn't moved in months, but I got there, to the tray, one step closer to my freedom, and to Lawin getting what he so deserved. I grabbed the gloves first then snapped them on. My hands shook, but it didn't matter. I could do it shaking. I could do this blind. I lay back on the table, angled my knees up, and said, "Watch this, asshole." I bit down on my own tongue to keep from screaming, then I peeled the tape away from my thigh, the catheter's anchor point, and exposed the tube where it entered my urethra. The ache flared again. That deep, internal pressure I'd tried to block out but couldn't any longer.

I inserted the syringe into the balloon port and pulled the plunger. Saline filled the barrel, faster and heavier than I expected. The balloon inside me deflated with an audible pop I felt more than heard.

I closed my eyes. "Do it."

Then I pulled, slowly. Controlled. Every inch of movement set fire to my insides like a hot coil scraping its way out of me, nerve by nerve. The pain stole my breath, but I didn't stop. I *would not* give him the satisfaction no matter how much it hurt. I nearly vomited when the end finally cleared, but I held it in and threw the tube against the wall with a satisfaction almost as strong as when I'd murdered Tommy's killer.

Now the other.

I rolled to my side and reached behind me. The fecal tube was shorter but rigid, secured with tape and a plastic flange sealed to my skin. I peeled the adhesive gently, even though each millimeter of release dragged a fresh ripple of nausea through my gut.

I pulled the tubing out. It wasn't as painful, but the sense of violation cut deeper than I had expected. I threw that one too. It landed beside the catheter, silent proof of the hell I'd been living in for God knew how long.

I scrubbed every inch of myself I could reach raw with the wipes. I didn't care that I was shaking. Didn't care that my knees buckled or my vision blurred. I was clean. Maybe not healthy. Not safe. Not whole. But clean. I leaned on the table to stand. My legs threatened to collapse, but I didn't let them. I didn't have the time to waste. I knew he was watching. I knew he'd unlock that door at the exact time he thought necessary, so I needed to move fast. To be precise in my actions. Because I was done being dissected, done being studied.

I snatched the surgical scissors from the tray and studied them quickly, noting their sharpness and how I could puncture his carotid if I got the angle right. The scalpel was better for precision, but the scissors gave me reach.

Lawin liked control, but I preferred leverage.

I searched the room again, both analyzing and waiting for his return. One door. Steel frame. Reinforced hinges. Handle on my side, locked from the other. No windows. No vents. No clocks. Though nothing in the room told me how long I'd been here, the bruising across my lower abdomen, the inflammation in my urethra, the pain radiating up my spine, those told me enough. It'd been days. Maybe more. "Your time has come," I said. "Your queen has made her move." I moved toward the door, crouched beside the hinges, and inspected them. No screws, but they're welded into the frame, and not a weak point. But the doorframe had a slight gap along the bottom. It was barely visible, but it told me one thing. I wasn't underground. The room had air exchange. Maybe even sound bleed. I dropped to my stomach, pressed my ear to the crack, and held my breath.

Silence. Then a shuffle. Fabric on tile. Maybe twenty feet away. He was out there. Close.

I sat back up and curled my fingers around the scissors. It wasn't the escape I wanted, but it would be the one I earned.

The lock clicked.

I stood.

The door opened.

He stepped through, calm, empty-handed, unafraid. I stood behind it watching him, knowing he knew exactly where I was, how I waited to make my move. He scanned the room once. His eyes landed on the empty table, then moved to the corner where I'd tossed his devices. He took in the gloves. The wipes. The fact that nothing bled. And then he smiled. "A textbook removal," he said, closing the door behind him.

I stayed where I was.

"You've always been smart, Rachel. Thoughtful. Methodical. But I wasn't sure you'd still be *you* in here." He motioned to the room with a lazy sweep of his hand. "This space tests people. Peels them back. I'm impressed."

I didn't answer.

He stepped closer. "I gave you everything you needed. And you passed."

I barked a laugh. "Passed what, exactly? A trauma response lab exam?"

"No," he said. "Predictability. It's a tool, not a weakness. And you're exceptionally reliable."

"Don't bet on that, doc." I moved the scissors slightly in my grip. "You want to see how predictable I really am?"

"I already have."

He was close. Not close enough to strike, but close enough for me to smell the antiseptic on his skin, the faint trace of citrus from his soap, and the fear brewing inside him.

"I smell your fear, Lawin. It's bleeding out your pores."

"Is that so?"

"It's obvious. The acrid tang of adrenaline, of fear. You try to mask it, but I see it. My years as a detective have trained me to detect the faintest chemical signals of stress."

"I fear nothing, Rachel. Why would I?"

"You want me to believe you're invincible, but I see it. I smell it. That scent is a tell, a tiny crack in your carefully constructed persona, and it confirms your vulnerability."

"Does that feed into your confidence? If so, I'm sorry to say you'll fail."

"I don't fail."

"Ah, but you do. You failed to save Tommy. That second of pause is your biggest failure, Rachel, and you've never moved past it. It dictates your life."

"You're right. It does dictate my life, and you're going to see just how."

He looked down at the instruments in my hand. "You won't use them. Not yet."

"Try me."

"You won't," he repeated as he stepped just a little closer. "Because deep down, you're still trying to outmaneuver me. You want an outcome, but not my death. You want *control*. And using that now would give me exactly what I want. Proof that I broke you."

I didn't blink.

He held out his hand. "Give it to me."

I smiled. "Nice try, asshole."

He nodded. "Now I see the real you coming through. You want out?

Then outthink me. Escape me. But don't reduce yourself to *this*," he said, gesturing to the scissors.

I saw it in his eyes. The glint. He *wanted* me disarmed. I smiled. "Your psychological bullshit." Then I stepped back.

His brow lifted, amused. "You think you're on offense now?" he asked.

"No," I said. "I think I'm not bleeding in a diaper anymore. Which is a hell of an improvement."

He laughed—cold, hollow, like none of this mattered. "I'm looking forward to tomorrow."

He turned his back. The sound of his shoes against floor burned into my skull. That arrogant rhythm. That practiced confidence. Like he owned the air in the room. Like I was still strapped to the table, still too broken to strike. He didn't deserve to walk out of there unmarked.

My pulse detonated in my ears.

He reached for the door.

I moved. "You won't have a tomorrow." My voice came from somewhere deeper than rage, a place quieter than fury, but worse than the pit of hell. I aimed the scissors where they needed to go to keep him alive, but give me the upper hand, then I drove them hard into the soft notch between his shoulder and neck. The wet crunch gave me an overwhelming sense of accomplishment. He staggered. His hand slammed against the wall. His fingers clawed at the handle. He spun toward me, his mouth parting, his eyes wide and shocked, not from pain, but disbelief that *I* did it.

And then it happened.

Finally.

I kicked him right in the balls.

25

Seeing him in pain, hearing the gurgle in his throat, and watching his knees hit the floor with a sickening thud, all gave me a satisfaction I hadn't expected. I surged forward with the scissors still clenched in my blood-slicked hand, then froze, intentionally slowing my breathing.

No, Rachel. You're not like him.

He tried to speak but could only gasp.

I crouched down and put my face next to his. So close he could taste my breath. "Still predictable, Doc?" I said in a low and steady voice. I felt calm in a way that made even me question my humanity. "Want me to show you what else I can do because damn, I'm ready. I'm ready to watch you die." I wanted desperately to stab him in the thigh, to watch the blood shoot from his body. To watch him suffer.

But I knew better. Jennifer Abbott and Gary Kinder deserved justice. Their families needed to see Lawin have his day in court, no matter how much I wanted him to pay for his crimes in the same way they lost their lives.

"Where's Bishop?"

His head lolled back against the wall. His eyes, unfocused but still open, watched me.

"Answer me, damn it. Where's Bishop?"

He sneered. "You'll have to work harder for me to answer that."

I punched him in the face. "Where is my partner?"

He swallowed.

"Is this how you want to play it, Lawin? Please say yes. Please."

He didn't speak.

"That's what I thought. You act all tough, but you're not. You're a worthless, pathetic excuse for a human. You're the middle school bully, Lawin. The one that caves the second someone stands up to him. You believed your king's ego was untouchable, but it's crumbling. You thought you'd removed me from the board, but all you did was clear the path for the queen to strike."

He sucked in a breath. "You can't save them, Rachel. You're not good enough."

Them? "Who else have you killed?"

"You'll know the answer to that, maybe one day."

I held up the scissors. "Are you sure about that?" I pressed the tip of the blades against his cheek. "Try me."

He stared into my eyes like he couldn't believe the queen had flipped the board.

I grabbed his shirtfront and yanked his body forward. "You like control, but let's see how you like losing every goddamn inch of it."

He gurgled something unintelligible, but I didn't care.

I listened to him whimper as I dragged him across the floor. The blood trail he left behind painted a broken artery's worth of red across the sterile tile. It smeared under feet, all thick and sticky, but I didn't flinch. I hauled him toward the gurney; the same gleaming steel prison he'd attached to me and heaved him onto it.

He screamed, but I still didn't care.

I kicked the gurney to reposition it. The metal legs screeched across the floor. He whimpered again.

I ripped a sheet he'd left on the table and tied his right arm to the leg of the gurney. He moaned.

"Oh, I'm sorry. Is this painful?"

"Stitch me up. You don't want me dead. How will I pay for my crimes?"

"Shut up." I yanked his other arm to tie it to the gurney.

He winced.

That arm went down with more resistance. His body bucked as I wrapped the ripped sheet across his forearm, but he didn't have the strength to fight me.

"Oh, good. That nerve still works. Sadly, you're not dying yet," I said. "You don't get mercy."

The scissors had done their job. They'd put me in charge. The queen had taken down the king.

He would recover. I hadn't hit in a kill zone because as much as I wanted him dead, I needed him alive. He could have victims, still alive, waiting to be found. We needed to know.

I strapped both ankles down and pulled the pieces of the sheet until they bit into bone. He let out a noise, but not quite a word. His chest heaved. He was fading. I needed him conscious. I slapped his face. "Stay with me, Lawin. This next part is important. And even though I want you dead, we'll let the court decide if that should happen."

I pulled his phone from his coat pocket and hit the side button. Locked. Of course. I shoved the phone in front of his slack face. "Smile for the camera."

His head turned just enough for the camera to register and unlock.

"Good boy." I went straight to the call history. Bishop's number was already there. I tapped it. It rang. And rang. Each second stretched like skin over a bone, tight and painful. My grip on the phone trembled.

Come on, Bishop. Pick up.

But he didn't.

My chest tightened. I turned toward Lawin and slammed the scissors into the metal tray beside his head. "What did you do to him?"

He smiled. God help me, that piece of crap smiled.

"Redirection," he rasped. "You weren't the only one on the board."

I gripped his shirt again, then leaned in close enough to smell the copper and antiseptic and that goddamn expensive cologne. "If you touched him—"

"Checkmate," he whispered.

I nearly drove the scissors into his other thigh. Instead, I stood and called 911. "This is Detective Ryder. I need the chief now."

Dispatch sent the call without another word.

Jimmy answered immediately. "Ryder? Where are you?"

I didn't answer his question. I didn't breathe. I just asked, flat, steady, and sharp. "Is Bishop okay?"

Silence. Just for a second.

Then, "Rachel, where are you? Are you safe?"

I swallowed. "Answer the question."

"He's... he's not at the station," Jimmy said carefully.

Everything in me twisted. The bile rose fast.

"Rachel—"

"Find him," I said. My voice cracked, the edge no longer steel but splintered wood. "Jimmy. I need you to find him now."

"Where are you? Are you hurt?"

"I'm okay." I looked at Lawin. "Where are we?"

He laughed.

"I don't have a problem walking out of here and leaving you for dead. So, if you want to live, tell me where the hell we are."

Jimmy yelled into the phone. "Rachel, what's going on? Who are you with?"

"I don't know where I am. Trace this number but find Bishop first."

Lawin laughed again. Weak. Dry. More wheeze than voice. But it still cut through me like shrapnel. "You lose the knight and the Queen crumbles."

"Wrong game," I said. "Wrong queen."

"Tell me who you're with," Jimmy said.

"My doctor. Torey Lawin. Find Bishop." I tossed the phone onto the ground and grabbed a roll of medical tape from the nearby tray. "This is your last chance to work with me, Lawin. Where's Bishop and where the hell are my clothes?"

He said nothing.

"Your choice." I wrapped it around his mouth. "It's going to hurt when I rip it off, and I can't wait."

He moaned low as I wiped my hands on his coat.

"Stay alive, Lawin," I muttered. "You don't die until I say you do."

I leaned against the wall and sucked in a breath. My knees finally started to buckle as the adrenaline shifted into tremors. My mouth went dry. My vision blurred at the edges.

And everything went dark.

26

I tried to open my eyes, but I couldn't. I moved my lips, but no words formed. Where was I? Had it all been real? Did I stop him, or was that my imagination? I couldn't tell.

Tired. I was so tired.

The sound reached me first. Distant. Too distant, like a dream crawling through molasses. A low hum, then a stutter. Tires maybe? No, engines. Diesel engines grinding against pavement. Was it delivery trucks or construction equipment? Familiar, but wrong. For a second, I thought I imagined it.

Then it came again. Closer. A horn. Short. Impatient. A car? A truck? I couldn't parse it. My brain, soaked in whatever cocktail Lawin had given me God only knew how many times, refused to fire in sequence. Every thought came fractured.

But something felt different. Something had changed.

Memory hit me in jagged flashes. Scissors. Rope. Blood. I'd stabbed him. I remembered the crunch, the sound his body made as it hit the wall. I remembered kicking him, hard, right in the center of the thing he thought made him powerful. Then I remembered tying him to the gurney. Had I finished? Had I passed out before I got the last knot?

Had he gotten free? No. If he had, I wouldn't still be breathing. "Lawin," I finally muttered, barely audible.

A groan echoed through the space. Not mine. Not involuntary. Male. Low. Weak.

That sound grounded me. It reminded me I'd hurt him. Reminded me I'd fought.

I heard another sound. Metal on metal. A ram. The door. They'd found me.

Voices barked commands. The scrape of boots on cement helped me focus. Static from a radio.

Then, "Rachel!"

I knew that voice. Knew it in my bones.

Jimmy. I whispered, "Over here."

Another crash, then another until the door gave finally. The air changed instantly, moving faster and freer. I sucked in big breaths as tears slid down my cheeks. My body reacted. My chest hitched. Not pain, not quite, more like recognition.

"Clear left!"

"Hostile restrained!"

"Jesus Christ—Rachel!"

Kyle.

More voices saying my name. I knew them all. Michels. Levy. All but Bishop. I whispered his name.

I wanted to shout. I wanted to sit up and grab their arms and scream that I was fine, but my body wouldn't play along. My limbs ached with a hollowness that came from prolonged stillness. My skin burned from inside out. My vision, barely functional, flickered with shadows and spots.

Jimmy yelled, "Get her vitals, now!"

"I'm on it, Chief."

I felt someone's fingers press against my neck.

"I'm okay," I whispered. "Bishop."

"She's awake," the person said. "Pulse weak but stable."

The man, one I didn't recognize, checked my eyes, nearly blinding me with a flashlight. "Pupils reactive."

"That hurt," I said softly. "Where's Bishop?"

"Let's just worry about you right now, Detective." He spoke to someone on my other side. "She's been drugged. Get her fluids started. Now."

Hands on me. Dozens of them. Fingers checked my pulse again. A flashlight flared in my eyes again, but I pushed it away. "They did that already." I blinked and flinched. The pain in my head surged. But I welcomed it. Pain meant I was still alive. "Bishop."

"Rachel." Kyle's face appeared above mine. I tried to smile when I saw the sweat cutting through the dirt on his brow. "Can you hear me?"

I nodded. "Where's Bishop?"

His face softened. "He's right here."

Lawin moaned from the corner. I turned my head, just enough to see him bound, bloody, but conscious.

"You did that?" Bishop asked from my other side. "You tied him?"

Tears slid down my cheeks. I raised my hand and touched his cheek. "You're okay."

"And so are you, partner."

Jimmy crouched beside me and let out a breath. "Hell of a job, detective."

But I didn't care. I needed to know. "Is everyone okay? Are there any more bodies?"

"We're all okay," Kyle said. "No more victims."

I closed my eyes and then opened them again. "Bishop."

Bishop leaned closer. "I'm here, and I'm not going anywhere."

A tear slid from my eye from the goddamned overwhelm of it all. The burn. The noise. The air. The fact that I wasn't strapped down anymore. That I was safe. That he was safe.

That I'd survived. But not finished. Because Lawin still breathed, and I had questions. Lots of them. "Don't let him die. I'm not done with him yet."

I woke up again, but not in the storage facility, in a hospital bed, wrapped in a thin white sheet and freezing to death. I shivered. "Is it winter?"

"Not even close." Kyle stood at the side of the bed and smiled. "It's ninety-six outside."

"What day is it?"

"It's Tuesday."

I tried to do the math, to recall when Lawin had taken me, but the head fog hadn't cleared. "How long did he have me?"

"Four days, and you've been here two."

"Two? Why?"

"Lawin drugged you with a combination that should have killed you, Rachel. The ER doc couldn't believe you had the ability to remove your catheter and fecal tube, defend yourself, and secure Lawin to the gurney."

A nurse walked in. "We're all in awe," she said. She adjusted something on my arm, making me instantly nauseous. "We've all worked with Dr. Lawin, and no one can believe he turned out to be a serial killer."

I swallowed back the nausea. "Where is he now?"

"He's in ICU. You did a lot of damage, but he's going to survive."

I wasn't sure how I felt about that.

"We've got multiple officers on him," Kyle said.

The nurse smiled. "Don't worry, honey. We nurses have made sure he can't escape." She winked at me and then left the room.

I watched her leave, then said, "Make sure you don't upset her."

He laughed. "You have another visitor. Are you up for it?"

I wasn't. I wanted to crawl under the thin sheet and hide, but I knew I needed to let everyone know I was okay. "Of course."

He kissed me on the forehead and held the door open for Savannah.

She stayed completely calm until he walked out, then raced to me and sobbed. "We thought you were stuffed into a suitcase somewhere!" She wiped her eyes. "Don't you ever do that to me again!"

Tears streamed down my cheeks. I bit my bottom lip, hard, completely unable to speak knowing I would sob as much as her.

She dried my tears with a tissue. "Are you okay? I swear on my ancestors' graves I will murder that man with my own hands if he ever comes near you again."

I had no doubt. "I'm okay. I promise." The thing was, I wasn't okay. My hands shook so hard, I hid them by wrapping them together. Flashes of Lawin moving those damn chess pieces, adjusting his medical equipment, and alluding to Bishop's death played on repeat in my head. I wanted

Lawin dead. I wanted him to suffer like Jennifer Abbott and Greg Kinder. I wanted him to pay for his crimes at my hand.

But that wasn't justice. Justice was allowing the Abbott and Kinder families to see Lawin in court, to watch him be sentenced. To know there had been closure for his crimes, to see Jennifer and Gary mean something, not to be victims, but humans who mattered.

Still, I wanted him dead. Bringing up Tommy like he had. Warping my pain to fit his game. Only a psycho would do that.

"Don't lie to me, woman." Savannah squeezed my arm. "You're not okay."

I sucked in a breath. "He used Tommy's murder to manipulate me."

Her normally sweet, sassy eyes darkened. "Whatever you decide to do, I'll support. I'll be your alibi. He does not deserve to live."

"No, he doesn't, but we both know how it works. Even if we hate it."

"What can I do? How can I help you through this?"

"Tell me the truth. Is Bishop okay?"

"He's fine. Nothing happened to him. Lawin lied to you, Rachel. They haven't found anyone else either. I think it was all a game to get to you."

"What about the parade?"

She hesitated before speaking, but finally said, "Seven people died."

"The driver?" My stomach flipped.

"Lawin's nurse. Rebecca Lister. She sustained multiple injuries, but will survive."

Bile raced up my throat. "How—what—oh, my God. He manipulated her. She wouldn't have done that on her own."

"Listen," she said, "you need to get some rest. I know you, and I know you're going to want to see this through, but Jimmy won't let that happen if you're not well enough." She brushed a hair from my face. "Call me if you need me."

I stood strapped to the gurney, my arms stretched above my head, my legs splayed and immobile and not touching the ground. The restraints cut into my skin, too tight and coarse, cutting off circulation. Fluorescent lights hummed above me, so bright and sterile, they burned holes into my retinas. The pain searing through my body paralyzed me.

No. No. What happened? I had him. I was okay. I was free.

But the pain said otherwise.

Lawin stood over me with his gloved hands moving in a calm and calculated manner. A surgeon's calm. A butcher's delight.

"Rachel," he said, almost kindly, like a doctor explaining a procedure to a nervous patient. "I want you to stay still. It'll only hurt more if you don't."

My chest heaved. I tried to scream, but no sound came. My throat refused to work. My vocal cords strangled by the fear of what I knew would come. More pain. More blood.

My death.

A scalpel glinted in his hand, already slick with something dark and warm. Blood. Mine.

He smiled. "You're awake. Good. I wanted you to feel this. The queen must feel the pain of her defeat. It's important to the finality of this."

My abdomen burned. I looked down and gasped. My heart pounded hard enough to rupture. He'd cut into me leaving my abdomen a yawning red cavern. Tubes snaked out from the edges, and my own intestines glistened under the light like coils of sausage laid out for inspection. "Oh, God," I tried to say, but nothing came.

"You always thought pain was power," he murmured as he gently pried something free from inside me. My liver? My stomach? I couldn't tell. He set it on a tray like a trophy. "But pain is simply the tax for being alive. And I need your currency."

He turned and tapped on a monitor beside the gurney. Tommy's face flickered on the screen. So young. So strong. So alive. His smile hit me like a blow.

I choked on my saliva. "What—what are you doing?"

Lawin turned back. "He's waiting for you to give him everything. If I take the parts carefully, precisely, we can keep him alive. You don't want him to die again because of you, do you?"

"Tommy." His name came out in a gasp.

"Yes," he said, tilting his head like a priest delivering last rites. "He didn't deserve to die. You know that. You've always known. But you let him. And now, you can fix it. Give him what's left of you."

My body bucked. The pain was unbearable. Fire tore through my abdomen as he reached his hand inside my body. I felt everything. The pressure. The twisting. The detachment. When something ruptured. Searing white hot agony flared from my ribcage. I screamed.

"I think this is your spleen," he said casually. "You didn't use it much, but Tommy will need it to survive. He'll need everything from you." He snickered. "That's how it works, Rachel. The queen must be sacrificed to save her king."

"Stop. Please. You're killing me." My words came out as a whisper. "Please."

He took my lungs next. "Just one," he promised. "Tommy doesn't need both, and it's a fair trade, really. Your life for his. You wanted this. You said so many times."

The monitor beeped. Tommy blinked. His chest moved. The machine was keeping him alive. Because of me. Because of what Lawin was stealing from me.

"Don't you want him back?" Lawin asked, eyes locked on mine. "This is what love demands. Sacrifice."

"No," I whispered. "He's gone. You can't save him."

"Maybe you can't because you already chose this," he said. "When you froze. When you let him die. But I can fix him. The king controls the board, Rachel." He shoved something deep under my ribcage. A needle. Or a blade. I couldn't tell, and it didn't matter. My vision exploded with black.

And then I saw it: Tommy, standing at the end of the table, not behind the glass. Not on the monitor. Real. Alive. Wrong. His skin had become waxy, his eyes hollowed. Blood trickled down his chin.

"You let me die," he said softly. "And now you'll die for me."

"No—"

"You're already dying," he said. "You just haven't accepted it."

I screamed and thrashed against the restraints, letting them rip my skin. My hands tore at the gurney. My muscles burned. "No!"

Lawin leaned his lips to my ear. "Say goodbye, Rachel."

The lights surged—white became red—alarms blared. Blood filled my throat. I choked, drowning in it. My vision fractured. Everything turned to shadow.

Then I shot up in bed, screaming and drenched in sweat. My hands flew to my abdomen. I sucked in a breath when I felt it still intact. But my lungs still heaved, each breath clawing through my throat like broken glass.

"Rachel!" Kyle's voice broke through my cries. He placed his hands on my shoulders and grounded me. "It's me, Kyle. You're okay. You're safe."

I couldn't speak, couldn't move. I stared at the wall across from the bed and then leaned to the side and threw up.

He pulled me into his arms. My face pressed into his chest, into warmth and safety I so desperately needed. I closed my eyes and saw Tommy again. "I saw him. He...he wanted to live." Tears poured from my eyes. I couldn't breathe and felt myself beginning to hyperventilate. "I need air."

He stared into my eyes. "Breathe, Rachel. I've got you. It was a dream."

"No. It was real. It was Tommy." I swallowed hard. "He was alive. But wrong. And Lawin—he was cutting me open. Piece by piece. He said it was to save Tommy."

Kyle's jaw tensed, but he said nothing.

"I felt it," I whispered. "I felt everything."

His fingers brushed damp hair from my face. "It wasn't real. I promise you, honey. It was just a nightmare."

I nodded, having begun to understand that. "It felt so real."

"I know."

I leaned into him. I wasn't sure I'd ever stop shaking. Maybe that was the point. Maybe Lawin didn't need a scalpel anymore. He had planted himself into my mind and I couldn't escape him. "I want to go home."

"I know you do." He pushed a button that moved the bed upright and sat beside me. "But it's going to be a few days. They need to make sure you're okay."

"I don't know if I can do this, Kyle. I can't close my eyes again. I can't see Tommy like that. Lawin messed with my head. I can't think straight."

"You will, Rach. I promise you'll be okay. We'll get you whatever help you need."

I swallowed back more tears. "I'm sorry."

"For what?"

"For being a jerk. For letting you walk out instead of telling you I understood your feelings. I shouldn't have worried you like I did. I got mad at you for loving me. I'm sorry."

He smiled. "Don't apologize. Next time, you'll be the one to worry. We can trade off."

I smiled, but only for a second, then the magnitude of it all hit me again. "I shouldn't have gone to the parade. I should have known he would do this."

"Babe, stop. You had no idea who killed those people. None of us did, but we sure as hell didn't expect it to be your doctor or that he would mow down a crowd of people to get you. You can't blame yourself for someone else's actions."

"I need to be there when they question him. I need to be a part of it."

"Do you really think Jimmy will let you do that?"

"No, but Savannah will work on him for me."

He grimaced. "Then I guess you'll be there for his questioning. Jimmy's scared of Savannah. All men are."

I laughed so hard it hurt my bladder. I winced and pressed my hand into my abdomen. "That hurts."

"You have an infection from the catheter."

"From removing it?"

He shook his head. "They think it was put in without being cleaned."

My stomach flipped.

28

They released me three days later. The night I arrived home, I woke drenched in sweat, the sheets twisted around my legs, my throat raw, my lungs fighting for air I couldn't draw fast enough. The scream tore out of me a minute earlier, and Kyle was already there, sitting upright beside me in the dark, with one hand braced on the mattress, the other reaching toward me cautiously. Like he didn't want to startle me. My heart hammered against my ribs so hard it felt like I'd cracked something loose.

He didn't say my name at first. He just sat there, watching me catch up to the room—the bedroom, our bedroom, with the dresser I'd chipped with a handcuff case, the edge of the quilt folded down exactly the way I left it, the fan overhead spinning slow enough to see each blade move. Not a storage room. Not *that* room.

Not with Lawin.

But my body couldn't adjust. It couldn't comprehend my safety or the fact Lawin no longer held me captive. My skin burned while my cotton shirt clung to my back, completely soaked through. I pulled it away from my stomach and blinked hard, trying to keep the nightmare from clinging like the sweat. I still saw Tommy's face—too perfect, too still—his eyes empty, and that voice behind me whispering clinical reassurance as a scalpel traced the outline of my sternum.

Kyle finally moved closer. "Are you okay? You were screaming," he whispered.

I swung my legs off the bed slowly, wincing at the pain under the brace around my abdomen and ground my feet against the cold hardwood. Every inch of me ached. My back, my gut, the inside of my thighs where the restraints had rubbed my skin raw. My right hand still twitched without warning. My fingers cramped as if the tendons didn't remember how to work. I rubbed my palm against my thigh and stood carefully, ignoring the pull in my lower abdomen. The doctors told me the catheter should have stayed longer, but I hadn't waited. I'd ripped it out in that room along with the fecal tube, tied Lawin down with one hand while the other bled, and while my legs buckled. The nurses called it extraordinary, but they didn't understand my desperation.

Kyle stood too and watched me, giving me the space I needed but staying his protective worried self. I walked to the bathroom but didn't bother with the lights. I turned on the cold tap and splashed water on my face, letting it run down my neck until the sting in my scalp eased and my breath evened out. My reflection looked worse than it had the day before. My pale skin, chapped lips, and too-wide pupils alarmed even me. There were deep grooves under my eyes, bruises left from days I didn't remember. I looked like someone who hadn't slept in years, not hours. I felt like that too.

I stayed that way for a while, with my hands gripping the sides of the sink as if the porcelain could ground me more. My body still trembled, but at least it was barely perceptible unless I looked straight at my own shoulders.

I didn't need the mirror to feel Kyle leaning in the doorway behind me. I had felt the shift in the air, the tension in the silence. I hated how well he read me. "Same one?" he asked, voice low and even.

I dried my face with the edge of a towel and kept my eyes on the faucet. "Yeah."

He didn't press. I appreciated that. I turned toward him and walked past into the kitchen, flipping the switch as I went. Warm light flooded the space, too warm for how cold my skin felt. The chill hadn't left since the hospital. Not even with socks and sweats and heat pumping. It wasn't temperature, it was trauma, and I hoped Kyle didn't see it.

"I'm getting water," I said as I reached into the cabinet.

He opened the fridge instead, grabbed a bottle, twisted off the cap, and handed it to me.

I took it and thanked him. The water went down hard.

He watched me.

"It's just dreams," I said. "They'll stop."

He raised one brow. "You've had them since you woke up at the hospital."

I exhaled through my nose. "Bodies don't reset overnight, Kyle. Neither do brains."

The vein in his forehead swelled. It happened sometimes when he held back his anger. "You're not talking about it."

"There's nothing to talk about."

"You were screaming," he repeated, more pointed that time. "Have you told the therapist about this?"

I set the bottle down on the counter and braced my hands on the granite. "I was asleep. Now I'm not, and yes. I told her. She said they're dreams, Kyle, and I'll process them."

"You said his name. You said Tommy's name too. It's the same dream, isn't it?"

I turned and looked at him. "Does it matter? Dreams don't make sense. They twist shit up."

"Rach—"

"I'm fine," I said, sharper than I meant to.

He went still. Not withdrawn, not angry. Just still. Waiting again. Kyle had always known when to push and when to pull back.

I respected him for that, but that night, I needed the pullback. "I didn't say I wasn't shaken," I added. "But I'm not unraveling."

"I didn't say you were."

"I know what this looks like," I said, then regretted it, because I'd given it away, how I felt, more than I meant to.

He stepped closer, close enough for me to feel his energy coming off his skin. "Tell me what I'm looking at then."

I shook my head. "You're looking at someone who hasn't had more than a few hours of good sleep in days, who's still recovering from being tied to a table with a catheter shoved in one hole and a tube in the other, and who's a little pissed that she's not back at work yet."

"I'm sorry."

"Don't be. I know you want to help, but I'm going to be okay, Kyle. I promise."

"I know. Those nurses said they'd never seen anything like you."

"That's probably not a compliment."

"They said you shouldn't have been able to walk, let alone take him down."

I met his eyes. "He underestimated me."

"So did the hospital."

"Well, I'm here now. And I'll be back at work soon. Jimmy's already trying to hold me off the case, but he can't do that for long."

Kyle didn't argue. He knew better. I wasn't going to stay benched. I walked past him and dropped back onto the couch. My muscles throbbed from the short walk, and my head ached with something deeper than dehydration or lack of sleep. I closed my eyes to recalibrate.

Kyle stood a moment longer, then came around to sit on the edge of the trunk, facing me.

"You don't have to lie to me," he said quietly.

"I'm not."

He gave me a look.

I shrugged. "Not really."

He reached for my hand, wrapped his around it, but didn't squeeze. He just held it. "You're not alone in this."

"I know that."

"You don't have to prove anything."

"I'm not trying to prove anything," I said. "I just want to stop waking up thinking I'm back in that room."

He nodded once. Didn't say anything else.

29

———

The department required quarterly psychological assessments for the detectives, so I recognized Anna Kane's voice the minute she spoke.

I let her know how I felt before she had a chance to ask any questions. "I'm doing okay. Nothing personal, but are you really necessary?"

She smiled. "I won't take that personally."

She should have. I wasn't in the mood for a deep conversation. "I really don't want to do this."

"I know, but you've been cleared for a short session," she said, calm as ever, as she dragged a chair from the corner to the side of the bed. "If you want me to go, you'll have to say it directly."

I stared at the wall. "Is it too late to fake a coma?"

"Probably."

"Damn."

She didn't laugh. Of course she didn't. Anna was unflappable in that deeply annoying way therapists always were, like they'd gone to school to learn how to smother your sarcasm with silence until they suffocated it to death. Most of me had already been too close to death for comfort, I didn't want to lose my sense of humor as well.

She sat and waited. I hated that.

"I'm not in the mood for this," I muttered.

"I know. That's why I'm here."

"I'm not joking."

"Neither am I."

I sighed. Loudly. "Seriously, Anna. Can't you harass someone else today? Maybe some guy in a neck brace who murdered his wife? That seems more your thing."

"You're alive, Rachel. That's my thing right now."

"Yeah, well, that makes one of us."

She didn't flinch.

"You don't want to talk," she said gently. "But you're still talking."

I hated when she read me better than I read myself. I hated when anyone did that. I turned toward her then, finally giving her my eyes. "You think I'm going to have some kind of breakthrough, don't you?"

"I think you already have. I just don't think you've admitted it to yourself."

"Oh, how poetic."

She leaned forward slightly, then laced her hands in her lap like a damn monk. "Tell me what you're thinking right now."

I laughed. "Really? That's how we're starting this?"

"Yes."

"Right. I'm thinking that this is a colossal waste of both our time."

She tilted her head. "Try again."

I closed my eyes. She wouldn't stop pushing until I gave her something, and all I wanted to do was sleep and forget. "Fine. I'm thinking about how you're going to keep pushing until I snap, and then you'll nod and write something in your little notepad about anger being a valid stage of trauma."

"I didn't bring a notepad."

"Even worse. You're memorizing this shit."

She let the silence stretch again. I hated how she was so patient with me. It made me feel small. Weak. Exactly how he wanted me to feel. My jaw clenched.

"There it is," she said softly.

"What?"

"That shift. Your body went rigid. Your tone flattened. You're either about to explode or implode. Which one is it?"

"Neither. I'm fine."

"Try again."

"I said I'm fine."

"You were held captive. Drugged. Bound. Psychologically tortured. Lied to, manipulated, and exploited by someone who knew exactly how to get inside your head. And you're 'fine.'"

"Yep." I crossed my arms. "Gold star for surviving. Let's move on."

Anna studied me. "You know what I think?"

Great. The analysis had started. "Please, enlighten me."

"I think you're afraid that if you actually say it out loud, say what he did to you, and how it made you feel, it'll be real. And if it's real, then it happened to you. Rachel Ryder. The one who always survives. The one who's never the victim."

My laugh was sharp and humorless. "Victim? No. Try bait because that's what I was."

Her silence showed her approval.

"I was his pawn," I added, as bitterness poured out before I could stop it. "Just like Tommy was his opening move. He used him to reel me in. To chip at me. He knew exactly what to say, what buttons to push. And I—" I broke off before I would lose it. I clenched my fists in the scratchy blanket and took a breath. "I walked right into it. I let him see me."

Anna nodded once. "You're angry."

"No shit."

"At him?"

"Of course at him. But also…" I looked away again, swallowing the lump that tried to rise. "At myself."

"Because you didn't stop him?"

"Because I didn't see it. I'm a detective. I'm supposed to read people. I'm supposed to be able to see through the lies. But I didn't. He got under my skin. Got into my head. He knew my guilt over Tommy still eats me alive at night."

"And he used it."

"Like I had allowed him to by trusting him." The anger in my chest expanded until it pressed against my ribs like a fist. "I wanted to kill him. There was a moment right after I got free when I saw him bleeding, cuffed to that gurney, and all I could think was how easy it would be to finish it. Just one quick motion. I wanted to watch the light leave his eyes."

Anna didn't recoil. She didn't judge. She just listened.

"But I didn't," I whispered.

"Why not?"

"Because I needed to win," I said. "Not just survive. Win. And killing him would've made me just like him."

She nodded slowly. "You wanted to take back control."

I swallowed hard. "Yes. He made me feel weak. That's what I can't let go of. Not the ropes or the drugs or even the humiliation. It's the way he looked at me."

"How was that?"

"Like I was a victim."

"And that's unbearable."

"No," I said. "It's infuriating."

I shifted on the bed. "You know what the worst part is? I still hear him when I close my eyes. That smug voice. That fake calm. I feel his voice in my soul."

"That must be awful."

"It is. He made me doubt everything I knew about myself. I questioned my instincts, my strength, my resolve. I fought tooth and nail to stay alive, and I won. I did it, but somehow, I still feel like I lost."

"Because he attacked your identity," Anna said. "Not just your body. Not even just your mind. He went after the foundation of who you are."

I hadn't thought of that.

"And you still beat him."

My throat tightened. "I don't feel like I did."

"But you did."

I looked at her then, all the armor stripped bare. "Then why do I feel so violated?"

"Because you were, and on multiple levels, Rachel. He violated your trust, your privacy, your strength, your memory of Tommy, and even your belief that you could see the darkness before it got too close."

I nodded slowly. "I keep thinking about how Lawin knew Tommy was the softest place in me. How he reached right into it and twisted everything I'd told him as a patient."

"He broke your trust."

And maybe my soul. "I already carry the guilt every day. Guilt that I didn't save Tommy. That I didn't see what was coming. That I let myself believe I had time. And Lawin took that pain and turned it into something cruel. He *fed* on it."

"That's what predators do."

"And I hate that I gave him anything. Even a single piece of me."

"But you didn't. Not really. He stole it and there's a difference."

I scoffed. "It doesn't feel like it."

"You're not broken, Rachel."

"Are you sure? Because I don't feel whole either."

"You don't have to yet. But you will."

"Jesus," I muttered. I dragged a hand down my face. "This is exactly why I didn't want a session. I'm turning into a Lifetime movie."

"You're processing trauma. That's how we survive."

"It feels like a lot of crying into a pillow and drinking tea while people tell me to relax."

She gave me a faint smile. "You're allowed to be angry."

"Oh, I'm more than allowed. I *am* angry. I'm furious. At him. At myself. At the universe for giving him the opportunity. At every person who didn't see it coming, including me."

"That anger has a place," she said. "But so does forgiveness."

I turned to her sharply. "You want me to forgive *him*?"

"No. I want you to forgive *you*."

That stopped me cold. I looked down at my hands. They were pale and trembling slightly. Lawin had burned so much strength out of them.

"I don't know how," I whispered.

"You start by admitting that you are human. You made the best choices you could with the information you had. And then you let go of the rest."

My voice cracked. "That sounds too easy."

"It's not easy," Anna said. "It's the hardest thing you'll ever do."

I wiped at my eyes with the heel of my hand. "He saw every crack in me and filled them with his poison."

"But you're still here."

I let that sit. Let it start to sink in.

"He doesn't get to live in your head anymore, Rachel," she said. "You're not his playground."

I swallowed hard. "It's not that simple."

"No. But it starts with telling the truth. And you just did."

We sat in silence again until I finally said, "I still want him dead, and I want to be the one to do it."

Anna nodded slowly. "Then we'll start there."

30

———

Four days had passed since I left the hospital. Kyle stayed with me when he wasn't working to find Lawin's drug dealer and Savannah stayed with me the rest of the time. She brought the kids twice but only for short visits.

"You should be with the kids," I told her. "I'm fine, really."

"Yeah, that's a no. You're not fine, and no one expects you to be. Besides, I need the break from the little tyrants, and my mother-in-law cheered when I asked her to stay with them. So, think of this like it's a girl's trip without the trip. I get to hang out with my best friend and not chase two crazy kids around all day."

"I'm glad someone looks at this with a positive slant. I never thought I'd hate my own home, but I'm starting to. I need to get out. Bishop called and said the doctor's released Lawin to the department. I need to be there."

"I know you do, and Jimmy's coming over in a bit to discuss it." She walked into the kitchen and poured me a glass of water.

I stared at the TV and laughed. She'd put on Walker Texas Ranger, one of Lenny's favorite shows. I considered it an old people's program, but I secretly enjoyed it because who didn't like Chuck Norris?

She set the glass on the wooden trunk. "How was your therapy session yesterday?"

"Same as every other one we've had." I sipped the water. "I'm not sure I can do it much longer."

She sat beside me and placed her hand on my shoulder. "I can't imagine what you're going through, but you need to work through this. Lawin's in your head, and you won't be right until you get him out."

"I want him dead."

"We all do, but even that won't fix what he broke inside you."

"I'm not sure anything can."

"She's helping you. I can tell."

I acted tough even though I still didn't feel that way inside. "Maybe."

"She's not Lawin, Rach. She's a good doctor with a solid reputation. She can help."

The doorbell rang.

"I've got it," she said. She walked over and peeked through the peephole. "It's my man. I'll give you two some space."

I pushed myself upright on the couch, wincing as my ribs flared with pain. The brace cinched tight around my torso made breathing feel like a damn chore, let alone moving. I hated it. Hated the stillness, the waiting, the way every minute passed in hours. Even with everyone taking care of me, I felt helpless and defeated, but I would not let them see that. I couldn't.

Jimmy stepped inside and shut the door quietly behind him. He wore our department-issued khakis and navy polo, but his face looked different. Less lines, more color. Maybe a full night's sleep or a sense of relief, things I wasn't sure I'd ever experience again.

"Brought you something," he said, lifting a paper sack. "Egg salad from Davidson's. Light on the mustard. No celery."

I gave him a half smile and took the bag even though I had zero appetite. "Thanks. Are you trying to bribe me into feeling better?"

"Nah. Just trying to keep you from murdering anyone out of boredom."

I wanted to laugh, but it just wouldn't come. "You're about a day late."

He sat beside me. "You look better than you did a few days ago."

"Thanks, but that's not saying much."

"Fair." He leaned forward and placed elbows on knees. "You sure you're good to talk? I can come back."

"If you don't stop worrying about me, I swear to God I'll throw something at you. I'm fine, and I'm ready to come back and finish this even if that means doing everything but leaving the office."

"We'll get to that in a bit."

I reached for the glass of water on the table and gritted my teeth as my side protested. "What's going on with Lawin?"

"We've got him on holds for now. Unlawful detainment, use of controlled substances in the commission of a felony, first degree homicide times two, attempted murder."

"And what about the parade? I still can't believe he manipulated Rebecca Lister to drive through the crowd of people. Bishop said she's in custody. Did she talk?"

He nodded. "She needs serious therapy and based on our interview, she's going to do time, but we're adding conspiracy and solicitation to commit murder, as well as assault and battery to Lawin's charges."

"There's got to be more we can charge him with."

"There is, and we will."

"And Lister's charges?" I asked.

"Similar, manipulated or not. Aggravated assault/battery, murder, among other things. She'll spend the rest of her life in prison."

"Kyle said his team has traction on the supply side," I said. "Has he updated you today?"

"Kinder played a bigger role than we thought. He went through multiple channels to gain access to the drugs. Kyle said his contact at Emery worked with Kinder for several years and watched him deteriorate."

"So it was him giving Lawin access to the drugs."

"Rachel, we think Lawin's got connections in several states."

My lungs deflated. "And that means multiple victims."

He nodded. "We're looking at everything, but this is bigger than just Hamby, and the feds will come knocking soon enough."

My skin itched. That meant movement without me. Pieces shifting on a board I wasn't allowed to touch even though I had been one of the main characters in the story. "We'll still be involved though, right?"

"I've already contacted the governor about it, but I can't say for sure."

"It's our investigation, Jimmy. We deserve to close it."

"And we will, at least what's in our state. Don't worry about this. You just focus on you."

"Has Lawin said anything to help move the investigation or is his lawyer stopping him?"

"Based on what he's said so far, which isn't much, he's telling his lawyer what he wants him to say," he said. He followed it with an eyeroll. "We're interviewing him tomorrow."

I wanted to be there, but I didn't bring that up. "Lawin thinks he's smarter than everyone, so that fits."

"It won't work much longer." His neck cords stiffened. "Arrogant prick still thinks he's playing the long game. But Bubba and Nikki gave us leverage."

"The other victims?"

"Yes."

I sat up straighter despite the pain. "Were there more than we thought?"

Jimmy handed me a folder he pulled from his bag. "Four states. Missouri, Alabama, Tennessee, and Florida. So far. Bubba traced the trail using Lawin's online aliases and burner phones."

"His what? How did you find those?"

"Zach Christopher took the death penalty off the table for Lister so she would talk. She bought the phones and set up his aliases and handed them to us on a silver platter."

"Never piss off a woman," I said.

"I'm married to Savannah. Trust me, I know that."

He got a smile out of me for that.

"Nikki cross-referenced the crime scene M.O.s with photos sent anonymously to police departments. The poses, wardrobe, even the language used in the messages. It matches what he did here."

"Checkmate."

"Every damn time. Same signature as the one he left for us." Jimmy's eyes darkened. "The FBI is classifying him as a multistate serial killer. They're trying to get jurisdiction, but I don't think they will. If we can prove the timeline and find corroborating physical evidence, he doesn't have long to live."

"And if not?"

"We will." His tone left no room for argument. "You know we will."

I flipped open the folder and skimmed photos and case numbers, all laid out in Bubba's usual grid format. Names of victims. Age, location, date of death. Each image cut like a razor. White robes, lipstick, obscured faces. "How many total?" I asked.

Jimmy hesitated. "Sharma thinks there could've been thirty-four. Total."

My stomach turned. "Jesus."

"We're still working on it. But she broke it down for us and it makes sense given his chess obsession. It's clear chessboard logic."

I met his eyes. "Lay it out for me, please."

"I think I should let you rest. We can do this another day."

I grabbed his arm as he moved to stand. "No. I need to know everything. I don't need the kid-glove treatment, Jimmy. I'm fine."

"Okay." He reached into his back pocket and pulled a notepad then reiterated what I already knew. I was the queen, Lawin the king, blah, blah, blah.

"Tell me what I don't already know, please."

"The pawns. She thinks most of the victims in other states fall under that category."

I traced a finger along the edge of a photo. "What about the rest?"

"Rook. Power enforcer. That was probably the tech guy he killed in Missouri and maybe the courier in Alabama. Bishop, alignment, and thank God not our Bishop. I don't quite understand her theory on this, but Sharma suspects one of the female victims in Florida symbolized that."

My throat tightened even though I already knew. "He made me his endgame."

"The only way we're going to know that is if he tells us, but I'd still like more details about your time with him, when you're up for it, obviously. Sharma said he shifted tactics because of you. The abduction, the manipulation, it was all about removing your moves from the board. Forcing the checkmate."

"He could have picked anyone." I exhaled through my nose. "But he picked someone who flipped the board over."

He grinned. "Damn right you did. Maybe he didn't think you could."

"He didn't. He thinks I'm weak."

Jimmy laughed. "Then he's not as smart as he thinks he is."

"I'm not sure about that." I tipped my head back to stop the tears and sucked in a breath. "I feel broken, Jimmy."

"Of course you do, Rachel. Who wouldn't after what you've been through? But you're not. You'll come out of this stronger than before."

"I'm not so sure."

"I am. Listen, are you a little messed in the head? Sure, but you've been that way since I met you." He smiled.

"That's a valid point."

We both laughed. I needed it. A silence settled between us.

"What else did Sharma say?" I finally asked.

"That the king—his ego—was never meant to fall. But the illusion cracked the moment you escaped, and we got to him before he could reset. She said he's psychologically fractured now. Cornered."

"Good," I said. "He deserves to rot in that corner."

Jimmy let that sit for a beat. "She also warned us not to underestimate how he'll try to reassert control."

"He's in a cell."

"Yes, but you know how these guys work. The mind's the battlefield."

I nodded slowly. "Then we don't give him room to play."

He leaned back into the couch. "We're trying to locate the remaining pieces. Sharma thinks there's symbolic value in doing it. We finish the game on our terms if we find the other victims he believed filled his roles."

I tilted my head and shook it. "She thinks that's closure? Because it's not."

"It's the best we can do."

I swallowed the lump rising in my throat. "Do you think we'll find them?"

He didn't lie. "I don't know. But Bubba's already cross-indexing cold cases, and Nikki's building a victim profile grid using Sharma's analysis. If anyone can pull the threads, it's them."

And I wasn't there. I stared at the folder again, trying to read between the lines, to connect patterns they'd probably already drawn. The ache in my ribs was nothing compared to the burn in my chest. "I hate this," I whispered. "I hate sitting here while everyone else does the work. I hate that he took that from me, even temporarily."

"You didn't lose anything," he said. "You're the reason we've got him, Rachel. And you bought us time. Gave us the final piece we needed. Without what you did in that room, we'd still be chasing shadows."

I looked at him. "Thanks, but that doesn't make this feel better."

"No. But it's the truth."

I closed the folder and set it aside. "What about Bishop? What's his place in all this?"

"Right. Sharma's still working through that, but she believes Bishop resembled his original therapist. One he killed and never linked. Lawin had treatment records from five years ago with a referral in Tennessee. His therapist disappeared shortly after Lawin worked there." He handed me a photo. "Look familiar?"

"My God. He's practically Bishop's twin. That's not a coincidence, Jimmy."

"Nope."

"Did they ever find his body?"

"No, and so far, there's nothing to prove Lawin killed him. Just a hunch on our part thanks to Bubba."

"Dear God," I muttered. "How long has he been killing people?"

"It takes a while to master a skill. It could have been going on for years. Each step was another move on his board, and since he may have already murdered the therapist, it's possible Bishop was going to fill that space in the game." He paused, then added, "Until you broke the pattern."

The clock ticked on the wall above my fireplace, marking time I could have spent out there with them. I hated every tick. "What do I do now?" I asked, and it wasn't rhetorical.

Jimmy's voice softened. "You heal. Then you write the report. Then you take every piece of this psycho's delusion and turn it into a profile that stops the next nut job who comes at us."

I clenched my jaw. "I don't want to write. I want to move."

"I know."

He reached into his bag again and pulled out another folder. "One more thing."

I opened it. Inside were grainy surveillance stills from security cams across town. ATMs, gas stations, the places I ran, and Lawin, in different towns, different dates. Always alone.

"I can't believe I didn't sense him."

"Why would you? Even Kyle didn't."

"How did you get these pictures of him? Tracked from financials?" I asked.

"Partially. Bubba scraped loyalty card data, too. Cross-checked it with debit card charges and travel logs from rental companies. That gave Nikki enough to geo-fence the timeframes."

"They're machines."

"They're the best," he said.

I ran my hand over my face, then rested my head against the back of the couch.

"Rachel," Jimmy said after a pause, "you did more than your part."

"Doesn't make this couch any less claustrophobic."

"No. But it makes this case solvable."

I looked at him. "Promise me you'll let me in on this when I get my medical release."

"I can't do that. The feds are involved, and I'm not sure we'll get to keep him."

"The feds can suck it. This is ours, Jimmy. We deserve this."

"I'm doing what I can to stop them, but this is big, and you know that. We don't have country-wide jurisdiction. It's one thing to take over a case in a neighboring city, but multiple states is impossible."

"Can't we work with them?"

"Maybe."

"I want to interview him. Please. I need to hear him, to see his face."

"I'm not sure that's a good idea."

"I need this, Jimmy. I can tell the feds if he's lying. Please don't take this from me."

"I'll think about it." He patted my hand and then stood. "In the meantime, eat something and rest. And for God's sake, don't try to do push-ups or something stupid. We need you at full capacity, not flat on your ass again."

31

———

The smell in Anna's office gave me a raging headache. Why did she have to fill the small space with so much nasal noise? I wasn't in the mood for neutral tones or slow-ticking clocks. I wanted steel, hard light, a cold chair and a metal table. Interrogation. That I understood. That fed my desire to heal a lot faster than talking about my feelings.

I didn't want to be there anymore, but Jimmy insisted, Kyle had seconded it, and Bishop had backed them both. And I was tired of people watching me out of the corners of their eyes like I might lose it if they looked away.

So, I went and came back. Multiple times.

Anna Kane sat in the chair opposite mine, one leg crossed over the other, with a tablet in her lap and her glasses perched low on her nose. She didn't look like a trauma psychiatrist anymore. No cardigan, no clipboard, no furrowed brow. She wore black pants, sandals, and a sleeveless blouse. Her eyes were sharp. She looked like a friend.

I analyzed her each time we met, looking for something that connected her to Lawin. A shared style of talking, maybe a reference he'd made. I had finally stopped searching for something I couldn't find, but it wasn't easy.

"So," she said, after letting the silence settle a little too long. "You've been home for a while now."

"It feels like it never happened."

"Right. You expect me to believe that, yes?"

"Yes."

"And how are you sleeping?"

I shrugged. "Same as before."

"Which means?"

"Two, maybe three hours if I drink enough water and take a muscle relaxer."

She didn't write that down. She just watched me.

"I don't want a prescription," I added, before she could offer.

"Good to know."

More silence.

I crossed my arms. "You're not going to take notes?"

"I don't need to. We're just talking."

"But you always take notes."

"I will again. When you stop trying to control the conversation."

I leaned back in the chair. "I'm here, aren't I?"

"Physically. What's changed, Rachel? Our talks have been good. You've made progress. Why the sudden switch?"

I pressed my lips together. "The feds took the case."

"And how does that make you feel?"

"Pissed off."

"That's understandable. Tell me more."

"Why? I can't control what the feds do. I can only control my feelings. Isn't that what you keep telling me?" I stood and paced behind my chair. "I don't mean to sound ungrateful, but I'm over this. I need to get back to work. I need to be a part of the investigation."

"I understand, Rachel, but you still need time to heal."

"I can multitask. Why can't I heal my way through the investigation? Wouldn't it be good for me to help find his other victims? To bring him completely to his knees?"

"Possibly, but I'm not sure that's your goal."

"What the hell does that mean? Of course it is. It's my job."

"You know this room isn't for me," she said. "It's for you. You're not here to impress anyone. There's no bar to meet. You don't get a medal for surviving better than expected or hiding your feelings."

"I didn't realize survival had qualifiers."

She tilted her head slightly. "You made sure everyone at the hospital knew you pulled out your own tubes and restrained him yourself. That's not typical behavior for someone who had been sedated for days."

"I did what I had to. Why does that matter now?"

She paused. "You performed for them because you wanted them to see you as strong, not as a victim."

"What's wrong with that? Fake it till you make it, right?"

"Not in this case. Rachel, you're performing for me now."

"No." My voice came too fast, too sharp. I exhaled. "I feel like people want me to fall apart. And I'm not interested in giving them that."

"Why not? It's human to feel weakness after what happened to you."

"It's a waste of time."

"Because falling apart means he got to you?"

My jaw clenched. "Yes, and because I'm tired. I'm tired of feeling weak, of watching everyone treat me like I'm damaged."

"We're all damaged on some level."

"That's not what I mean, and you know that." I fell into the chair and cursed. "I just want to move forward, and the only way to do that is to get back to work."

"Rachel, I'm not here to pick at wounds. But if you're going to get past this—"

"I *am* past it. Mostly."

She waited again. She was good at that. Too good. "You want to talk about what's keeping you up at night?" she asked finally.

"No."

"But you will."

"Yes, just not today."

"I think you already are. We often talk around things to talk about them."

"I need you to sign a medical release, please."

She leaned forward slightly. "Lawin said you were predictable. The way you're acting now is just that."

I flinched. "We've already talked about this. He was wrong. I showed him that." My throat burned.

"Yet I feel you want to show him again. Normally one acts that way when they haven't worked through their emotions."

"I don't care what he said about anything including Tommy," I muttered. "I care that he's still alive."

"Confronting him isn't going to change what's happened, Rachel."

"I know that, but I still need to do it. Dr. Kane, he sat there with his little monologues about strategy and structure, talking like he was moving chess pieces while I was tied to a table. And the whole time, I kept thinking if I can just understand the rules, I can beat him. And I did, but something's missing. I have to figure out what it is."

Anna nodded. "You believe you need this to help you heal."

"Don't you?" I drummed my fingers on my knee to maintain some kind of composure. "Isn't that why rape victims confront the rapist? How is this any different?"

"I'll give you that. I do think confronting him will help you, but I'm not sure of the timing."

"The feds are taking the case. We won't have him for long."

"I understand but answer this for me. As his queen, what did turning the tables give you?"

"Give? Nothing." I looked her dead in the eye. "Reversing our roles gave me power. He wanted to beat me, to destroy me, but he couldn't. I took that from him."

"And do you believe that?"

I crossed and uncrossed my legs. I knew where she wanted to go with that, but I didn't want to. "Believe what? That I took his power? Yes."

"That's not what I asked."

My voice dropped. "Fine. I don't know if I believe it, but I'm here now, and he's in jail, so you tell me what I believe."

"Maybe that's why you feel the need to forget about the pain, and to confront him, because you can't understand why you let him get to you."

I stood abruptly because I couldn't sit still. Pain shot through my abdomen from moving so quickly.

"I want to look him in the eye and make sure he knows he didn't break me," I said. "That's justice."

"Are you sure it's not revenge?"

"I'm not looking for revenge. I'm looking for closure."

"Closure doesn't always come in the form you want."

"Don't quote bumper stickers at me, Doc."

She let that one slide. "Rachel, we have more to discuss, of course, but I want you to think about this because ultimately, this is your kryptonite."

"What is?"

"Tommy. You're not obligated to carry his death forever. Lawin couldn't have done this without that guilt."

"That's where you're wrong. I am obligated."

"You were his wife. You weren't God."

"I made a choice," I snapped. "I paused. I should've—"

"No. You reacted to a surprising and alarming situation. The people who killed him are responsible. Not you."

I turned my back to her. "It doesn't matter. Whether it's true or not doesn't erase the fact that I feel it."

"Feelings aren't facts."

"Maybe not, but they still shape what we do."

"Rachel, I would like to give you a prescription for something. It will help you work through all this and make things easier."

I shook my head. "I've survived too much to let a pill do my thinking."

"It wouldn't."

"No. I'm ready to work cases," I said. "I need to be sharp."

She didn't respond.

"Please give me a release and don't force me to take meds. I need to be *me*."

"Maybe you don't know who that is anymore."

"I know exactly who I am."

She let the silence stretch again. "You're angry," she said at last.

"I'm focused."

"You're scared."

I turned toward the window. "Who wouldn't be? But fear's not useful unless it's functional."

"And when it isn't?"

"Then I manage it."

"By pretending it's not there?"

"By compartmentalizing. Which is what I've always done."

She closed the tablet. "Maybe your coping mechanisms got you through, but they won't get you *out*."

Damn it. I didn't want reasoning. I needed permission to do what I had to do to recover. "Why do I have to do it your way when my way works for me?"

"I'm not saying that. I'm saying you need to allow yourself to heal."

"Healing will happen when I can get in front of Lawin."

"I believe that's how you feel." She stood, walked to her desk, and handed me a printout, but I didn't take it. "It's not medicine. I won't bother with a prescription I know you won't take. It's simply a summary of grounding techniques," she said. "Just tools."

I took it, folded it and shoved it into my bag.

"I'll give you a return-to-work letter, but I want to see you once a week for an undetermined amount of time. If you don't show up, then you'll be removed from duty."

"I'll be here."

32

Jimmy and I sat at Starbucks sipping our coffees as if I hadn't been held captive five days earlier.

He tapped his fingers on the table.

I leaned back and crossed my arms. "Go ahead. Say it."

"Say what?"

"You're not going to let me interview Lawin." I sucked in a breath then released it. "I have to do this, Jimmy."

"I know you do, but I'm not sure that's going to happen."

"Why? You have my release letter. I can do this. You know I can."

"Rach, you already know the feds have it."

My heart raced. "I know, but I thought you would push back on that."

"I tried, but I didn't get a say in it."

I shook my head. "No, Jimmy. That's BS. This is ours. We caught the bastard. We own this."

"You know how it works."

I walked into the pit to a standing ovation I didn't deserve or understand. I'd survived a serial killer, not had a baby. It didn't feel like something to celebrate. A welcome back sign with purple balloons taped to it hung across the outside of my cubby, and Bishop and the team stood in front of a cake with a knife stuck in it. I smiled. Police humor, as morbid as it had to be sometimes, could be the best therapy.

As uncomfortable as the celebration made me, I sucked it up and pretended to enjoy it. The department needed it, and I knew, somewhere deep inside I needed it as well.

Levy wrapped me into a hug then whispered in my ear. "I'm here if you need me."

Michels pointed to the cake. "We thought the knife would fit the mood."

"Can I take it into the interview?" I winked.

"You think the feds will let you talk to him?" he asked.

"I'll make sure they do."

"Then you can, but only if you'll let us watch."

Bishop didn't hug me. He did give me one of his worried looks instead. He had disagreed with me coming back so soon, but he also understood it was what I needed. "If this happens, I'll be in the room with you."

I shook my head. "I need to do this alone, but I want you all on the other side."

"I can't do that."

I placed my hand on his shoulder. "I appreciate your desire to protect me, and yes, I would want to be there for you, but if I let you in, Lawin wins, Rob. I can't let him think I need my bodyguard or a pacifier to talk to him."

He exhaled. "If he says anything that—"

"Then I'll handle it." I wrapped my arms around him. "Thank you for being you, but please, let me be me."

He squeezed tighter. "As if any of us have a choice."

"All right," Jimmy said. "Enough partying. We've got work to do."

The team followed him into the investigation room.

I wasn't surprised to see the assistant District Attorney, Zach Christopher at the head of the investigation table.

He stood and shook my hand. "Good to see you, detective."

"You too." I poured myself a cup of coffee then turned toward him. "Lawin deserves the death penalty, Zach, and I'm happy to be the one to administer the shot."

"I think we'd all like to see that happen. Jimmy's updated you on the case, yes?"

"You mean the feds taking it over?" I nodded. "I think it's BS."

"You're not the only one."

I sat beside Bishop. "There are multiple possible victims across the country. We should be the ones to find them."

"I agree, but we don't have control over what happens next."

"So, we're done?" I asked. "That's it? The POS kills people here, and we catch him, but we're done?"

"We don't make the rules," Jimmy said.

Right on cue, Susan opened the door. "The feds are here, Chief."

Jimmy stood and scrubbed a hand down his face. "Send them in."

The men walked in like they'd come straight from a *Men in Black* remake, dressed in black suits with grim expressions plastered on their faces and steel in their eyes. One older, one younger. Neither looked experienced enough to handle Lawin.

The older one introduced himself. "Special Agent Dominic Hale. FBI. This is Agent Trevor Murphy."

He paused and scanned the room, but his eyes landed on me. "Detective Ryder?"

I raised a finger. "That's me."

"We're glad you're okay."

"Thank you, but I'd be better if you didn't steal our case."

"Detective," Agent Murphy said, "with all due respect, there are thirty-four pieces in a chess game. You're delusional if you think Lawin hasn't played every piece."

Murphy's words barely finished leaving his mouth before Bishop was on him.

His chair scraped hard against the floor. "Say that again," he snapped, his voice low but sharp enough to cut. "I dare you. Come on tough guy."

No one said a thing.

"You think you can sit here and call her that after what she's survived?" Bishop's face reddened. "After she's been in that bastard's hands and still came out fighting?"

Murphy opened his mouth, but Bishop's glare froze him in place.

"It'll be a cold day in hell before you have the right to talk to her like that," he said, each word clipped and deliberate. "She singlehandedly took down a serial killer after being held captive for days. What the hell have you done?"

"Rob," I said.

"No," he replied. He looked back at Murphy who had somehow shrunk in height. "You're not the one who saw what he did to her. You're not the one who's been piecing this case together while she was barely able to stand. So either you show her some damn respect, or you keep your mouth shut."

The silence after that was thick enough to choke on.

"I believe you've been misinformed," Hale said. "We aren't taking over your investigation. The FBI has authority to join an investigation under the Federal Serial Murder Initiative, when murders are suspected to be linked across jurisdictions."

"We understand that is how it's supposed to be in theory," Jimmy said. "But reality is a different story."

"It won't be with us. We've already found connections to Dr. Lawin in multiple states," Agent Hale said. "That being said, we're here with a request for a joint investigation. The Bureau would like to offer resources such as profilers, lab techs, VICAP access, and analysts. Of course, we request access to the suspect, but for now, he will remain in your custody."

He set a folder on the table. "Here's how this works." He smiled at Jimmy. "In case you've forgotten." He cleared his throat. "We've got a Memorandum of Understanding in place. As you know, that means we're officially forming a joint task force. My team will be deputized locally so we have jurisdiction here and select Hamby detectives will be issued FBI credentials for the duration of the investigation."

Jimmy leaned back in his chair. "Select? I want them issued to the entire team. We've all worked on this investigation."

Hale ignored the tone. "Understood. As I was saying, case files will be merged into a secure system for cross-comparison. You'll have access to anything directly related to the Hamby murders. The out-of-state cases will be filtered through my office to determine what's relevant."

I felt my partner's jaw tighten beside me. "So, you get all of ours, but we get yours only if you decide it's useful?"

"That's standard protocol," Hale said.

"Standard protocol sounds a lot like a one-way street," I said.

Hale gave me a thin smile that didn't touch his eyes. "Detective, you've got your lane. We've got ours. My job is to coordinate so we don't waste time chasing dead ends."

"We've already got the guy who started this," Jimmy said. "That's not a dead end."

Hale's smile faded. "Then I guess we'd better make sure we're not stepping on each other's toes."

I bit back the first response that came to mind. His version of coordination felt a lot like control. "I'm interviewing Lawin."

"It's my understanding your department has already interviewed him. We will handle any additional interviews."

My blood boiled, but I couldn't show it. If I didn't stay calm, the feds would find a way to take complete control of the investigation, and we'd end up with nothing. "Agent Hale, I have a personal relationship with the suspect. I know how he thinks, and what he's aiming for. I will interview him, and your investigation will benefit from it."

He eyed Jimmy.

"There is information we still need for our victims, Agent Hale," Jimmy said. "And Detective Ryder is the best one to get it."

"Very well," he said.

33

I walked into the interrogation room and closed the door without a sound. Torey Lawin sat at the table, calm and patient as if he hadn't murdered God only knew how many people in multiple states. He didn't look at me. He didn't move. He wanted me to make the first move.

I pulled the chair out and sat across from him. "Hey, Doc. Long time no see."

He lifted his eyes. "No recordings?" he asked.

I pointed to the ceiling. "You're the star. I'm sure you love that."

He smiled. "I'm glad we have this opportunity to talk."

"This isn't a friendly chat, Lawin."

"That's too bad. I've always enjoyed our friendly chats."

"I haven't."

He smiled. "Interviews have purpose. What's yours?"

"To make sure you get the death shot." I paused and flipped open the file as if I didn't already know it by heart. "I reviewed the recent notes in our investigation. You know, the ones I wasn't there for."

"While we were spending time together."

"Right. That's how I think of it too." I slid the manipulated photo he'd first sent to the department toward him. "That fake tattoo, the photoshopped image of a real woman into a staged scene, the blurred face. You meant it all as deliberate deception, a profound trick. Your knight's play was designed to mislead and disorient us and to jump directly into my personal space, to draw me into your game. You expected us to fixate on the obvious, didn't you? The superficial details, like the unmatching tattoo, to waste our time while you perfected your masterpiece."

"You've learned so much from our time together."

I ignored that. "I want a name."

He didn't blink, didn't even speak. He just sat there with a sick smile plastered on his face.

"Let's stop with the games, okay? You paraded her like she was the first move in the game, though I'm confident she wasn't. Your test case. You watched us chase our tails through a maze you built around her, and all that time you never told me who she was."

His smile disappeared, but his mouth twitched. "You never asked nicely."

I didn't flinch. "I'm being as nice as I can be."

He waited before responding. I had learned everything was always a performance with him. "Taylor Jennings."

My hand shook slightly as I scribbled her name in my notebook. "Why? Was she just another pawn on the board?"

"I am saddened, Rachel. I thought you understood, but I was wrong."

"Then explain it to me."

"I wanted to prove my control over your mind and your predictable reactions."

"Interesting. What did you want me to do?"

"I wanted to see if you were truly the opponent I believed you to be. And you proved yourself worthy, Detective. You deduced the intricate connection, didn't you? You related to her. You pictured yourself in her shoes."

No, I hadn't, but I refused to answer his questions because doing so played into his God complex. "How did you know her?"

"She was a patient a few years ago. I diagnosed her with Creutzfeldt-Jakob Disease."

"Which is?"

"A rare, degenerative brain disorder caused by prions, misfolded proteins that trigger other normal brain proteins to misfold and clump, leading to rapid brain damage. There are several types of CJD, but Ms. Jennings suffered from what's referred to as Sporadic CJD, the most common type. The disease advances swiftly, and death is often quick."

"Is there a cure?"

"Unfortunately, no. After her diagnosis, she came to me hoping to disappear. I gave her purpose instead."

"You used her."

"I sculpted her. She understood her place in our story and willingly accepted my request to join in it."

I forced my jaw to relax. "What about her family?"

"She was an only child whose parents had passed four years ago. She didn't want to die alone in her apartment only to be found months later. She needed my help." He held up his hands as if he wasn't to blame for any of it. "I offered her a solution."

"You wiped her identity. No hits on DMV, no passport, no facial rec. We ran social scans but found nothing. You blurred her face in the photo and added that fake tattoo. You wanted her to be a ghost. If she agreed to be a part of this, why do that?"

"I didn't want her to be a ghost. I used her as a riddle, and with her approval. And for the record, she had no social media presence. She suffered from anxiety, and social media scared her."

"Where did you leave her remains?"

He leaned back, then forward again. "I believe it's time to tell you that. After all, I did promise she would be handled with respect and grace."

"You mean from someone other than you."

"You'll find her at Fort Knox Climate Storage on Holcomb Bridge Road in Roswell. Unit 217. Don't worry, it is temperature controlled, and I have her on ice."

"Which has obviously melted."

"She's in a freezer in a suitcase."

"She wasn't a message," I said. "She was a person."

"She was the beginning of our game."

"No," I said. "She's the reason this ends."

He nodded, slowly. "Our game, yes."

I ignored that and pulled the file from under my arm and then dropped it on the table. "And that wasn't your only masterpiece of disappearance, was it, Lawin? Not the first time you helped someone completely vanish because you saw what others missed. Your game of control, your knight's play, it began much earlier, didn't it? Like with your therapist in Tennessee, the one who disappeared five years ago. The one whose vanishing act was so perfect, so untraceable, that no one could prove a thing. You truly *removed* him from the board, didn't you? A precursor to your plans for Bishop, perhaps? Another way to prove your invincible control. Which, we both know, never happened because you weren't strong enough to take down my partner."

"I never intended to. He was just a tool."

"What happened to the therapist, Lawin?"

His eyes darkened. "He is at peace."

"I need more than that." I wanted him to tell me for multiple reasons, one being so the feds didn't find him on their own.

"He carried the weight of so many. He needed to release that pain. I simply helped him."

"Is he in a suitcase like your other victims?"

"He is buried in one, yes, just outside of Knoxville in the Grainger County backwoods. It's a quite deep, rural area, heavily forested and sparsely inhabited. Really, it's an ideal location."

"Do you know the exact location?"

He laughed. "Of course, I do." He described a specific tree where he'd carved the Greek letter Ψ. I eyed the camera, knowing someone would move on that immediately.

"Why?"

"Why what? I help people, Rachel. I've already explained that."

"That's an excuse, not an explanation. I want the real reason you've murdered all these people. Now."

He shifted in his seat. "Because no one else ever noticed."

"Noticed what?"

"I see things in my patients no one else saw. I treated what others ignored. I kept them out of hospitals and stopped their suffering. I rewrote outcomes. And it never mattered."

"Your therapist never saw, did he? That's why you killed him."

He nodded once.

"I get it now. You want credit."

"I wanted accuracy, but if someone rewires the machine, the least you can do is acknowledge the new circuitry."

"And when they didn't?"

"I stopped asking and showed them instead."

"By killing?"

"I didn't kill to prove I was right. I killed to help, as I have said numerous times already."

"But that's not the only reason, is it?"

"No. I killed to prove I understood what everyone else missed."

"Of course that makes sense to you."

"It's completely sensible. The systems were broken, so I simply exposed the weakness. Each subject revealed a failure point."

"These people had families."

He tilted his head. "So do the people you've arrested."

"Our jobs are not the same."

"Ah, but they are. You help the victims of crimes. I help the victims of illness. I helped them leave behind what ruined them."

I tightened my jaw.

"You see yourself as efficient, but I see a serial killer."

"I see myself as honest. You're the one pretending this world isn't already engineered for decay."

I kept my voice steady though I felt as though ants were crawling under my skin. "Tell me about the hotel photo. The robe. The number on the sleeve. What's the purpose of the performance?"

"I think the numbers are clear. They're a count, Rachel. I would expect you to understand that, though I will say they start over in each state."

"You mean New York and Arizona." I acted as if I hadn't considered the number of pieces on a chess board and how that could relate to multiple victims in multiple states.

"I am licensed in several states, Rachel, thirty-four to be exact."

Bile shot up my throat. Holding back wasn't possible any longer. "How many, Lawin? How many victims total?"

"Do you have a pen and paper? I'm happy to provide the details."

I glanced at the window knowing someone would bring one.

"I'll continue while we wait for the materials," he said. "But first, you must understand, I did not look for these people. They came to me, just like you."

"I didn't come to you to be a victim. I came to you for medical treatment."

"Isn't that the same?"

"No."

"Very well. Though you are right. They didn't all come to me for medical treatment. Many came to be relieved of their pain, their emotional pain."

"How would they know about you?" I asked.

"The internet is a wealth of knowledge. There is a multitude of sites for people looking for compassion and help."

"You manipulated sick people on the internet. You—"

He cut me off. "Released them from their pain, and for that, I deserve recognition. With Ms. Jennings, I wanted to see how long it would take before someone questioned whether it was real."

"And if we hadn't?"

"Then you weren't the person I believed you were."

"You wanted my attention."

"I already had it. I wanted your action."

"Why would you wrap me into this chess game with a group of sick people? So I could figure it out?"

"I do enjoy a good game, but this wasn't all about you, though I may have said that a time or two. My patients needed relief. I just used their treatment to take down the queen. It all worked quite well. In each game I played."

"Maybe in the other states, but I'm still here, and you won't be much longer."

He didn't argue.

"What other states?"

"I will write it all down for you, Rachel. As promised."

I looked down at the notes. My handwriting had tightened into cramped rows. Every time he spoke, the press of old instincts, control, detachment, resolve, began to slip. I pushed them back into place. "You manipulated me to fit into your little game."

"You're personalizing this now. Is this to help you heal?"

Maybe it was. "You manipulated them all, didn't you? No one agreed to your game. You forced them into it."

"Like with you, I listened to them. You volunteered. Just like the others."

"Bullshit, Lawin. I didn't volunteer for anything. You used my grief."

"You carried it too long."

"You exploited it."

"I made it useful."

"I didn't need your help."

"You needed something. You just didn't know what it was."

"You broke laws. You broke lives. You don't get to decide who needs what."

"I don't decide. I reveal. Must we continue to repeat ourselves, Detective?"

Levy walked in and set a pen and paper in front of Lawin.

He looked her in the eye. "Thank you."

When she left, he smiled at me. "There are several. This will take some time."

I forced myself to act unimpressed, but my heart rate soared. "Let's not waste time with this back and forth, Lawin. There are thirty-four chess pieces. You claim to be precise, so tell me about the others. Where are they? Tell me about every single one of your pieces, you narcissistic bastard. You murdered them, and you will give me every detail."

An evil smile stretched across his face. It made me sick to my stomach. "I didn't keep notes."

"Bullshit."

"Rachel," he said, softening his tone. "You're trying to treat this like a procedural. It's not."

"I don't care what it is. You confessed to murder, and we both know there are more than nine victims. I want them all."

"Not murder," he said. "Resolution."

"Where did you leave the bodies?"

"Some were found. They're just not yet connected."

"Then connect them for me."

"That's up to the FBI now, isn't it?" He smiled. "You want me to tell you everything so they can't investigate. You want to be the one to take me down, don't you?"

"I already have."

"Only in part. You'll never have closure unless you recover every victim. You personally. But I won't let that happen."

I clenched the pen in my hand so tightly the plastic cracked. "You don't get to stand behind riddles now, Lawin. If you want a deal, you're going to need to stop talking in circles and tell me what we want to know."

"I'm not hiding. I'm giving you a puzzle you're already solving."

I stood.

He sat still. "You should ask the last question."

"I don't care what you want."

"You will."

I paused at the door. "What did you want me to do? Fall apart? Break down?"

"I wanted you to understand that you're not immune. That even the strongest ones have soft spots. I just pressed harder than anyone else."

"You think this makes you brave."

"No. It makes me honest."

I opened the door.

"You're still carrying him," he said.

I stopped but didn't turn to face him.

"You won't put him down until someone forces you. I tried to help you do that."

Finally turning, I looked at the pen and paper and said, "All of them, Lawin." I walked out before I remembered how much I wanted to slam the door.

34

I needed a moment to collect myself after the interview.

Levy met me in the locker room. "How're you holding up?"

I stared at my face in the mirror. When had all the age lines around my eyes appeared? "I've had better days, but I'm working on it."

"I'm here if you need me."

"I know." I tightened my ponytail. "Right now, I need to nail this bastard to the wall."

"Then let's do it."

We walked into the investigation room to Murphy talking.

"He wanted her thinking about herself."

"Yes, he did," I said. "But I wouldn't let him focus on me."

"Quit psychoanalyzing the wrong person," Bishop snapped. "Our victim's in a box in Roswell. We need to find her. Right now everything else is noise."

"Roswell PD secured the facility for us," Jimmy said to me. "Nowak secured our warrant, and Roswell will assist. We have authority to access the unit, plus search adjoining ones for exigency, and seize any items in plain view."

Michels said, "The manager confirmed the account's been paid monthly, cash, under James O'Hara. The lease opened 2017."

"O'Hara doesn't exist in Georgia state systems," Bubba said without looking up. "No driver's license, no utilities, no voter reg. Manager said he photocopies IDs so we'll prove it's the doctor."

Jimmy cut a look at him. "You already asked the manager something I didn't hear?"

"I sent him an email." Bubba shrugged. "Faster than walking out there to ask permission."

Murphy shifted. "Next time, the request runs through me."

"Cute," Bubba said, and kept typing.

"Why are we here?" Levy asked. "We need to be at that storage unit now."

"She's not going anywhere," Murphy said. "Let's review what we know."

"It's a storage unit," Levy said again. "They're all the same. Temperature controlled, low-traffic, uniform layout, easy to sanitize."

Bubba printed out a map of the location and handed us each a copy.

"Limited entry and exit," Bishop said. "One camera per corridor if they're cheap. Two if they're cautious. A single roll-up door between you and the thing you can't unsee."

Jimmy studied the map. "We know this guy obsesses over presentation. The robe photo. The slit. If he's telling the truth, assume he staged the body to be found. But I want every safety box checked before we roll that door."

"Explosive hazard," Hale said as he slid a list toward me. "Trip lines. Irritant dispersal."

Michels lifted a brow. "You think he rigged a coffin with a flash-bang and glitter?"

"People have done worse," he replied. "I'm not underestimating a man who turned a murder scene into a showroom."

I pictured the interview room again. His stillness, his eyes. How he saved his words for impact. "He won't waste the reveal on confetti. He doesn't want chaos. He wants my reaction. He's got the victim in the freezer in the suitcase. He's too proud of that to lie."

Murphy steepled his fingers. "That makes sense." He glanced at me again. "You ride point because you were point in the room. He set this up to yank you through the door. If he's waiting to see how you react, he might have triggered the place. We can't put you at risk. The safest place for you is behind the shield, not in front of it."

Bishop's mouth lifted. "You're trying to protect her now?"

"I don't need your permission to stand where I stand," I said.

"I'm trying to stop him from directing the choreography," Murphy said. "He's already chosen the stage. Let's just make sure you're right about him."

I felt the heat rise in my throat and forced it back down. "He put the stage under a roof of sheet metal. That's the only power he has left. We still decide where to put our feet."

Jimmy straightened. "Enough. We're done debating who's smarter at chest-thumping. We move in five."

He pointed as he talked, using his hands to cut the air into assignments. "Michels, Levy—scene perimeter with Roswell PD. Block media two blocks out if you see a lens. Bubba, stay on comms with the manager and pull every second of footage he still has including old drives, cloud, anything. If he cries about retention policy, I want his vendor on a conference call with a signed letter in five minutes. Nikki, kit for cold storage and long-term wrap. We don't contaminate because a rookie lifts a lid too fast. Bishop—"

"On her hip," Bishop said.

"No," Jimmy said, then saw my face. "Fine. On her hip. But you both follow procedure."

Hale reviewed the map. "One entry hallway. Unit is third on the right. Camera nodes every other door. Two emergency exit stairwells at each end. One freight elevator. Loading dock to the south."

"Walk it," Jimmy said. "Slow."

We rolled as a group. The FBI Suburban looked brand new and smug. Our unmarked cars looked like they'd actually lived a life. We pulled onto the storage property in a line with our lights low and no sirens. How the media hadn't found out about it surprised me. But they would.

The manager stood by the office door with a clipboard tucked against his chest. He wrung his hands.

"Inside," Murphy said to him. "You'll stay with one of my agents until we clear the unit. No calls. No statements."

He nodded quickly and disappeared.

A woman dressed in an FBI jacket was already there and walked over when she saw us.

"No mechanical tampering," she said. "No telltales at the seam. No dust drags that suggest a line. No trip under the runner."

"Why the hell is she here already?" I asked Hale. "This is ours."

"She's the expert in safety. Trust me, you want her."

No, I didn't.

Bishop behaved and asked her, "Mirror under the door?"

She nodded and slid a mirror along the bottom lip. The glass reflected concrete, dust bunnies, and the bottom edge of something metallic a few feet inside.

"Box," she said. "No lines."

"Open," Jimmy said.

"On me," she said, and everyone listened.

She took the handle and lifted the door a foot, then checked again with the mirror. Nothing. She pushed it shoulder-high, then rolled it to the top until it rattled into the stop.

Cold air draped over us. The unit stood nearly empty yet everything about it felt familiar. The concrete floor, the walls, everything except the freezer elevated on a low dolly.

Nikki exhaled, a thin line of sound. "Whoever rolled that in did it clean."

"Step back," the agent said. She swept the box with a vapor wand, then a handheld meter. "No volatile reading. If he wanted a puff, he'd have used something kitchen-shelf. I'm not getting anything obvious, but we still treat it like it bites."

"We could do this on our own," I whispered to Bishop.

"I know."

She ran her gloved fingers over the latch. She found nothing. No putty, no tape, no wire. So, she stepped aside and let Nikki kneel.

Nikki snapped on fresh gloves and opened her kit. The lens cap clicked off. She circled the freezer, shot, then circled again. I watched her rhythm; it steadied me. Measure, record, touch. Nothing else. Nothing extra.

"Record begins," Nikki said. "The freezer industrial. Aluminum. Standard. Serial scratched. Two single handles on front. No side locks. No visible tampering."

Jimmy looked at me. "Ready?"

No. Yes. I nodded.

Nikki opened the door. Metal clicked. She pulled slowly, pausing halfway to listen. We all listened but heard nothing. The dead speak, but never with their voice.

She opened it fully.

The smell rolled out and smothered everything else. It was both sweet and chemical at once, decay laced with the sterile bite of cleaning agents. My stomach knotted. My mouth watered with the urge to gag. I forced myself to breathe slowly and evenly.

A woman stared from the inside with eyes that didn't see. He'd wrapped her in clear plastic wrap from shoulders to toes, as tight as a second skin. Dark hair slicked against her skull. Her throat bore a single, precise line like the others.

Nikki didn't flinch. "Female. Mid-thirties. Approx five-five. No obvious lividity through the wrap. He cleaned the field."

"Any pooling under the plastic?" Murphy asked.

Nikki angled her light. "No. Like the others she was either exsanguinated elsewhere, or he cleaned postmortem. The wrap's new. No dust. No degradation. The box is dry."

Murphy shifted to the side to see but didn't look too closely. "At least he put her on ice."

"Clinically," I said, voice steady because I forced it to be. "He preserved the reveal which is basically what he told me."

Bishop's hands curled and uncurled at his sides. He stood close enough that our sleeves brushed. "He kept her near you."

"Chain of custody, Chief," Murphy said, his voice quiet and edged. "She goes to your lab if you insist, but we ride the whole way, and my people step into the autopsy."

"She's ours," Jimmy said.

"She's a homicide with interstate implications," Murphy shot back. "Pretend you don't hear the word task force if it helps you sleep, but it exists, and so do my requirements."

"Both of you shut up," I said, looking down at her. "Not in front of her."

The corridor stilled.

Nikki resumed. "I'll photograph, then swab the freezer's interior, the edges, the handles, and dolly wheels. We'll pull castings if I get an impression. Then we'll peel the wrap by inches and bag separately to preserve any trace trapped between layers."

"Bag her hands," I said.

"Already planned," she said.

Reagan, the intern, crouched at the threshold with a small black box and a camera lens. "I've got particulates on the concrete. Two sizes of grit. Different treads. The dolly's polyurethane wheels did most of the work. The push prints are deeper toward the back. No deep scuff from the heels. Barely any cadence change. Lawin didn't hurry."

"He didn't have to," I said. "He rented a corridor with silence."

Reagan continued collecting granular ghosts from a floor that would never be clean again no matter how many times the manager ran a mop over it. The mask of professionalism held, but the tension bled out in small, human ways. Michels rolling a shoulder. Levy pressing a knuckle against her lip. Bishop's jaw ticking as he counted each evidence bag under his breath, matching Nikki's numbers like a second set of hands.

Hale stood near the threshold, giving instructions into a low mic, not loud, not dramatic, but beyond frustrating. He didn't posture or crowd. I filed that away.

Murphy drifted closer to me until we stood side by side, both staring at the victim's face, the way the plastic clung to cheekbone and chin.

His voice dropped. "You kept it together in there."

"In the interview?"

He nodded once. "He likes your edges. He wants to sand them. Don't let him."

"He already tried." I kept my eyes on the body. "He failed."

"He's counting on you to carry Tommy back into the room," Murphy said. "Don't carry him. Carry them. His victims."

I didn't answer. I didn't trust anything I might say to a man who had called me delusional hours before. My anger at him lived under my tongue. But the words were true, and truth didn't need a decent messenger to stand.

"Ready for movement," Nikki said finally. "Hands bagged. Wrap secured. Primary photos complete."

Jimmy gave the nod. The Roswell sergeant backed a gurney into the unit. We lifted in silence. Though not touching the gurney, I guided her down the corridor, past the blinking camera, past the uniform numbers, past the manager's office where a man pressed his palms to his cheeks and pretended not to see because pretending was easier than knowing.

The heat hit like a wall outside. A few bystanders and reporters had gathered behind tape because they always did. One held a phone chest-high, filming. Michels stepped in front of the lens and stared until the phone lowered. The man swallowed and looked away.

We slid her into the van. Nikki climbed in and shut the doors. The lock thunked. It all felt so final. So contained.

Murphy turned to Jimmy. "We'll follow."

"You'll ride," Jimmy said. "One in the van with Nikki. One with me. Ryder rides with Bishop." He pointed to him. "You follow with Levy and Michels. Bubba, you stay here and get anything else you need from the manager, and get it signed."

Bubba snapped a mock salute without looking up.

Murphy didn't argue. He walked to the van and knocked twice for Nikki to open the side door, then climbed in and took the fold-down seat.

I stared out the passenger window as Roswell blurred past. The taquerias, nail salons, a park where a kid in a bright red shirt chased a soccer ball and fell and laughed and popped back up, it all sped by. Life went on, indifferent and relentless, the way it always had.

Bishop drove with both hands on the wheel and his jaw set. "You did good."

"Doing good means nothing if no one finds the others."

He nodded once. "Copy that." After a short pause, he added, "He stared at you in the interview like he owned you."

"I know."

"He wanted you to feel him staring now."

"He doesn't get to come with me," I said. "He stays in his box."

"Good." He glanced at me. "Keep him there."

A beat passed. Then another.

"Murphy isn't wrong about everything," he said as reluctant as a man chewing gravel. "He knows the chessboard. He just likes to tell people he knows it."

"He called me delusional," I said. "He can know things from the back row for a while."

His mouth twitched. "Fine by me."

We took the exit for the morgue and fell into the familiar grid of the area with its strip centers and churches and traffic lights too short for the amount of traffic they pretended to manage. The van pulled into the back lot and backed to the loading bay. We parked beside it.

We moved Taylor Jennings into the morgue with the same care used to lift her from the box. Nikki peeled back the first edge of plastic, The chemical smell sharpened and hit us all with a mean little sting. I didn't cough. I didn't step back. I watched.

"Here," Nikki said. "There we are."

Hale stood beside her. He wore a mask as if he wasn't used to being around dead bodies.

"Our doctor will be here soon."

A booming voice from down the hall stopped Hale from saying anything more. "My ass don't wait for nobody," Barron said. "Your guy wants in on this—" He checked his watch. "He's got exactly ten minutes to get here before the door locks. And if he makes it, he's only observing." He mumbled something I couldn't make out, but I understood his tone. God, I loved that man.

Murphy took a step toward me, then stopped like he'd thought better of it. His voice stayed level. "We'll need your full notes on the interview by end of day."

"You'll get them," I said. I followed the gurney to the autopsy room then turned around and asked Murphy if he was coming inside.

"I'll wait out here," he said.

"I figured."

Inside the room, Bishop's shoulder touched mine and anchored me into place. He didn't speak. He didn't need to. His actions said it all.

Behind us, Hale's phone buzzed. He checked it, eyes flicking over whatever bad news lived there. "Knoxville just called," he said. "They found the therapist."

Good.

EPILOGUE

The FBI hated being stuck in a coordinator's role, but lucky for us, every single murder belonged to a state. Not one landed in federal jurisdiction. Murphy and Hale hadn't hidden their frustration, and none of us hid our joy. If Lawin's list had pushed his crimes to the federal level, they would have run it from top to bottom, but Lawin, as smart as he claimed, didn't know how to play that piece. And that was good for us because it meant we controlled the narrative. The Bureau's only job was to link the cases in Arizona, New York, Tennessee, and Georgia, and make sure the right people talked to each other.

To their credit, they did it well. Evidence moved between jurisdictions in hours instead of weeks. Nobody hoarded information. Lab reports, photos, and case notes all went into a secure system we could access instantly. We worked side by side, local detectives, state investigators, and the FBI. I still couldn't stand Murphy, no matter how many times he apologized for calling me delusional. The man could hand me a winning lottery ticket, and I'd still roll my eyes, but at least he didn't sabotage the work.

We all cheered when we learned Georgia had Lawin first.

The trial moved fast. A week of testimony, three hours of deliberation, and a verdict everyone expected. Guilty on all counts. The jury returned for sentencing and never flinched. Death. The judge signed the order with a smile on his face.

That verdict shifted the ground for the other states. Arizona, New York, and Tennessee had their cases ready, but they had to decide if putting more families through the agony of trial was worth it. Two states chose to wait, keeping warrants active in case our conviction collapsed on appeal.

Tennessee refused to wait. Their DA announced they would prosecute, not for the sentence but for the closure. They wanted their families to look him in the eye and hear the word guilty in their own courtroom.

New York had no death penalty to offer, only life without parole, but they kept their case open. Arizona stayed quiet in meetings, though I saw the signs they would not shelve their file without a fight.

The task force kept meeting for months after the cases officially closed. We planned contingencies while waiting for appeals to run their course. Until then, Lawin lived inside a concrete cell with a clock he couldn't control.

I liked that best. For the first time, he didn't control the game. We did. I walked out of the last meeting with Murphy and Hale knowing Georgia had ended it, and nothing he did could take that away.

Jimmy and Savannah had added an inground pool and a covered patio I would have given my right arm for, to their backyard. He invited us, no, ordered us to a cookout the night after the judge made his decision.

The grill sizzled under the late sun while their kids chased each other through the sprinkler, shrieking as if the last few months hadn't happened at all. Who needed therapy when they could watch the joy in an innocent child's face?

I leaned against the back porch rail and held a sweating glass of sweet tea while watching Michels trying to flip burgers with one hand while batting Bishop's hand away with the other.

"Backseat grilling's a federal offense," Michels muttered. "Don't make me call our buddies from the Bureau."

"If you'd stop flipping them every twelve seconds, they'd cook even," Bishop shot back.

Jimmy chuckled. He held his beer in his hand and sipped it. "Let them burn. They'll be fine once you drown them in sauce."

"You're all wrong," Kyle called from the picnic table. "Grill marks are an art form."

"Keep telling yourself that," Levy said. She nudged him with a cold can from the cooler.

Everything felt normal but me; I still felt displaced and distant. I still met with Dr. Kane, and we'd worked through a lot of my issues, particularly the nightmares where I watched Lawin shoot Tommy. She had said my brain used Lawin as a stand-in for the danger and loss I had felt when Tommy died, and the nightmare was my mind's way of trying to process that trauma and helplessness, even if the facts didn't match. I had agreed, but I didn't think the guilt would ever disappear.

Kyle walked up behind me and slipped an arm around my waist. "You good?"

"Yeah, mostly. It feels good knowing Lawin's fate is the same as his victims, but—" I tapped my temple. "There's still a lot going on in here."

He kissed my temple. "What can I do?"

"Stop asking if I'm okay."

He nodded once. "I'll work on that."

"I'm working through it, babe, but I need everyone to stop walking on eggshells around me. I can't stand that."

"I'll make sure that message's clear."

"Thank you." He headed for the cooler. I let him go. He'd earned a minute of lightness.

Savannah caught my eye from where she was helping her daughter with a popsicle wrapper. She gave me that look, that one part question, one part demand one she gave when she knew something wasn't right and tilted her head toward the side yard.

I followed her past the fence line. The fireflies hadn't come out yet, but the sky had started to bruise, and once the sun set, they'd be there, lighting up the night like mini fireworks.

She didn't waste time. "Are you sleeping?"

"Enough."

"That's not what I asked."

I sighed. "Some nights are better than others."

Savannah crossed her arms. The sleeves of her designer T-shirt pushed up as she narrowed her gaze. "It's going to take some time to work through this, Rach. Give yourself that."

"I know."

"But yet, it's still eating at you."

"Yes." She stepped closer and placed her hand on my arm. "You can't save people you don't know are in danger."

"I know that, but it doesn't mean I can accept it yet."

"You've got a good man," she said after a beat. "Don't let Lawin take what you've got left."

"I won't."

"You say that now," she said, "but I've seen you bury things too deep. Just don't forget the way out."

I gave her a half-smile. "I didn't realize you were handing out wisdom with the watermelon slices."

Her eyes lit up when she smiled. "Wisdom looks good on me. Like pearls and a fresh blowout."

We walked back just as Nikki let out a laugh-snort so loud it startled Zach Christopher's labradoodle. It took off running. Nikki's cheeks turned a bright shade of pink.

The food hit the table in waves. Charred burgers first, then grilled corn, baked beans with too much bacon, not made by me, and someone's potato salad that tasted like the times Lenny took my best friend and his daughter, Jenny, to Door County, Wisconsin, to camp.

The kids hovered like bees, each sticky and loud, grabbing watermelon and juice boxes with the urgency of a sugar crash on the horizon.

I sat at the long outdoor table next to where Savannah always sat. Kyle handed me a paper plate full of food. "I'm not clearing your plate if you don't finish it."

"Guess I'll eat it all then."

Across the table, Bishop tipped his drink toward me and winked.

We all ate as we chatted about everything except Lawin and his victims, acting as if none of it had happened. But it had, and even pretending couldn't make it go away.

As the sun dipped and the fireflies finally blinked to life, Jimmy flipped the background music to something soft and southern. Savannah danced with her daughter. Michels and Bishop argued about football. Jimmy held Carter on his lap while he slept and tried to eat a burger with one hand. Carter ended up with mustard on his face, but he never budged.

"To sleep that soundly would be incredible," Levy said.

Jimmy laughed. "Fresh air wears them out."

"I bet," she said.

And I sat there, with the people who mattered, and felt the trauma I'd experienced lift a little, just enough to breathe easily.

How They Were Taken
Jenna Wyatt Book 1

In Atlanta's shadows, where secrets fester and the missing stay buried, one woman's quest for truth threatens to unearth her own haunted past...

Jenna Wyatt thought she'd left her demons behind when she traded her GBI badge for a private detective's license. But when a desperate mother's plea echoes the unsolved mystery of Jenna's own missing sister, she's pulled into a labyrinth of deceit spanning decades.

Reluctantly partnering with Jack Parks, a magnetic ex-NCIS investigator, Jenna probes into Atlanta's underbelly, uncovering a chilling pattern of abductions and murders. As they peel back layers of lies, Jenna and Jack find themselves trapped in a deadly game where every revelation brings them closer to danger—and to the ghosts Jenna has spent a lifetime trying to outrun.

With lives hanging in the balance, Jenna must confront her darkest fears and decide: how much is she willing to sacrifice for the truth?

USA Today Bestselling Author Carolyn Ridder Aspenson delivers a heart-pounding thriller that will keep you guessing until the very last page.

Get your copy today at
severnriverbooks.com

30% Off your next paperback.

Thank you for reading. For exclusive offers on your next paperback:

- **Visit SevernRiverBooks.com** and enter code **PRINTBOOKS30** at checkout.
- Or scan the QR code.

Offer valid for future paperback purchases only. The discount applies solely to the book price (excluding shipping, taxes, and fees) and is limited to one use per customer. Offer available to US customers only. Additional terms and conditions apply.

ACKNOWLEDGMENTS

I want to express my deepest gratitude to the incredible team at Severn River Publishing for their unwavering support and belief in my work. A heartfelt thank you to my amazing husband, Jack, for your endless encouragement and patience, and unwavering support. And a special acknowledgement to my expert of all things law enforcement, Ara, whose invaluable insights and expertise have been instrumental in bringing this story to life. Your collective contributions have made this journey possible.

ABOUT CAROLYN RIDDER ASPENSON

USA Today Bestselling author Carolyn Ridder Aspenson writes cozy mysteries, thrillers, and paranormal women's fiction featuring strong female leads. Her stories shine through her dialogue, which readers have praised for being realistic and compelling.

Her first novel, *Unfinished Business,* was a Reader's Favorite and reached the top 100 books sold on Amazon.

In 2021 she introduced readers to detective Rachel Ryder in *Damaging Secrets. Overkill,* the third book in the Rachel Ryder series was one of Thrillerfix's best thrillers of 2021.

Prior to publishing, she worked as a journalist in the suburbs of Atlanta where her work appeared in multiple newspapers and magazines.

Writing is only one of Carolyn's passions. She is an avid dog lover and currently babies two pit bull boxer mixes. She lives in the mountains of North Georgia as an empty nester with her husband, a cantankerous cat, and those two spoiled dogs.

You can chat with Carolyn on Facebook at Carolyn Ridder Aspenson Books.

Sign up for Carolyn's reader list at
severnriverbooks.com